CIRCUS ABSURDUS

A Novel By

Robert Tyler

Naked Acres Books

Cover design: author concept illustrated by Jeanne
Hospod (http://www.jeannehospod.com/)

CONTENTS

JESUS BOOTS

Sputnik Debris

Northern California, 1970

At the center of his soiled underwear and raging hallucinations, Forward rides accused. He raises his Jesus boot, mashes the tops of his bare toes against the gear lever, and lifts to fourth. The shovelhead coughs and swallows, screams, and the road ahead thins under the tensile pull of the faster tire.

The sirens, man, the sirens! Forward is trying to hang on in so many ways right now, and the sirens are messing up his grip. The nasal shriek sticks to him like fast-flung snot, decibels of it soaking through his pores and registering like the insistence of a thirsty baby. And the lights, man, the spinning lights. The red light is everywhere, strobing the asphalt, slapping the evergreen trees, casting pinky fog over a fire that's bringing everybody and everything, dressed or not, out into the long hall of an underwater whorehouse. Man. Man, oh, man.

The only stability Forward carries as he moves through the rapidly changing worlds around him is his understanding of the tragic circumstance in which he is embedded. Though any deeper thoughts on his predicament are willfully muted, Forward does understand he is being pursued. He understands he needs to get away.

The sheriff deputies behind him are alongside each other now, close and closing as they tow the nasal circus with them. The headlight of the Harley gets lost in it all, struggles to cast a guiding beacon out in front of all this mess, but—

Bear! Smokey the Bear has stepped from the forest … and dissolves just as quickly.

Man. Man, oh, man.

The bandanna slides down Forward's brow, and he raises his clutch elbow to deal with it. But his adjustment is clumsy, and the bandanna whips off of him. Now his long brown hair flies straight out behind him, tugging on his scalp, stretching his face back from his nose, all of that air friction holding him in this awful headwind he needs to escape.

Curve coming up. Forward pushes down the gearshifter with his tire-tread sole and drops into third. He bends into the arc, comes out of the lean, he's ironing the curve, toes ready to lift back to fourth, and—

Cake fire! Red cake fire, fiery red cake coming right at him, catapulted off the spinning lights of the oncoming patrol car. The new siren hits Forward even before the light does, crawling into his ear like a mosquito. *A mosquito's in my ear, man!* Forward shakes his head, but the mosquito won't go away. He points his ear into the wind, but it won't go away. He raises a shoulder and whips his neck back and, man, his rose shades fly off. Now the red lights are closer, and worse.

There's a side road coming up. Forward raises his clutch arm to block the oncoming light. Yeah, the road looks real … and it's angled like he should take it.

He takes it.

The chopper has no suspension for this kind of situation. The thin wheel way out there in front piles into loose gravel, and the forks move in and out like trombone tubing. The whole thing is slop. Pull any front brake, and he and hog will be doing Jack and Jill. Forward pushes his right sandal down on the brake lever and locks the fat rear wheel, sending his jewelry into an electric panic. The halted chain is flailing around in the sprocket case, the peace medallion around his neck is knocking coin slots into his forehead, the love beads are ecstatic, his tasseled vest has come alive, and every bolt on the bike has loosened a quarter of a turn.

... And then the headlight goes out. Man.

The spinning red lights behind him shine even pinker through the dust storm. Forward hopes the low-beam filament is still there. He smears the thumb switch... It is. But dim and nearsighted, the low beam isn't telling the front wheel up there anything it doesn't already know. The reek of his soiled underpants finds his nose despite the commotion, man, and the pink haze around him turns back into the blood circus as the patrol cars continue to gain on him.

And he can't go any faster. Each fuzz has four wheels on the ground; he's barely got even one, bouncing around like a marble fired into the Taj Mahal. Parts are falling off his hand-built bike, and he wonders how much longer it will be before he and a remaining handlebar skid to a halt.

Just get off the road, man. Forward glances at the forest on his right ... then on his left. For an instant, Bambi, in fawn-spot fidelity, runs alongside the bike, ears tucked, sprinting like a slow-motion greyhound, whole back and butt involved. The Little Prince is stationary relative to the stars, and each thrust of his tiny hooves torques a new spin for the planet beneath him.

The thicket, Bambi, run for the thicket!

Forward is no stranger to altered states, and even this weapons-grade drug he is experiencing could be a manageable adventure. But when moving between realities, setting is everything. In this case, he knows that the cartoonish phantasms sprouting around him are generated by his own need to distract himself from the trauma of the image he holds of beautiful Breeze, her head on the pillow beside him, her eyes still and fishlike. *Just get off the road, man.* Forward looks again at the forest on the right ... then the left. One of Maurice Sendak's wild things is there, standing on one leg, giant ankles crossed, pine trunk in hand like it's a bus pole, grinning with an underbite of triangular teeth. Like the forestry bear, it dissolves almost as soon as Forward notices it. Man. Man, oh, man.

The creek! A trickle of water over a river of silt. *Take it, man. It's all you got.*

Forward enters the shoulder and hits the berm. The forks compress, bringing the front wheel all the way back to the tachometer, then shooting forward in a cannon fire of dirt clods and mountain flowers. The bike follows like the ass end of a Slinky.

Everything's delightfully suspended in the air for a moment —the bike parts and dirt clods and mountain flowers, all orbiting together like Sputnik debris—and then the crankcase slaps down on the bed of silt. Forward pulls back on the reins and locks the back wheel. The chopper plows a hook-shaped furrow into the earth as it spins around to a stop.

He is now in a riverbed, facing the road ... watching the excited deputies clambering out the doors and windows of their damaged patrol cars. And even though the cars are now stopped, the red lights continue to spin. Man!

The river of silt threads beneath these cars through a galvanized steel culvert under the road. The ribbed tunnel is a Trojan worm, its tiny eyes looking at Forward expectantly. *You're already pointed this way. Everything happens for a reason. Choose your movie, man. Take it!*

Clutch fingers pull back. The left Jesus boot clicks the shifter down to the ground floor—no, wait, up a click and a half; second is better. The clutch pops, and a rooster tail of silt screams out behind the chopper as it surges forward. Third gear, six thousand RPM, three miles an hour, the motorcycle enters the metal tunnel.

Man. Man, oh, man.

The deputies are clambering down to the noisy hole where the motorcycle went. But now the bike's chrome-spoked wheels are up on top of the silt, hydroplaning on the moist film. The chopper shoots out the other end of the tunnel and rockets away down the creek bed.

Chuck Wagon

"I said to send in the dogs, Arnold. Now, why didn't you do like I told you?"

"I was going to, Sheriff, but Deputy Marley, sir, he, uh…"

"Deputy Marley called off the dogs? Who the… Marley, you there?"

Deputy Marley holds his steering wheel by the horn. He lowers the volume on the angry speaker in his car and then presses his microphone. "Yes, Sheriff. I'm driving up … North Timberlane, I think it's called. Where are you?"

"Me? Where are … where am I? I'm at the station, dammit! Now, I wanna know—"

"The suspect has lost his exhaust manifold, Sheriff. We hear him fine. Dogs are not yet required. Did you retrieve hairs from the bed?"

"Hairs? Wha—well, yeah. Albertson's got them in a little baggie here. Now where—"

"Are the hairs chestnut brown?"

"Chessnut what?"

"Brown."

"Are the hairs brown? Well, I guess they're brown, but I don't know about—"

"How long are they?"

"How what? You mean the hairs?"

"Perhaps you can remove a ruler from your desk drawer

and measure one."

"We can measure the damned hairs later, now—"

"No we can't, Sheriff. Please measure the hairs now."

There is a moment of silence before the sheriff returns. "Twenty-one inches, alright? Now—"

"How curly, Sheriff?"

"Curly!" The little speaker becomes indignant. "How in the hell am I supposed to tell you how cur—"

"Hold the hair by the follicle, Sheriff; let it hang. I assume the last number you gave me was for the hair stretched out straight. Now I want the length of it hanging freely."

The Sheriff goes silent again, then grudgingly comes back with a second number: "Sixteen, okay? Now—"

"Thank you, Sheriff. I suggest you send the dogs to stand by at the … Kamner Road crossing. Deputy Jessup has gone to retrieve some dirt bikes he believes a farmer can loan us—"

"Elbert, sir. They're Frank Elbert's son's bikes. I got 'em right here in the trailer. This is Jessup, sir."

"Sheriff, I suggest you survey your deputies to determine which ones are capable of riding a dirt bike, then send those deputies that can ride a dirt bike to the Kamner crossing as well. Marley out."

◊◊◊

Man, oh, man—only a gentle slope, and the fat wheel can't grab any of it. As it spins on the slick pine needles, bike and rider arc around the front wheel like it's the needle leg of a drawing compass—lots of noise, but no momentum. Then the heavy bike falls on its side again, the headlight pointing at nothing, the fat wheel spinning in the air...

Ah, man... Ah, man! Ah, *man! Man! Man! Man! Man!* Forward tries to pull his leg out from under the bike, but the counter sprocket has grabbed one of the bells of his bell-bottoms, pulling on the fabric, reeling in his fleshy sandal... *Man! Man! Man! Man!* The sprocket swells to three feet in diameter, teeth like something out of Big Ben. *It's trying to eat my leg—man! Man! Man!*

Forward lunges his torso up and pulls the kill switch. Everything stops; the light goes out. He collapses back onto the pine needles.

... And now the sound of two-stroke engines. Many of them. Coming from below. Frantic and deliberate, they climb up toward him from the valley. The pigs got chainsaws... Man, chainsaws! *The pigs are coming after me with chainsaws!*

Forward squirms under the heavy bike, but he can't free his bell. He releases his macramé belt—*let the hog have 'em*—and slides out of his pants. Standing upright now in his stinky boxers, he looks down at his chopper—man!—then turns to scramble up the pine-needled hillside in his sandals.

◊◊◊

Deputy Marley comes to a halt and calmly shifts the enduro into neutral. The other bikes pull up behind him. He reaches into his coat.

"Sheriff, every time you radio me, I have to stop."

"Oh. Yeah. You find him? Over."

"No, Sheriff. We're following his tire tracks up from the creek. His engine is off now, so he's moving slowly. I'll let you know when we find him. Out."

◊◊◊

It's not really rain, but it's cold and wet and lives in the air. Forward is thickly soaked despite being clad now in only a leather vest and thin undershorts. Going uphill is slow because the pine needles are slippery. But uphill is where he must go. Up, up, up. These are the instructions that ring into and through him.

The harmony Forward hears calling him through the forest is faint, but it guides him. He knows that the world wants

7

him to escape. He knows that he will escape. The manner of his escape is one he cannot yet predict, but if he leans into the harmony it will be revealed to him. Lean into the harmony. Just as he was trained to do in the Brotherhood. Harmony, the inner music, it's everywhere in the world. Sometimes hard to hear. Here, his situation is so out of tune that the direction from which he hears the harmony is very crisp.

Forward stumbles onto a campground.

There's somebody … something. The unnatural object sticks out amid the forest shapes. Forward moves toward it, then slows, stops. The thing is bulbous, curiously metallic, glowing. He accelerates, falling like a moth into the event horizon of the lit attraction.

◊◊◊

It takes three deputies to lift the fallen chopper.

"Slowly," Marley insists.

The deputies follow his instructions carefully.

"Stop. Just hold it there."

The deputies strain and grunt, but they hold the bike up while Marley inspects the denim pants twisted around the motorcycle's crankshaft. With his flashlight, he illuminates the patched bell-bottoms from all angles, closely studying the manner in which the denim has been ingested by the counter sprocket and chain. He motions for the deputies to set the bike back down.

The deputies do so, then stand looking at Marley, who has turned to gaze toward the crime scene in the mountain town below. Even with his war-scarred face pointed away from them, he commands respect. They do not interrupt his moment. When he turns back, his eyes are mournful, glossy, professional. "The suspect is not injured. He can run. We can't track him on these pine needles; we'll have to split up. Each take a different direction; include the one we came from. Miller, radio the sheriff and have him run this plate. Then search the engine and frame for any numbers and radio the sheriff again with those. Let him know that this bike has been chopped, so any one of these numbers alone is insufficient; he'll need to check every number you find. One of you take the belt off those jeans and run it down to the station. Call ahead to..." Marley cannot remember the name. "... your forensic doctor." Straddling the enduro, he almost sighs. "The doctor who's examining the victim's body." He kick-starts the engine and climbs the hill.

◊◊◊

"There's no 'you' in 'penis,' Herb."

"... There isn't?"

"Well, maybe in Mexican. But not in English. Our board is in English, Hon. Now do it right. Just pull the 'ewe' out... There you go... Now slide the 'eye' in. See there?"

Oh, man. Forward has been listening at the aluminum door. He rubs a forearm across his wet face, trying to shake these new images out of his ears. Then, raising high the little green shovel he just found, he reaches out and knocks.

From inside, the sound of surprise. "Who could that be?" Footsteps... Then the door creaks open, yellow light leaking out. Forward has been running through a moonless night, navigating by subtle shades and shadows—and now radioactive mustard screams into his retinas. It seems for a minute that he has knocked on the door of a giant refrigerator ... a giant refrigerator from outer space. And someone has answered. Oh, man ... man, man.

An elderly woman stands in the doorway, but Forward can't really see her. There's only her silhouette as it stands firm in the flow of light escaping the big metal box. Forward holds an arm over his brow; his other arm holds the shovel.

The woman looks down from her metal step at his tie-dyed boxers. "Good evening. May I help you, young man?"

Forward doesn't think he's really that young. On the other hand, he's not at all old ... but that really doesn't matter right now. His feet and mouth stutter where he stands, little shovel in the air, arm over his brow. The light, man, the light! ... He's trying not to be swept backward by it.

"... Young man?"

Forward still isn't that young. And it still doesn't matter.

"Do you need something?"

As color slowly bleeds into the lady's silhouette, Forward discovers that she's green and may have short antennae protruding slightly from her blue hair. Oh, man. Man, oh, man.

"Did you want to borrow that shovel?"

Man, man.

"It's quite alright if you do. You know, there's also a toilet seat folded up against the tree—right over there where you found the shovel. Just bring both of them back when you're done." She starts to close the door.

No, man, I don't want the... Oh, man. Forward wants to speak, but gill slits have opened up on the lady's neck. Man, man, *man!*

"... Who is it, dear?" In Forward's interpretation of the light entering his eyes, a second alien appears behind the first —this one probably a male. The two aliens trade places in the doorway. The male notices the collapsible shovel Forward has raised in the air, then nods toward the tree. "The fold-up seat's right over there. You need a flashlight?"

The spade of the little shovel rattles on its hinge. Forward says something ... sort of.

"What did he say?" the alien in front whispers to the one behind.

"I didn't catch it, either." Whispering: "I think he's a stutterer, Herb."

"You think so?" Whispering: "Maybe he's hiding a harelip under that beard."

"Oh, yes ... dear ... you could be right."

"Key. Key. I just need the key. Just give me the key, man." Forward is still rattling the shovel in the air, but he just can't look up for very long.

"Key? Did he say 'key,' dear?"

"Key? Yes, I think he did. Did you say 'key,' young man?"

Forward is certain by now that he's really not that young —man, the key, he just wants the *key*!—and he wants to communicate more effectively, but speaking into the bright light is like staring into the sun.

"Oh, see there, Carol? He did say 'key.' "

"This thing, man. Just give me the key—the key to this whole thing." More shovel rattling.

"Whole thing? … You mean our motor home?"

"Yeah, man. The … man, the key. Man, give me the *key*!"

"Well, it's got three keys; which one do you mean?"

"Four, Herb." The smaller alien points a finger upward.

The big alien thinks about the little alien's pointed finger for a moment, the direction of it seeming to surprise him. Then he eagerly agrees, "Oh, yes, the storage box! You're right, my love, I forgot about that. Carol's right: there are four keys."

Forward eventually gets the keys—*just give me, man, give me* all *of them*—but as he backs away from the door, something is bothering him about the feel of the keys in his hand. Perhaps he expected they would all be on a ring together. They're not. Each of the four keys is on its own rabbit-foot key chain … and now all four rabbit feet have come into coordinated spasms in his hands, front and back pairs trying to gallop across his palm, surprising little toenails buried in that soft fur. Kind of hurts, man.

"The patio chairs." Whispering: "He means the patio chairs, Herb."

"He wants us to go sit down?" Whispering: "Why would he want that?"

"Herb, hon, whatever he wants, it's clear he wouldn't be at our door looking like this if we weren't supposed to help him."

"You're right. As usual." The two giggle politely over this, and then the male addresses again the young man at his door: "The patio chairs? You want us to sit down over there … over there on our patio chairs?"

"Maybe you should tell him to screw the shovelhead down

11

a little better. That's why it's clacking so much."

"Why does he hold it up and shake it at us like that?" Whispering: "Is he cold? He's not wearing much."

"Would you like a sweater, young man?"

Forward's too occupied with the galloping paws in his hand to contemplate a sweater. He backs away, then around the front of the RV, over to the driver's side.

The latch, where's the door latch? Forward searches for … for the door, where's the door? Man, where's the *door*?

Forward steps back to widen his view. But there's no door —just an outline of the continental U.S. with some downed states painted in red, and a sticker of a cartoon face with a halo. The eyes on the face seem to stare right at him.

"You can't get in from over there," says Herb, speaking a little loudly so he'll be heard from his patio chair. "If that's what you're trying to do."

Forward comes back around the RV.

"There's only the one way in." Herb points helpfully. "Right there—the same door we came out of." He means the refrigerated portal that still leaks radioactive mustard. "But there's no Porta Potti in there, you know."

Forward looks into the maw of alien light, then turns to keep his face on the patio-chair-seated couple. Shovel still rattling above him, he backs his way up the fold-out stairs and into the vessel.

Forward finds the driver's seat, and the right key—*No, it's this one, man*—and starts the engine. But he can't get it into gear. He pulls the shifter; he's even pretty sure he sees the little pointer is on *D*. But when he presses the gas, nothing happens; the engine just revs loudly.

Man! Man, man!

Herb pokes his head through the door. He has his toy poodle in his hand. "You're not trying to pull out in this, are you?"

"Gear. Man, the gear! Man, how do you get it in *gear*, man?"

"Gear? Is that what you said? You want to put it in gear?"

Herb strokes his dog. "Getting it into gear isn't your problem, son. The problem is that the wheels are off the ground."

"Man, *what*?!"

"Yup, I blocked her up. You'd think they'd grade these camping spaces down level, but—"

Oh, man. Man, man, man!

"But why do you want to put it in gear? Do you need to go into town, son? Why don't you just borrow our motorbike there?" The green alien shifts the fluffy space maggot to his other arm and points outside.

◊◊◊

Technically, footprints don't form in pine needles. Even so, occasionally Deputy Marley brings his flashlight to bear on a clump of forest floor. He hunkers down almost onto his stomach. With a penknife, he prods the ground for tiny clues.

◊◊◊

Minibike. The old man meant "minibike." This is a minibike, man.

Forward looks down at his feet. They've grown enormous on the tiny foot pegs. And right in front of his feet are his fingers; he's pinching the little handlebars, operating the tiny controls, trying to maintain a straight course on the narrow footpath along the river he wishes to get across.

There's something in the distance... Maybe it's a bridge. He slows, pulls in the clutch. The baby engine falls to an idle, and the magneto-driven headlight sinks down to a candle flicker. He revs the engine—*rev rev rev*—and the distant structure climbs out of the darkness. Idle—it disappears again. *Rev rev*— it appears. Idle—it disappears. *Rev rev.* Idle. *Rev rev rev rev.* Idle. *Revvvvv rev rev.* Idle. *Rev rev.* Idle.

Revvvvvvvvvvvvvv! The headlight gains intensity and casts its dopey gaze upriver, but Forward is still not sure if the structure is a bridge. He needs to get closer. He twists the throttle—*REVVVVVVVVVVVVVV*—lets out the clutch, and—*REVurpurpurpurpurp*—the screaming little light is swallowed by its engagement with the drive chain.

Putt-Putt the circus bike rolls up the footpath.

◊◊◊

"Marley here."

"Sir, this is Arnold. I've just seen some light signals, flashing like some kind of code—bright and dim, bright and dim, pausing, then bright again. Sort of like maybe Morse code, or—"

"Where?"

"Coming from the south bank of the Coulot... The Coulot's the river that flows—"

"Yes, I studied a map. Where on the Coulot, Deputy?"

"You did? ... I mean, just upstream of the rapids, sir. I figure he's maybe got a rendezvous, someone come up from the campground. Or maybe... Sir? Are you there, sir?"

◊◊◊

The bridge is three mossy logs wide ... no handrails. Forward goads his circus bike to climb up the approach, then eases the front tire out onto the structure. He looks down at the swift-moving river, then back up along the bridge. But he can't go yet. He's got to wait for the clown in front of him to get across first. With tutu and balance pole, the clown's not moving fast.

Go, man!

The clown is across; it's Forward's turn. *Just keep the wheels on the center log. Don't look down.* Forward knows this. *Just keep the headlight on that rock over there. Watch that rock. Go straight for the rock.*

How fast he should go is another matter. Too fast, and he won't have control; too slow, and he won't have gyro balance. It's a trade-off that depends on the weight and geometry of the bike. But whatever the optimal speed is, Forward hasn't had a lot of experience with it—not on this thing. And at the midpoint of the bridge, he becomes distracted. The roar of the river drags his gaze down to the front wheel, rolling so precariously along the ridge of the slick, slimy log…

The wheel skates off and into the crotch between the logs —and the logs open up to swallow the front of the bike. Forward tries frantically to correct his mistake. He looks again at the headlight beam; he wants to put it back on that rock, that rock over there, like the imagined clown told him to. But the beam is gone. It's not on the rock, not in front of the rock, not behind the rock—not anywhere over there even *near* the rock. Instead, there's a strain in his wrists as the front of the bike falls, then WHAM!

He feels a metal shoe strike his forehead. He's been kicked by a horse—right in the center of his forehead.

Forward lifts his head off the log. Is he fainting, or is he *not* fainting?

The horse with the heavy shoes gallops away—across the bridge at first, and then, fuck the forest, it just runs up into the sky. Forward's head raises further as he watches it go.

His peace medallion peels off of his forehead and falls back down to his chest. Is he fainting, or is he *not* fainting? He sits up, bringing his hands to his damaged face. Blurry, dizzy… He is even weightless for a moment.

Splash.

◊◊◊

Deputy Arnold is leading Deputy Marley down the footpath. "Right down here, sir." Arnold has three lanterns set up on the bridge. "Right over here, sir." He looks back at Marley, then down the path at the bridge, then back at Marley, then back at the bridge. "Here it is, sir." He's sort of walking sideways.

Marley looks at the tiny motorcycle. It's in a headstand, caught in the bridge logs.

"You see, sir..." Arnold's looking proud about something. "... I figure this is just supposed to throw us off."

Marley inspects the landing side of the two logs that have separated.

Deputy Arnold follows him around. "Look at that, right there in the middle. See that, sir? Perfectly over the center of the river. What's the chance of that?"

Marley points his flashlight along the crotch of the log separation; he's looking at the moss that has ripped apart.

"He wants us to think he's drowned." Deputy Arnold is almost giggling. "He wants us to think he fell in and went downriver and maybe even over the falls—but it's too perfect. It's too perfect, sir! Look at that: right exactly, precisely in the middle of the bridge. What's the chance of that? I bet you he probably just used a crowbar to pull the logs apart."

Marley is not listening, having crawled out onto the bridge. He has his penknife out and is applying it to the log with the care of a clockmaker; he's collecting long strands of hair and bloody grains of wood. There seems to be a peculiar symbol notched into the log's velvety surface: a peace sign. Marley pauses, straightens his neck, then measures the diameter of the engraved peace sign with his penknife.

"Or ... or maybe if he didn't have a crowbar with him, he could have, he could have just used a—"

"Bring me a small bag, Arnold. Or a jar."

◊◊◊

The tassels of Forward's leather vest splay outward like tentacles in lazy exploration of their new environment. Forward feels the ice-cold water all around him, and he sees that he's in a river now. As in a dream, recent events have been discontinuous. He remembers he was on a bridge ... on a motorcycle, a tiny motorcycle—something a little circus dog might ride. And now he's here. It's like a dream, but it's not a real dream. In a real dream, he might open the refrigerator—and suddenly, there's the garage. It's not something he would say he was expecting, but he would step through unfazed. Fussy presumptions concerning a logical customary arrangement of the material world would be suspended. He was going to get a beer, but now he's loading laundry; no reason to be startled. A dream understands the caveats underneath the grand illusion, and anyone not ready to relax these tenets simply wakes up and returns to the flat world, rested and having learned nothing.

◊◊◊

"Where are Sampson and Metzger?" asks Deputy Marley.

"They should be about a half mile upstream by now, sir. Sampson went up the left side; Metzger's on the right. See, because I figure if the suspect wants us to think he..."

Marley looks at Arnold's extended arm—at the finger, and at the place where the arm connects to Arnold's body. Then he turns, leaves the bridge, and heads down to the water.

Arnold follows. "You see..." *Splash splash.* "... you see, the way I figure it, sir, he tried to make it look like an accident; he's trying to make us think he fell in and now he's drifting *down*stream..." *Splash splash.* Arnold hops to keep up with Marley as they enter the water. "... when what he's..." *Splash splash.* "... what he's really doing..." *Splash splash.* "... what he's really done is gone *up*stream."

◊◊◊

There's no moon, but just enough starlight—enough for Forward to hear the many fish that fight their way upstream around him. They behave so much like ordinary salmon that at first their symbolism escapes him. And to be sure, the cold water has slowed his focus. His sleepy heart pumps blood through his body like sap through a winter tree, and he can't quite keep his eyes all the way open.

It's only when the starlight coalesces into Ursa Minor—

wet paws in the shallows of the rapids, connect-the-dots maw open and ready, Pisces swimming in—that he understands. Now Forward sees the fish he had previously only heard. They're everywhere, hundreds of those crossed parentheses wildly flapping their glittering forked ends as they fight the frothy current to reach an immaculate conception upstream. As Forward floats downstream, barely conscious at the center of his tentacled polyp state, he finally realizes that Jesus is trying to tell him something.

◊◊◊

David Marley's flashlight grows dim. Both deputies now have their gun belts around their necks as they wade around rocks and peninsulas of riverside brush. Marley turns toward Arnold, who still chatters.

"Sir, I'm not saying it's not a good idea to check downstream too. I mean, it probably is a good idea to check downstream too. All I'm saying is—"

"Give me your flashlight." Deputy Marley reaches over and exchanges flashlights with Deputy Arnold. He turns and continues down the river. Arnold, now with a dimmer light, follows, *splash splash.*

◊◊◊

Forward raises his head off the mattress and wipes his runny nose. He sets his head back down, but he can't get to sleep. He needs *so* much to sleep … but he can barely feel his body. Everything's frozen. And the loud roar, man. He can't sleep next to that loud roar.

Opening his eyes, he raises his head again, scanning the piles of soggy refuse, then slowly climbs up onto his forearms. He pulls himself further up onto the mattress, further out of the cold water. He needs to wake up. This is what the fish told him. Only in a real dream can he rely on an awakening to rescue him.

This is what the fish told him.

◇◇◇

Deputy Marley returns from the base of the waterfall below. "He didn't go over."

"He didn't?" Deputy Arnold squints. "How do you know? I mean, sir, you don't think someone could have gone over the falls?"

Marley turns to glance very briefly at Arnold. "Someone, yes; him, no. He must have come out of the river over there by the trash pile." Marley walks toward the pile.

"Oh, I looked all around that pile, sir. There's nothing fresh."

Marley wades out to a half-submerged mattress.

Arnold follows. "But can you believe this?" *Splash splash.* "What kind of people drive up here and dump their trash in the river? Who knows how much of this crap has gone over the falls? Did you see a bunch of trash down there?" *Splash splash.* "Down at the base of the falls, sir? Was there a bunch of trash?"

Marley leaves the mattress and heads back to the riverbank.

Arnold, *splash splash,* skips to follow him. "It's like throwing a Coca-Cola bottle out the car window. You know what I mean, sir?" They move to another promontory in the trash heap. "You pull off the road to fix one flat, and suddenly you got two." *Splash splash.* "All because somebody couldn't just drop the dang bottle in a trash bin. You ever get a flat like that? Winds up not even being about littering." *Splash splash.* "You know what I mean? ... Sir?"

Marley has stopped suddenly at a spot along the peninsula of garbage that enters the water. He studies a tire print in the sandy gravel. "Take a cast of that, Arnold." He stands up, buckles his gun belt back around his waist, and marches out of the river.

◇◇◇

Forward knows he's leaving a trail, but he can't help it. The mountain slope is steep, and there's nothing soft moccasin about the heavy soles of his open-faced Jesus boots. He's rolling up pine needles. But he can't help it. The mountain is calling him.

◊◊◊

"This is Marley, Sheriff. Suspect is on foot, headed up the south slope of the mountain called Quarter Horse. It's time to bring in the dogs. I suggest you bring them up to the Coulot River Campground. Out."

◊◊◊

Forward's jewelry is *so* loud. He sounds like a chuck wagon. He hadn't known this about himself. All along, man, and he never noticed. He stops in the starlight, gazing down at his fingertips that have risen to his clavicles, and considers how he became this way. *I'm, man, I'm a chuck wagon.*

Forward takes off his jewelry—all of it. A hemp cord comes off first. It has a little leather bag tied to it that contains a special pebble with grand and mysterious powers. He opens the bag and shakes the pebble out. The tiny rock falls to the ground, leaving him without making even the tiniest noise. Next is an American Indian choker thing, picketed with some kind of bones like piano keys; he pulls it off. Then, just two more necklaces: the one from Arizona with the turquoise nugget framed in boney baguettes, and the simple peace medallion. After that, he has a few rings; he sucks them off of his fingers. Finally, a leather wristband with beaded embroidery. The knot breaks easily.

Forward searches himself. It's all off. A bush now wears his jewelry—and in much the same way he did. It's all right there, right there in front of him, suspended and waiting. He could have it all back with just a dive through the bush, like a ghost swooping back into its material body.

He backs away with reluctant steps. And the bush just stands there, rooted and wearing his load, waiting for him to go.

Forward rushes back to the bush. He wants his peace medallion—just his peace medallion. It will be fine by itself. No noise, no chuck wagon. Just the peace medallion.

◊◊◊

"Deputy Marley? This is Albertson."

Albertson? Which deputy is that? Marley thinks. *Oh, yes, the old clerk.* "Yes, Deputy?"

"Oh. Um … Doc Norrel called. He measured the width of the bruise on the victim's neck, like you asked. And he said he did find macramé fibers in the skin. Looks like we got a match with the belt you found."

"Thank you, Deputy. Marley out—"

"Say, wait… Deputy Marley…"

"Is there something else, Albertson?"

"Uh, no, sir. I was just, uh, wondering … you know, curious. Did I hear right that the suspect got his britches caught in his motorbike?"

◊◊◊

Forward is out of breath. The slope gets steeper and steeper, the altitude higher and higher, the air thinner and thinner, the trees sparser and sparser, the moon…

Hold on … there's no moon tonight. Forward has just put it together. No moon, man; that's why it's so dark. That's why he's been bumping into things. There's just starlight once in a while in the brief meadows between trees. The rest of the time, he can only make out the objects around him by their infrared projections, the slight differences in temperature between soil and bark and leaves and rock. They appear as surreal colors, a Dali forest displaying the lagged relationships of the objects

21

with the sun, everything dressed in thermal inertia. And he's running through it, bumping into things because he doesn't have much experience hiking through such paintings. In any case, there's no time to learn, because the chainsaws are coming.

Hold on... Forward tries to hold his breath to listen. No, man; no chainsaws. Stopped ... or, no ... wait ... wait, man ... what's that? Holding his breath to listen is very hard. Forward squats down. He holds his breath, holds his heartbeat.

Dogs.

Dogs, down by the campground. *Dogs.* They're coming this way.

Dogs. Man, they got dogs. *Dogs! I'm being hunted by dogs!*

Forward stands and runs. The horrifying sound of the dogs now takes over the whole forest, transforming the Dali landscape into something darker, something gothic.

Wurarh wurarh wurarh...

Dogs! Man! Dogs! *The dogs are after me!*

◊◊◊

Marley mounts a boulder. "Baker, report?"

"This is Baker."

"Did you get your extra men?"

"Affirmative. Three from Campbell Lake, and Bainsville sent up four. Sir, we've got three teams spread out; he's pretty well trapped. There's nowhere for him to go except up the mountain. And unless he's got technical climbing gear with him, he's not going to get much further."

"Has anyone ever free-climbed this side of Quarter Horse?"

"Not that I'm aware. It'd be challenging even as a technical climb with full equipment ... and did I hear he lost his pants?"

"We don't know what else he might have had loaded on his motorcycle. Call over to ..." Marley consults his map. "... Hallersville and have them get their men ready; if he makes it over, he'll still have to come down the other side."

"Deputy Marley, sir, there's no way he's going to make it over. Hallersville's twenty-five miles away by road, and all the men are sleeping. It was hard enough getting the ones I got from Bainsville and Campbell Lake, and we've shared deputies before. What are we going to tell them in Hallersville—that we're worried some hippie is coming over the top of Quarter Horse in underwear and sandals, so they should—"

"Baker, this is the sheriff. This is a murder-rape case, and we'll wake up whoever we goddamned have to. Now just do like Marley says and call Hallersville. Have them get their dogs ready too."

"Yes, Sheriff. Baker out."

◊◊◊

There's thousands of them. Coming from all sides.

Wurarh wurarh wurarh...

Everything has turned gothic. Dark and black. Leaves fall from jagged branches.

Wurarh wurarh wurarh...

Forward stumbles into a clearing on the high slope. Gasping, he has to stop again to lay his palms on a rock and find air.

Wurarh wurarh wurarh...

The dogs are no longer dogs; they're becoming gargoyles. Their grotesque sound is so close that he can see their transformation. Their fur becomes wiry, their paws become talons, their fangs lengthen and drip, and their eyes... No longer the eyes of dogs, their pupils become goat-like, ovaloid, shimmery cold. *Wurarh wurarh wurarh...* And their giant nostrils, thousands of giant nostrils, sucking in his scent, closing in on the sweat he can't mask and the soiling he can't control. Monsters hunting down his drug-poisoned body.

Wurarh wurarh wurarh...

Get out of the vest.

Wurarh wurarh wurarh...

Get out of the vest, man.

Wurarh wurarh wurarh…

It's his own voice, but piped through the sky and trees.

Wurarh wurarh wurarh…

Get out of the vest, man; you've been wearing it since the Summer of Love.

The voice is right; he has been wearing the vest since the Summer of Love, bare-chested and in every possible kind of activity. The vest is now grimy leather with soggy tassels —scent-radiating tassels. A pheromonic travel diary broadcast over a multi-tassel antenna. Hell, the vest smells more like him than *he* does.

He takes it off and lays it over a rock. Good idea. He turns to leave.

Button me up, man.

Forward stops.

Button me up.

He turns back to the vest.

Button me up, man.

Forward squats down and buttons the vest around the rock. He hesitates, then combs the tassels straight, like he would if he were dressing himself. He stands back up.

Now kick me.

Forward looks at the rock—the rock wearing his vest.

Kick me, man. Shove me hard.

He lifts the black tread of his Jesus boot and places it firmly on the vest. He shoves.

◊◊◊

"Deputy Marley, Sheriff Connelly! This is— *wurarh wurarh wurarh*—this is Morton. Listen, I'm just below Melber's Ridge. My dogs are going crazy—*wurarh wurarh*—they're hot on his trail. I'm trailing him *down* the mountain. *Wurarh wurarh wurarh.* I repeat, he's headed back *down*."

The sheriff crackles—an exclamation of some kind. Something about "running him down, now!" and "with all the dogs!" Something is now "as easy as tracking pork rinds."

24

"Morton, this is Marley. Send two of the dogs down, but keep the others going up."

"What! Who the [*crackle crackle*]! I said to [*crackle crackle*] a dog's nose is [*crackle*]..."

"Our reception of you is poor, Sheriff. Marley out."

◊◊◊

Forward climbs. Following the call of harmony, he just keeps climbing, further and further up the mountain as the slope turns into rock face. All those gargoyles, those thousands of goat-eyed gargoyles, *wurarh wurarh wurarh*, clawing their way up the mountain, towing their pigs... This will slow them down.

... At least until the transformation is complete, and the gargoyles gain their wings.

◊◊◊

"Deputy Marley! Deputy Marley! *Wurarh wurarh wurarh.* This—*wurarh*—Morton. I think I got him! The dogs—*wurarh wurarh wurarh*—crazy. I'm climbing down the col now."

"Understood. Everyone else, continue up. Marley out."

◊◊◊

Forward grabs fistfuls of the spongy rock face. He attaches his mucus soles to the granite—*pflock pflock*—and up he goes. The cliff face isn't hard to climb ... *if it would just stop breathing, man.*

◊◊◊

"*Wurarh wurarh wurarh.* Deputy Marley, this is—*wurarh*—this is Morton."

"Go ahead."

"Sir, um, I climbed—*wurarh*—down to the dogs. But—*wurarh wurarh wurarh*—just found—*wurarh*—big rock—*wurarh wurarh*—dressed in—*wurarh*—hippie vest."

"Korn to Marley."

"This is Marley."

"Sir, I've got Blue here. She's our best dog. She's hit some tracks. He's still climbing up."

"Up, confirm?"

"Yes, sir: up."

"How far ahead of you?"

"I'm not sure. Parts are turning to cliff, and it's getting slow finding a way around with the dogs."

"Let the dogs loose. Tell the others to do the same. They'll find their way up faster if they aren't tied. I'll take the east side; have Sampson take the west. We'll follow the dogs."

"Yes sir. Korn out."

◊◊◊

Wurarh wurarh wurarh...

The sounds of the dogs register optically in Forward's brain—fiery in color, eight feet tall, dripping fangs. Their goat pupils are ruptured and leak into the surrounding eye yolk. They can see through the gothic darkness. Forward lifts his sandal up to a higher foothold. They can see him, they can smell him, and they're finding their way up to taste him. They're coming around the cliff face ... from both sides. They're finding their way up. Thousands and thousands of them.

Wurarh wurarh wurarh...

And then he summits ... sort of summits. He feels like he has summited. But it's not a summit, just a bluff, a crag, a promontory in the sky. The mountain continues still higher. In any case, it doesn't matter; the gargoyles have him surrounded. They're racing in from both sides now. He has nowhere to go. The monsters will encircle him, eyeball him with their popped goat eyes, smell him with their giant nostrils, and then with their drippy fangs, they'll toss him around like he's a little lizard. *Wurarh wurarh wurarh...* Until he's just a juiceless leather sack.

Man. Man, oh, man. Forward pushes the bad-trip images

out of his head and tries to restore his perspective of the multiplicity of reality, his connection with the Cosmos. He calls upon his training in the Brotherhood to calm himself, hear the harmony's call, and allow himself to be further recruited by it.

He walks through the forest of the promontory now. Calmly. Serenely.

Below a magnificent sequoia, he sits in the pine needles. He pulls his legs into the lotus position. Now more than ever, he must come back to his training. The world around him is so awfully out of tune. He must calm himself, listen, and slide into the resonance.

Forward knows that he has been brought to this event, this place, for a reason. This movie is ending. He shuts his eyes. When the gargoyles arrive, he'll be far away in meditation. Dissolved back into the grand illusion. He'll go out like a cool cat. Like Jesus. Just—*wurarh wurarh wurarh*—empty his mind.

The night air grows viscous. Forward's legs are still folded into a fishtail. The hellish sound of the gargoyles is now murky, though close.

And then there is a sound from above. Motion. Commotion. For an interior part of Forward not limited by expectations or imagination, there is no mistaking the racket for what it is: a surfy froth of rope and wooden dowels tumbling down through the branches, twisting, turning, the rungs bumping excitedly into each other as they fight to overtake the knotted predetermination of their rank. When the commotion stops, a rope ladder reverberates in lazy torsional oscillations as it hangs from the sky above Forward ... a rope ladder stretching from the lap of his lotus position all the way up into the darkness of Heaven, up to his appointment with God.

I'm just like Jesus. I'm Jesus, man. Forward wrenches his fishtail back into legs and stands up. He puts a hand on the ladder. He climbs ... climbs. Hand over foot, hand over foot, he climbs, leaving the monsters to thrash in futility below, cursing their lack of opposable thumbs. Hand over foot, hand over foot, he climbs.

27

Woorarhwoorarh … woowoo… Forward now hears the gargoyle cacophony dissolve into music, harmony, but a composition more electric and modern than anything written for the sheep-horn-and-gut-string ensemble that may have accompanied Jesus's ascent, back in the days when they were still stacking rocks to build their churches. *Woorarh … woowoowoowoorarh … rarhwooowoooowooooo…* Why ascend to the tune of dead animal parts when there's a wah-wah pedal? A modern ascent merits distortion, and Forward's rise to Heaven is covered by none other than Jimi Hendrix … Jimi Hendrix on the electric gargoyles.

Hand over foot, hand over foot… Forward keeps his gaze straight up the ladder. He doesn't look around, he doesn't look down; just straight up the ladder. Not that he can see much— it's pitch black—but who knows what God's view is like looking down. And Jesus, for sure Jesus didn't look around to sightsee as *he* climbed the rungs to Heaven. Forward's not even a Christian anymore, but he wants to climb to Heaven just the way Jesus did. So, hand over foot, hand over foot, he climbs.

High up in the tree, there's an unexpected interruption in the hand-over-foot ascent to Heaven. A break in the ladder. A halfway house. A scrub station or something.

Of course.

Forward steps off the rope ladder and onto the platform. His eyes remain trained upward, gazing up at the moonless sky that leaks through the high branches. Then he feels an angel remove his sandals, his Jesus boots—a gentle nudge for him to shift his weight, and the heel straps peel down. The sandals slide off. The feminine hands reach up to his waistband, pause, then peel his boxers down and off of him. A moist towel glides over his body, caressing gestures that methodically collect and remove his spent shell. And then the towel spirals up a knee, opens high between his legs, a shoeshine motion. Hendrix is wailing on the gargoyles, setting fire to those winged dogs—a big sound. A gown comes down over Forward's head. He lowers his extended arms.

He's ready now. He's ready to meet God.

AWAKENING

Backward In Pig Shit

Vietnam, 1967

Knuckles in pig shit, backed up against the pen boards, and panting, panting hard, Major David Marley's eyes take inventory. Three, three of them—two on the left and one on the right; he counts his attackers. Browns and greens are coalescing in the blurry light: three green uniforms. Three green uniforms that scoot around a livestock pen, trade places, untangle legs, sort through links of chain, come down onto elbows, switch to other elbows. Three prisoners of war searching one another's knees for back support, simply trying to get comfortable again after being jerked by their ankle chains from their preferred side of the pigpen—the side of the pigpen where the pig shit is not wet, as it is under the knees and knuckles of their chain-mate, who has just regained consciousness.

Although technically he has just regained consciousness, Marley is not yet fully situated behind the eyeholes of his face. A few internal matters remain as loud as his need to assemble a relationship with the outside world. In fact, the external and internal matters mix, leaving his priorities for the moment in dispute and therefore addressed simultaneously in some mixed, half-assed sort of sense. Discovering himself seemingly and so suddenly in a pig pen with three strange men—Marley notices now that there is also a pig in the corner—is startling. But even more startling was his scream. Marley's eyes take inventory. Had these soldiers heard it too—how it had blurted out of him?

Uncontrollably. Marley's eyes take inventory. Like a stepped-on bathtub toy. Marley's eyes blink once, note the shackles on his ankles, the chain connecting his ankles to those of the other men. Blink. A shriek—the sort of sound a man makes when his self-control has eloped with his dignity. Marley's eyes read the American military fatigues. David Marley has never once screamed as an adult. And a *shriek*? Not even as an infant.

The mental blizzard of snow glitter is settling down to reveal the little village now. A physical world has materialized from the tempest between conscious states, and Marley's panic subsides. His tongue runs over his teeth, checking the place like a nervous widow returning home from a trip. And then Major Marley can finally speak.

"One of you … one of you tried to lick me," he says. "In the face."

He knows it was the black man.

One of the men—the black man—is leaning on his elbow, and he looks up. "Well, I ain't licking you no more, that's for damned sure!" The other two nod understandingly. "Not after you bat me upside the head like you did."

Marley's eyes take inventory. Two of the soldiers seem familiar, but in an eerie, incomplete way.

"Bet you ain't ever kept a woman—and it ain't nobody's wonder. Probably jump up in the middle of the night while you was having a bad dream and strangle the unlucky broad."

The other two laugh—seemingly less in ridicule of the major than in appreciation of the poetry in the black private's dialect and word choices.

"Don't matter if they made me medic; let you reach up and lick the pig shit out of your own split-open head."

Split-open head? Marley's eyes, the eyes that take inventory, look around … and discover they can't see the head from where they are. But then his hand finds the blood dripping down from his own eyebrow. One finger and then the others come up onto his face and crawl around the perimeter of the injury. They gather information, then bring their Braille summaries to the insides of his eyelids.

"You're injured, man," says the private chained to Marley's left ankle—PFC Walker, according to the uniform. "Rifle butt, man." The private scoots toward the major.

"Rifle Buttman—hoo, that's him!" says the black man—PFC Yawn, by the uniform. He's chained to Marley's right ankle.

"They really got you." Walker leans toward Marley, his face expressing sympathy and disgust. "They got you with the … with the butt, man." He giggles.

All three privates are staring at Marley's forehead.

"Man, I don't know if that's really, you know … sanitary. You should let Eight finish licking it out." Walker nods toward Yawn.

On the left end of the chain line is an older, middle-aged soldier—well-groomed, brown hair with symmetrical graying, one PFC Edison, according to his uniform. Private Edison slides over and leans forward to closely examine Marley's face. Marley stares back. With the brow posture of someone who wears bifocals and the voice of a hobbyist, the older private finally summarizes, "Yeah… Huh… Can't really tell how deep it goes. Ooh… But Forward's right: you should let Eight finish licking that out."

"Nooo, not me," says Yawn. "Told you, I ain't licking pig shit off that pervert no more. Let him fester!"

"That pig crap is absorbing into his brain, man," says Walker. "You got to clean it out. You're the medic, Eight."

"Shit, Faw, wasn't anybody but you decided how that rock-paper-scissors shit supposed to work with three people."

"You lost fair and square. You're the medic, man."

"How you know us licking him is even clean?"

"Cleaner than pig shit, man."

Edison raises an index finger. "There must be a good reason animals lick their wounds."

"Yuh, their *own* wounds, Ed."

"Hey, man. My sister's dog used to lick my cuts."

"Growing up, I saw the cows lick each other all the time. They'd get cut on the barbed wire."

"See, Eight? Even the cows have medics."

"Ooh, and don't forget about hookworm. They'll burrow right in if you walk barefoot around the pigs."

"Hookworm, man! You got to lick the hookworm out of his brain. You lost, Eight. You're the medic."

"That don't make me medic forever. Be like you still being 'it' from when we were kids. How about you take a turn? Reach your own skinny white tongue over there and see if this crazy motherfucker don't bite your eyebrow off or some shit." Yawn shifts to his other elbow. "Don't know why you anyway sticking up for this peekaboo pervert. First we saw of him, he was coming out of that spy closet."

"His brain is almost coming out, Eight. Give him a break."

"A break? Faw, you got some kind of Mother Teresa shit going on! We got plenty of enemy right here in the pig shit with us. Don't need to be giving it a break."

"You're grouchy, man. How about lighting us up another spliff?"

"We done smoked it already. I told you."

"Really? Man, you don't have another one?"

"Told you; just packed the one. Didn't figure I'd be chained up with y'all."

"Man. Check your other boot. Maybe, man … maybe, man, you packed two and forgot."

"Faw, you telling me you think I packed weed in one boot … then forgot all about it by the time I was putting on the other, or some kind of shit like that?" Yawn first holds a look of incredulity and indignation, softening into offense, irritation. This blossoms into a new expression: crescent eyebrows, a pensive pucker, and finally a cheerful nod. "Hell, yeah … I suppose something like that could have happened. Around *you*, at least. Hold on, let me untie this mother and take a look."

"From what I can see by your uniforms, I'm you're superior." Marley's head has cleared enough for him to begin establishing control.

Private Yawn stops untying his boot. He looks over toward the major. His dark face reverses back through the previous sequence. "If you the su-perior, then how come you the one still on the pig-shit side of the pen, Major?"

The men laugh.

Except Major Marley. He doesn't react to the comment. He is not offended. Instead, he carefully observes the men, their small-eyed laughter and lack of realistic appreciation for their situation. Marley has recently received training on recognizing these symptoms. It seems that these men are indeed under the influence of marijuana cigarettes.

While Yawn unpacks his boot, Marley scoots out of the wet excrement. He takes dry dirt from the ground and begins to clean himself—efficiently and quickly, with no sign of embarrassment.

Meanwhile, Private Yawn has made a discovery: "Hoo-wee! Don't know how long this hobo been riding around in there all crumpled up." Yawn hands a mauled joint to Walker and begins to put his boot back on.

Walker carefully rolls the joint out on his thigh.

The middle-aged private, Private Edison, looks on, even leans over a bit. "Looks like maybe it got a little damp, what with being in your boot and all. Say, Eight, did you ... did you have it *inside* your sock? Or...?"

"Ed, you think I'd have it in there with my sweaty foot? You know that ain't no place to keep a sacrament like this."

"Not in this swamp weather, man."

"Especially not in this swamp weather! Can't be carrying the weed 'round in there against your sweaty foot. Got to show it some respect. Treat it like you would a communion cracker." Yawn tinkers with the reverse lacing of his boot. "Like I said, Ed, just got a little crumpled up in there. But wasn't in no sock with my stinking wet foot, dammit."

"Wow, it's got a few holes in it," says Walker.

"Holes? Holes ain't no problem." Yawn strangles his ankle, ties the lace, then sits up. "Just got to hold it like you would ... like you would if it was a little clarinet."

"A clarinet, man?"

"A clarinet. A little clarinet, and you playing something on it, blocking up the little holes with your fingers while you smoking it down."

Walker nods; he agrees. Then he pulls an unsafety match out of his private stripe and lights it against the railing of the pigpen. Soon the mutilated joint is making the rounds between the privates, stopping even at the mature Edison, each man carefully noting the correct finger chord positioning before receiving the little instrument.

"Men, you will notice our ankles are chained together," Marley begins.

"*I* noticed," says Yawn immediately, raising a single finger off the smoky clarinet.

"I noticed too, man."

Even the elder private has a slight grin.

Marley's eyes take inventory. In deciding how to engage these men, he must consider the drug's influence. But what model should he use? Should he treat them as drunks? Children? Mentally retarded? Marley's training has not yet given him clear guidelines. But he pushes on: "We are in a very serious situation. I'm in command, and I need you men to get it together."

Yawn looks toward his knees and slowly shakes his head. "Com-mand. Umh umh umh."

"First, each of you will brief me on—"

"Umh umh umh."

"Private Yawn." Marley turns his head specifically toward the private chained to his right ankle. "Do you see the oak leaves on my uniform?"

"Hard to see anything under all that hog shit, Major."

The men laugh, now in hearty ridicule, as they run exaggerated glances over the major's shitty uniform.

"Anyway, you think I'd be calling you 'Major' if I didn't? Maybe you need to take a moment and pull your own brain back in your skull before you start telling us what we got to do. Thinking you in com-mand and shit."

Marley observes this—no expression, he's just carefully collecting and analyzing.

Edison is the first to stop laughing. He hadn't laughed as hard as the other two. "Well, ya know, boys, he *is* an officer. I betcha he knows some nifty things we don't. Maybe he can even help us with that question we had earlier." Edison sounds to be from the Midwest.

"Oh, hey, you're right, man," says Walker. "We didn't ask *him*."

"Because he was still unconscious."

"That's right; out for the count."

Edison, representing the three privates, turns to the major and explains, "Seeya, Major, we were all wondering," he scoots closer, "before you, uh … before you woke up…" He raises his eyes again to the major's forehead. "Ooh… We were trying to figure out why they chained us together like this. Would you have any idea? There's something pretty peculiar about it, don't you think? See here, how our ankles are chained together one after another in a line like this?" Edison points at the three interior chain segments that each connect an ankle from one man to an ankle of another, and then at the two segments on the ends. "But our chain train isn't really chained to anything else, see?"

"Yeah, man—you'd think they would run the chain through, I don't know, the boards over there, or around a post, or something like that," says Walker.

"You mean, to keep us all from running out of here?" Yawn asks.

"That's right: to keep us from running out of here. See how peculiar it is, the way we're connected together, Major? But not to anything else."

"Nah, Ed, they ain't going to run the chain through no boards. They'd have to unlock all that shit every time they want to lead us around. Little gookas got things to do; can't be spending all their time pulling chains out of boards and shit."

"You think they want to lead us around, man?"

"Hell, yeah. Have us dig them a ditch or something."

"Or a trench, man."

"Same thing, Faw."

"Hmm." Edison scratches his head. "A trench. Sure, I can see that. But even so, you'd think they'd link in some kind of a weight, like a heavy ball, or—"

"Hoo hoo! And some striped pajamas too? You been watching too many cartoons, Ed. Where around here you think they gonna find a hea-vy bawull?"

"Well, then a cinder block or something."

"Man, I don't know about a cinder block. Couldn't we just smash that apart with a big rock?"

"Well, then a big truck wheel, say," suggests Edison.

"Or a car part, man."

"Truck wheel *is* a car part, Faw," says Yawn.

"What I mean is, what's to keep us from just climbing right out of this pen? We could all run right out of this barn, right here, right now," says Edison.

"Wait a minute, man; a truck wheel *is not* a car part."

"Seems sort of like putting a leash on your dog, but not tying the—"

"A truck part's a *truck* part, man."

"Faw, how come you pretending like you don't understand what I say?"

"Because you leave too much of the communication job to my side. Weed your own garden before you deliver the carrots, man."

"Maybe that's on purpose." Yawn's eyebrow raises accusatively. "Slow you down. Maybe I don't want anybody pulling up my carrots."

Edison's mouth and eyes constrict with curiosity as he composes a question: "So, what happens when you leash some dogs to each other, but not to anything else? Would they know better than to run around opposite sides of a tree? Would they get it together?"

"You mean get it together *together*, man?"

"Right. Will they get in tune, harmonize? Or at least keep their whole from becoming less than the sum of their parts."

"Hoo, those dogs take the wrong sides of the tree, they going to find out right away some one-plus-one-less-than-two shit."

Major David Marley has become impatient with this chaotic chatter. Precious time is being wasted. He speaks: "We wouldn't make it ten yards out of this barn. Right now, we need to—"

"How's that, Peek?"

"Yeah, man. You weren't even awake when we rolled in here. How do you know what's out there?"

Major David Marley is not accustomed to being interrupted —not irreverently, not even by his superiors. He logs this poor judgement as an effect of the marijuana cigarettes. Then he returns his focus to the task at hand. The privates do have a point. In consideration of this, he starts now with, "Did any of you men get a look at the camp?"

"Look at the camp? Hell, yeah."

"Well, it's really a farm, you know."

"Hear that, Peek? Ain't no camp; it's a farm."

"Yeah, man; all of us got a look."

Marley exhales.

"We didn't see too awfully much on the trip here." Edison looks toward the others to make sure this is fair. "On account of the bags they put over our heads. But when they unloaded us off the truck, over at the end of the barn over there, they took the bags off and, well, yes, we got a quick look. Quick look around, I mean."

"Lucky we even made it into the truck, after Peekaboo pulling his Yosemite Sam all over the house," says Yawn.

"Yeah, that was sure close," Edison agrees.

"He almost got us all shot, man," Walker adds.

This catches Marley's attention, causes him to listen very closely. In "all over the house," what does the private mean by "house"? That must be the brothel, the location of the experiments. And "Yosemite Sam," that's a cartoon character, used here as an archetype—maybe to suggest rapid, indiscriminate firing of handguns. But "Peekaboo"? Why does Yawn refer to him as "Peekaboo"?

"Old Phong took a bullet through the head," Yawn continues. "In one ear, out the other. All because of you."

"How long were we in the truck?" Marley asks.

"Do you mean while it was underway?" Private Edison asks.

"What do you mean, 'underway,' man?"

"Hell, the major's trying to figure out how far out of Saigon they brought us," Yawn explains.

"But maybe, man, maybe they just drove us around in circles to make us think—"

"Hoo, take a look at that ant there! Ain't a black ant, ain't a brown ant... Some kind of *auburn* ant or some shit."

"Wow, fella's pretty big too! Don't see that in Minnesota."

Major Marley stirs impatiently. There are very good reasons for a command structure in the military. The faculties of these men are so diluted by the influence of the marijuana cigarettes that they don't even understand the severity of their situation, much less the reprimands they are inviting should an escape be achieved. "I'll address you first, Private Edison," says the major, corporally turning toward the apparent senior of the privates. "I have two questions. My first question is the following: from the time that I fell unconscious to the pres—"

"Ah, Peekaboo, you *fell* unconscious alright, hoo hoo!"

Marley tries to ignore Private Yawn. He makes sure his eyes remain fixed on Private Edison. He has asked Private Edison a question, not Private Yawn. But Private Edison has shifted his gaze, immediately more interested now in Private Yawn.

Yawn lowers his head and voice like he's telling Cub Scouts a campfire story. "The major, the major, well let me tell you..." His lowered voice creates a contraction in the ankle chain as the men are drawn closer together to hear what Private Yawn has to say. "The major here, he took that rifle butt to the head and toppled straight down those little stairs, Yosemite Sam guns rolling down after him.

"But not before he took down a couple of them, umh umh." Yawn laughs. "Emptied both his guns all over the walls and everything else. Hoo, boy went down those stairs like some kinda gren-ade."

The privates, even the mature Edison, laugh. But Marley is not paying attention to this. The stairs? He had fallen down stairs...? Marley begins to remember.

Marley's mind evaluates two strategies for engaging the men. On the one hand, he wishes to push for discipline; these interruptions and lack of focus are costing valuable time. He can't let this chaos take over. But on the other hand, he recognizes that these unsolicited remarks have provided crucial information in reassembling his own fractured timeline. This protracted insubordination has, in some sense, helped him regain his consciousness. Only now does he remember rolling out of the black closet—the spy closet. The shoot-out in the stairwell... He shot four, probably killed two. He remembers the second Viet Cong team arriving from the rear of the building, the rifle butt crashing into his face. Marley recalls all of this now.

"We're at most a couple hours out of Saigon, Major," says

Walker.

Marley responds with a cautious, vertical nod of appreciation.

"Something else you should know: they got our trucks. They got our trucks out there, man. *Our* trucks."

Edison combs his hair with his fingers. "Yup. Hijackers. This is probably just a temporary camp they're making their raids from, is what I'd guess."

Marley turns toward Walker, toward Edison. His nod is circular. He sighs.

Private Walker—Forward—he sighs too. He leans toward his commanding officer. "You're not interested in the trucks? Major, we need to find out why we're here. What this movie's about. And you're slowing us down. We need you to open your mind, man."

Forward In Sequitur

Many discoveries come to Forward as he struggles to awaken.

For one, the world outside is very bright … even painful. Certainly painful. His eyes tighten, drawing back on the separation that is trying to dissolve. And a sound, a soft and expansive breeze, connects to a feeling of motion, a slow swaying.

But the most unavoidable discovery for Forward this morning assembles more slowly. It's deep, spiritual, gentle … and disappointing. As he struggles to awaken, as he is rocked by the strange swaying, as his ears fill with soft breeze and he blinks in the new light, Forward realizes with tender slowness that he didn't really die and go to Heaven after all.

The ferocious drug has left him, worn off, its rabid plans extinguished in foamy slumber. And now Forward understands that he is in a tree. Not Heaven ... a tree. Here on the pearly platform, where he stood like Jesus on Corcovado to be stripped and scrubbed for the Ascent, he now lies under a fluffy cover. In a beanbag bed. A granulated texture greets his cheek with the news of his celestial declination, his incomplete arrival in Heaven. It's a nippled texture that gently teases him about his aspirations and reminds him that he still slobbers in his sleep. Forward recognizes that though the world out there is very bright, he is still in the world of forms, separate from the One. He is merely a shell, a hollow shell, a mantel ready to cloak his soul and rise into the bright light, the strangely bright light beyond his flittering or maybe fluttering eyelids, the bright light beyond, where Context vaults through meadows and playfully waits to be hunted.

"Here. Food and drink."

Forward hears the voice, but he is not yet capable of looking for its source. Slowing the admission of the loud light beyond, his eyelids still flitter ... or maybe flutter.

Flitter and flutter are maybe no different from one another. Blink, on the other hand, is very different. Blink involves, even if very briefly, the full aperture of the eye. Blink provides an instant of the present by creating a discontinuity between past and future. And blink is what Forward finally accomplishes as he lifts his head from the beanbag bed and brings it higher to track the silhouette.

"Holy mayun, what a butt!" he whispers without certainty as the shape scampers up through the fiery light filtering through the tree branches. Unlike the seepy flitter or flutter, blink is luminously defiant of its own average; it's a stone block pushed out by a sandy pharaoh in his tomb, or an ice block pushed in by Chinese fireworks over boreal igloos. Blink is burning brightness and nomadic darkness all collected in the same bucket, a bold bite into the steamy core of a flash-cooled spring roll, black and white before the compromise of gray, the spectacular forms dancing in the uncollapsed, pliable magic of the incompletely specified. "Mayun, what a butt!" he says again, realizing now that he has seen absolutely nothing clearly of whoever or whatever that was. Blink is seeing the photons for what they are, before they've been forgotten and replaced by the averages in their train car. Blink is the spectacularly wealthy imagination while it's still too poor to afford analysis. And most importantly at this awakening moment, blink is a vital distraction, a panic response pushing his awareness to jump beyond his eyelids before consensual reality can land within him to build an unbearable despair out of the events of his recent history. At this moment of Forward's awakening, the only safe place for him is the present.

Forward has, this morning, just received some light … and he has, this morning, just received some sound, some food and drink … and he has, this morning, just fallen back into the beanbag bed to think about these gifts.

The voice he just heard—it was the scrubbing angel, from late last night. Forward's eyes had been skyward; he had only seen the angel as a peripheral whirr, a seraphic busyness that lowered his dirty boxers, removed his tire-tread sandals, cleansed him, and sat him down on a bag of beans to wait for God.

So, he hadn't really seen the angel. But he had heard her … or at least, in his last alert moments, when an internal quest for back support led him to lie back in the beans and study the treetop above him as it sparkled in the light of a rising moon, he heard the angel speak. Not to God above, nor to him in the beans, but to the gargoyles below. The angel had climbed down the tree to speak with the goat-eyed monsters. That's when the electric music paused, when the color of the moonlight in the treetop shifted to alabaster, and the angel could be heard to say, "Blue?"

Lap lap lap.

"That your name, girl?"

Lap lap lap.

"You a priiiddy girl."

Lap lap lap.

"Yeahuh … uh huh … Blue priiiddy girl."

Lap lap lap.

"You the leader, Blue?"

Lap lap.

"Blue leader girl?"

Lap lap lap.

"Blue priddy leader girl?"

Lap lap lap.

"Here, girl, let's try these underwear on."

EGRESSES

Tangled Tentacles

Deputy Marley is already at the station when the sheriff arrives this morning. He has been here all night, reading in closer detail through the thick intelligence reports on the commune—The Motel, as it is called. He had been an intelligence officer for a dark mix of agencies. And he quit. Despite that, he has had little difficulty in getting even the most classified reports sent to his new desk as deputy sheriff of this small mountain town.

He arrived in Ashton six weeks ago, and until now, he had not yet read through the reports in detail. Of course, in his previous reads, he was not seeking clues to explain a murder. He was not even urgently interested in the threatening counterculture that the reports center on describing. His views of the true threats to his nation's values have evolved. Indeed, at least in the case of the war effort, his support for it became shattered as completely as the ceramic toilet he smashed on a tarmac before leaving Saigon. When Deputy Marley requested these reports, his reasons for wanting to better understand The Motel and its hippie inhabitants were more personal and diffuse.

His reason for now having spent the night in the station studying these reports has as much to do with solving a murder as with avoiding the cutting penetration of the murder's significance. In his sparsely furnished apartment, there is little leverage for distraction. And it will be days before he is able to sleep. These reports have provided a needed distraction. Read in the right order, they are almost a comedy—a comedy that would have made him laugh under much different conditions, and if his physiology were capable of such a response.

While everyone calls it The Motel, it's really just a big house —a bunkhouse, a mansion, an estate, or simply a scrambled and sprawling one-story structure that never anticipated it would ever grow to become so big. At its core is a rough-sawn room that no longer has windows to the exterior. It is said that this room was once a cabin, built long ago from the very first trees felled in the mountain valley of this town that would one day become Ashton.

From this ovum, the initial growth may have followed a somewhat reasonable course, as a blastular level of organization can be seen in the surviving traces of the earliest additions to this first room. But today, most of The Motel is comprised of the many sections that have accreted—unmethodically, erratically, haphazardly, even cancerously—ever since. Each one of the additions is a defiant individual, a proclamation documenting the materials and design that were easiest to gather at the precise moment of its creation. Although The Motel is definably one building, it resembles a harbor of boats piled together on the beach by a storm. It's a delirious honeycomb waxed out over generations by highly adaptive bees responding to their immediate needs. Incrementally, it is a surprised and desperate response to each new landing of lumberjacks and millworkers. Collectively, it is an architecturally achieved portrayal of the Ashton Lumber Company's fabulous myopia when contemplating the consequences of its own expansion.

The Company had expanded the early Motel multiple times over its history to house increases in the number of seasonal workers. It was a cheap place to house a lot of people when you needed to. But eventually, The Motel didn't serve the Company very well. Eventually, there were few workers willing to even stay in The Motel, and those who did stay didn't stay for very long.

For one thing, the plumbing and electrical wiring of The Motel are incomprehensible by any usual schematic. Repairmen have indeed visited The Motel, but without their tools—a visit motivated purely by curiosity. Similarly, fire inspectors have visited The Motel—not because of the easy prey for their citation booklet, but rather because the spectacular use of extension cords has become a famous attraction: outlet multipliers plugged into outlet multipliers, sometimes extending out from the wall in a heap requiring brick support. It was an apt occasion for the inspectors to learn the correct plural of the word octopus. Tangled tentacles spread from the octopi, far and wide, stapled along baseboards, taped to walls, hung between light fixtures, run under doors, through bathrooms, under shower mats, into screwdriver-punched holes in the wall, sometimes finally reaching an appliance, sometimes just reattaching to feed a generational segment of The Motel's previously installed wiring. The Motel's electrical system is a dense and tangled web of metallic strands that the inspectors have decided should stay just as it is ... because in case of an earthquake—and earthquakes are undeniably common in this area—all those wires will be needed to hold the building together.

The real problem the workers had with The Motel wasn't the feral wires, nor that every flip of a wall switch was a major experiment with unpredictable and sometimes faraway consequences. The real problem with The Motel wasn't the tangled alchemy of plumbing that turned every instance of a clogged toilet into a community upheaval. And it wasn't the forced air in the quilted heating ducts that travels for decades without discovering a destination. Not one of these complaints was the reason the workers left. The reason the workers moved out was because The Motel was haunted.

Not haunted by ghosts; a different kind of haunted. The workers—the loggers and lumberjacks, the millers and their families—they didn't have the right word for what they meant, so they used the word haunted. But the correct word was supremely available to the new occupants who purchased The Motel from the Ashton Lumber Company for a pittance: the word was vibe. The earlier tenants had wanted to say that The Motel "had a bad vibe." Ironically, the new occupants possessed the appropriate word, but they didn't need it. The hippies that moved in didn't find The Motel to be haunted—not at all.

Previously, The Motel seemed to make folks get mad, causing the most violent behavior to flare up, even from the docile wife of a band saw operator. Folks discovered whole unneighborly attitudes in themselves that they had not previously known they harbored. By the time they started calling it "haunted," The Motel had already taken three lives and left dozens of others with permanent disabilities. Yet there were never any mysterious bumps in the night, no rattling chains or sourceless moans, no chairs seen rocking in empty rooms. Each of the three deaths, for example, followed a clearly witnessed sequence of events.

The first death was set in motion when one person hung laundry directly in front of the only usable window of another person's unit—which ended with a hot iron docking in the left temple of a third person, who took the wrong side in the laundry debate.

In the second death, one man had made firewood out of another man's hammock tree. When the first man refused, even under intimidation, to erect a pole or a post or a goddamned something else to replace the goddamned tree that was supposed to be there to hold up the other end of the goddamned hammock, the second man took offense and backed his truck through the living room of the first man's unit, killing a young girl who was busy on the floor with her homework.

The third death was initiated when motor oil was drained into what some considered to be the designated sandbox of the unofficial playground. This ended with some angry mothers pushing the offending car off its blocks at an unfortunate moment in its repairs.

In each case, the description of what happened was always frustratingly mundane, the line of material cause and effect clear—but as an explanation, it seemed ridiculous, absurd, out of tune. What was missing was the ethereal "why" that could account for the collective attitudes fueling these skirmishes. Some kind of ghost—and nothing of the floating-bed-sheet variety—was haunting The Motel.

The ghost only became properly illuminated when it suddenly disappeared—or in other words, when the hippies moved in. These new occupants didn't cut down trees, didn't own irons, didn't change their motor oil. More fundamentally, they used The Motel in quite a different way than the former occupants had. The former occupants had engaged in a constant struggle to draw boundaries. Because they were renters, they had a very strong sense of ownership and wanted to label everything in The Motel accordingly. The source of the skirmishes, as they understood it, was that the labeling was incomplete; it wasn't clear what belonged to whom. This, as they saw it, was the problem that needed to be fixed.

Unfortunately, The Motel didn't help them out very much in this regard. Perhaps if The Motel were anything like a real motel—with equanimously parceled square footage and compassionately comparable flooring, fixtures, views, and refrigerator space… If each parcel had an adjacent parking space, and autonomous control over its own lighting… If plumbing problems were not so gregarious … then maybe the model of ownership espoused by the former occupants would have been successful. But the harder they tried to parcel out The Motel, the more "haunted" it became, until finally they regarded the building as unlivable.

Since the hippies moved in, however, things have turned around; The Motel has entered a phase of harmony it never knew before. This has created something of a puzzle, because many of the people who now live in The Motel have previously lived in other communes, and living here in The Motel is so … so pleasant. Unusually pleasant. Consistently pleasant. Preternaturally pleasant. So pleasant that people come from far away just to see for themselves how pleasant it is. Reporters come to write about how pleasant it is; doctoral students come to study how pleasant it is; others just come with the expectation of reifying their conviction that such a dirty shared space couldn't possibly be pleasant. It seems that the same quirky attributes that made The Motel seem haunted to the previous occupants have made it blissful for the new ones. The hippies arrive seeking transcendence of the deep-seated societal model of privacy and ownership, and The Motel more than meets this need: the unparceled and unlabeled contorted tangle of malignant resources provide daily reminders of what the hippies hope to achieve. At The Motel, the challenges of living together are neither petty nor masked, and this seems to be important in how they are addressed.

Most everywhere else, the typical commune is becoming a loud example of the unrealistic expectations of the flower movement, a remarkable petri dish where idealistic young people are crammed together long enough to discover that they really do hate one another after all. The Motel has become a famous exception to the rule, fueling support for the continuation of this experiment in counterculture and the questioning of conventional behavior. But for the crew-cut dad who sits this morning reading the paper at the same kitchen table where he last saw his brassiere-less young daughter, right here in the kitchen where he delivered the "my way or the highway" ultimatum, the news of the murder at the famous commune in Ashton—the, hrumpf, "Mo-tel," as they call it—may be cause for celebration.

Reporting on The Motel has advanced past stale condemnation of its counterculture lifestyle and freakish living conditions. Respected journalists have progressed to reporting on the famous organic produce reaped from The Motel's ten acres of fertile soil—and on The Motel's annual Parallel Parking Contest, where the satirical aim is to sublimate the past tradition of associating manliness and virility with lower-dimensional skills such as very, very quickly pulling a handgun out of its leather belt caddy. Accordingly, contestants are awarded prestigious vegetable-basket trophies based on their prowess in parallel parking a standard VW bus.

But this morning, the crew-cut dad has something to smile about. Maybe he grins as he jabs his stiff bacon slice at the newspaper and exclaims, "I knew it!" Somewhere, he knows, his braless daughter is reading the same article. Maybe she's even at that gadfersaken "Mo-tel" right now. Maybe Dad's even wishing his daughter ill without realizing it. Maybe at this moment, he is jabbing his bacon into the black-and-white picture of the murdered girl and repeating with even greater satisfaction the second time, "I knew it!" as he beckons his wife over. Perhaps Wife is pouring orange juice right now but promises to come look as soon as she can. Perhaps the newspaper photo of the murdered girl is already marked for the wife with the grease of pig flesh.

Although it is from a different newspaper, Deputy Marley has an identical article and photo of the victim, carefully folded up in a pocket below his badge. The sun has risen. He sits now not behind the boxes on his desk, but in front of the Sheriff. In his office. In the guest chair.

The newspaper was delivered to the station before daybreak, by a boy on a bicycle, just as it was delivered to many places by many boys on many bicycles. A fabulously efficient news syndication has this morning taken Marley's shattered heart and shared it with the whole world.

"A raid? You want to raid The Motel?" he asks his sheriff.

"That's what I said, Deputy." The sheriff shows some irritation, maybe defensiveness. "Soon as Arnold gets here and goes over and gets the new gear, we'll suit up and head over."

Marley looks at the sheriff. "The justification being…?"

"Justification being that that Forward fella could have circled back and be hiding out in there."

One of Marley's eyes contracts. "So, you're saying that last night, he climbed up a mountain, reversed course, somehow got past the dogs … and then chose to hide out at the crime scene?"

"Yes, Deputy, that's what I'm saying. Didn't you hear Jessup? That hippie had our dogs running all over the mountain like a bunch of banshees." The sheriff's face is outraged. "Put his goddamned dirty undershorts on our lead dog. Blue, she couldn't help it. Fine dog from a fine line. Best-trained too. Other dogs, dumb as farm hounds. Chased poor Blue all over God's green acre."

Marley nods. "A continued investigation of the suspect and his connections at The Motel certainly makes sense, but a couple hundred kids live there, Sheriff. A raid of the whole Motel isn't warranted any more than raiding a whole block of houses would be just because a suspect lives in one of them."

"Deputy, I know you were some kind of big shot in the Agency, but maybe a small-town sheriff can teach you something about how things work in a small town. Not only do I get a call from above telling me I got to hire a new deputy I don't even need, I got the Lumber Company putting pressure on me to bring down The Motel. This is a lumber town, Marley, and the Company wants that Motel gone! Those beatniks been spiking the Company's trees and dumping sand in the crankcases of Company bulldozers. You have any idea what it costs to rebuild a D7?"

The sheriff pulls his sleeves back down. "Now. We have them for littering and for murder, maybe even for vandalism, but none of that's big enough to take them completely down. So. We go rooting through that Motel, and we're going to find some of that loco grass they've been growing. And that's all we need —all we need. It's Schedule I now. Mighty serious." The sheriff nods with a grin, appearing very satisfied with his plan. "The Company's sure going to be happy with us when we hand them a permit, so they can go take those same D7s they had to rebuild and raze right over that goddamned Motel."

Marley pauses, nods. "Understood."

"Good. Now how about instead of telling me how to be sheriff, you go in there and type up a warrant? Then you go across the street and get Judge Wallace to sign it. The victim— that Breeze girl—her real name, I found out..." The sheriff raises his reading glasses and consults a note on his desk. "... is Sarah Marley. Hey, and tell Arnold, when he gets in, that before we start the raid, he's gotta run over to the Company first. Company has some new riot gear they're donating to help out."

Breeze In The Trees

The breeze is still in the trees, but it mixes now with the brilliant blue falling from above. Not from far above though, for the nest in which Forward lies is nearly in the treetop. If this were a Christmas tree, there would be little more above him than some tinsel and a crowning star ... or so it seems when looking downward. Factually, the nest is more toward the middle. Not the top, the *middle*.

The platform is just a lip, a flange of sorts, a partial deck rolling out from the hull of sticks that holds the fluffy bed in which he lies. A tarp is rolled up and tucked away to the side, attendant for days when the blue does not fall from the sky as it does today. And the rope ladder that brought him here is now just a bouquet of rungs, a quiet bundle of sticks tied to the bottom of a branch.

The bed is a beanbag. Forward can feel the beans right now below his fluffy covers.

They're big.

And crunchy.

The beans are *crunchy,* man.

Maybe they're peanuts. Maybe Forward can even feel the double-breasted shapes under his cheek. He pushes his face deeper into the bed to decide about this.

When Forward awakens again, it's … it's probably late morning. Or early afternoon. The sun is not at its highest point. Forward has lost his orientation; he doesn't even know where the sun is headed or where it came from today. But there's an inexpressible quality to the light that makes him think it's late morning, rather than early afternoon.

That girl, the woman, she brought him the … the lunch box … and the thermos. As he first awoke in the bright morning light, she brought him these—the lunch box, and the thermos—and then she … she went somewhere else. Scampered off. Forward sat up to look over the nest edge, but she was already gone—nothing but the quiet branches of the pine tree. No apparent causeways, handrails, knotted ropes, or slotted bark. Just pine tree. *High* pine tree. She had scampered off through the branches like a squirrel.

So, Forward opened the lunch box.

A peanut butter sandwich.

Three stalks of celery—uncropped stalks, their leafy canopies curled around to fit in the box.

A cookie. A peanut butter cookie.

And a thermos.

Forward pulled off the cup-shaped lid of the thermos—Fred and Wilma Flintstone, Dino, and the Rubbles, all in barefoot pursuit of some kind of "Yabba Dabba Doo!" that can never be reached in the cyclic geometry of their path—and unscrewed the inner cap.

Tea. Still hot. Green tea. Forward drank the tea, ate the sandwich, ignored the celery, pulled the cookie back into the fluffy bed with him … and … and fell back asleep.

Somewhere during the path of the sun since, the cookie got crumbled. Forward has collected the bigger pieces and now sits eating them as he peers again over the lip of the nest. He looks down, more carefully than he had before. But there's just green branches, pinecones, and breeze.

Partial Riot Gear

Because of The Motel's shoddy patchwork construction, it would be difficult to lift the roof with any mere assembly of cranes. But such an impractical act is what Deputy Marley performs inside his head as he seeks orientation and perspective.

If the roof could be raised, the pathways could be examined. If the roof could be raised, it would be tremendously illuminating for the presently occurring police raid, this comical chase, this clown show lacking probable cause. The scene looks something like guinea pigs chasing hamsters through a hamster habitat —specifically a hamster habitat. And not just an old shoebox with a tired treadwheel, but rather a wondrous complex with all the tubes and tricks that only a resident hamster could know about. If the roof of The Motel could be raised right now, what might be visible are sleek hippies rapidly shuttling potted plants along complex passageways—pattering through hallways and bathrooms, directing their hugged loads around refrigerators to pass through unlikely doorways, sliding bunkbeds aside to hand the plants through once exterior windows that now connect interior rooms. And in this scene would be several deputies in partial riot gear, trying to follow the sheriff's plan for an organized east-to-west sweep of the building. Instead, they're moving in circles, backing up, bumping into each other in dark rooms, getting clogged up in the hamster tubes, and becoming very confused by the pathway gimmicks that only a sleek resident hamster could know about.

Despite his thought experiment, Deputy Marley stands at the center of this circus, as disoriented as the sheriff.

By the way it flies, it looks like a fat and feathery mosquito —the full-of-blood kind. But it is a chicken. A yellow chicken. Frantically batting its wings as it steams a low-altitude course through the room. It came from the passageway beside the broken pinball machine. Now it flies across the cluttered space, bangs into a tattered sofa, and goes up and out a window that once upon a time led to the outdoors.

"Son," asks the sheriff, scratching his ear, "you kids keep chickens indoors?"

"Oh, I don't know. They kind of—" The hippie has to take a step back to let the police dog pass. The dog, on the same course as the chicken, appeared from beside the pinball machine; it trampolines off the sofa and flies out through the relic window.

"—they kind of just live here, man."

"Sheriff, Sheriff!" It's Colmers, out of breath, riot helmet a little crooked. He too has come from the passageway beside the pinball machine. "Did you see Spinner come through here?"

The sheriff nods at the window. Colmers quickly climbs up the sofa and, utility belt scuffing a window frame made from the first tree purposely felled in the valley that would become known as Ashton, exits through the same window as the dog and chicken.

Sheriff Conneley and Deputies Arnold and Marley stand deep in the heart of The Motel, in the original room—the Big Bang singularity from which The Motel was brought forth. Very rustic, yet smooth. Rough-sawn knotty pine, through generations of traffic, has been polished to the texture of oiled driftwood. There are no exterior windows, but the room is surprisingly well lit; nearly the whole ceiling is covered with enormous lamps. The hippie on hand—Sparrow, he calls himself—explains that this is a congregation room, a sort of stage. A room where they come to … to recite poems and perform music, deliver skits, and stuff like that. Hippie Sparrow explains that this is what the lights are for.

The sheriff kicks at the oiled driftwood floor, glances again at the speaker set high in the corner of the ceiling, then interrupts Hippie Sparrow's description of *Gone with the Wind* and other stuff like that that they perform in this room. He points at the speaker: "Can you turn that off, son … so we can hear better?" If the sheriff likes a song by the The Monkees, it's not "Pleasant Valley Sunday."

"Humn … yeah … no, can't," Sparrow answers thoughtfully.

The sheriff forces a pleasant face. "How about turning it *down*, then?"

"No, *can't*, Sheriff. It's just a speaker. You can't turn down a speaker. I mean, it turns itself down sometimes, but it's just a speaker, and, well, who knows where…" Sparrow's broad wave points to a conceptual star in The Motel cosmos. "… where the—"

"Arnold, climb up there and see if you can disconnect a wire or something. Can't talk under this racket."

"Sure thing, Sheriff. I got a pocketknife right here."

"No, dammit, don't…" The Sheriff is watching his deputy mount an old wicker chair. "Don't *cut* it. Just see if you can pull a wire out, disconnect it or something."

"Sure thing, Sheriff."

The sheriff attempts, awkwardly, to form a question about … about atriums. "You kids have anything like that around here?"

Sparrow first thinks that the sheriff is asking about some kind of glass box. "Not for fish—I know that, man—but you mean for lizards or something like that?"

"No, son, not for liz—"

Everyone stops for a moment to watch Deputy Arnold, foot now through the chair he tried to mount, as he squeals and tries to hop away from the wicker-toothed animal that has seized his leg. Sparrow finds this enormously funny, laughing like a fourth grader until the deputy has finally freed himself.

Then the young man's face changes into an expression of confusion. "But why are you asking about lizards, Sheriff? What does that have to with Breeze?"

Pachink pachinK pachiNK pachINK …

A girl dressed like Pocahontas—except for the gypsy bells on her ankles and the large oven mitts on her hands—skids to a halt as she reaches the room. Several of the freshly baked cookies on her tray slide off onto the floor. Scared look. She turns and *PAChink PAChink PAchink Pachink pachink* scampers down another passageway.

One police dog. Then two more. They slide into the room over the oiled driftwood floor, scoop up the fallen cookie pucks as they make the turn, and skate down the hallway after the girl in oven mitts.

Pillow Room

"In there?" Deputy Marley steps forward to come between Sparrow and Arnold, pointing through what might be a hall, closet, or pantry. "That's the room you call the Pillow Room?"

"Yeah, man, that's the Pillow Room."

A couple of the police dogs have evidently fallen sick; they're behaving strangely, at least. Marley was happy to see the sheriff run off to check on that, and he would like to have ditched Arnold as well. But at least instead of searching The Motel for some kind of atrium with furrows of marijuana plants—or whatever indoor garden the sheriff is expecting to find—now Marley is back at the crime scene … the crime scene that was in fact only scantly examined the night before.

"In the statements, several of you—"

"We call it that because of all the pillows." Sparrow giggles. "See all those pillows, man? Isn't that crazy?"

Marley nods to show he acknowledges the many pillows. "In the statements that several of you gave, you said the only way in or out of this bedroom is through that room, the Pillow Room— is that right?"

Sparrow looks like he has been asked a chemistry question. His nod is round. "Yeah, man … I think."

"You're not sure?"

"No. I mean … I mean, how would I know what everybody else said in their statement, man?"

"That's correct," says a new hippie who has just arrived, apparently to help out.

Vertically striped pants with bell-bottoms, a purple paisley shirt, a stovepipe hat with plastic flower, ample donkey beads— the new arrival is exuberantly dressed. Marley examines a patch on the man's pants. It is not sewn on at a spot where one would expect much wear.

Marley turns back to Sparrow. "There's this connecting room," he points, "and the bathroom. Any other egresses?"

"… Eager what?" Sparrow asks.

"Egresses, exits; no other doors or windows?"

"That's right, Deputy; the Pillow Room's the only way in or out," says the stovepipe-hat hippie. Marley hears this but does not turn; he continues looking at Sparrow.

"Oh, you mean windows too? Yeah, the bathroom has a window in it," says Sparrow. But his confidence immediately erodes, his eyes rolling inward to think about this more deeply.

Marley enters the bathroom. The small window rises with difficulty. Through the window, he sees that a cinder block wall is only inches away on the other side. He lowers the window, steps back into the room with the others.

"The only egress is through the Pillow Room," Arnold agrees.

"Is that true? There is no other way in or out of this bedroom?" Marley watches Sparrow carefully and notes a slight hesitation. The boy's eyes trace the gaps between the floorboards, then tap the ceiling—one skylight, then the other —scanning, evidently, for egresses, whatever and wherever they may be. He seems unaccustomed to providing rigorous responses.

"Jig and Bunny were in the Pillow Room the whole night," adds Stovepipe, again without solicitation. "They could tell you who came in and out of the room."

Marley turns. "What is your name?"

"Martin. Kevin Martin, sir."

Sparrow laughs as he turns and looks at his Motel-mate. "Kevin? Your real name is Kevin?"

"So, what's your..." Marley can't quickly find the word. "What's your nickname?"

"Ken Doll!" blurts Sparrow. "His name is Ken Doll." Sparrow's laugh suggests his knowledge of the origin story of this name.

Marley turns toward Kevin Martin. Ken Doll. "Are you saying that last night at the approximate time of the murder in this bedroom, there were two people right out there in the Pillow Room?"

"Eight called you that." Sparrow's initial laughter has only increased. "Said you were as smooth as a Ken doll." He points at Kevin's groin, giggling like a cartoon chipmunk. "He meant down there."

Marley turns toward Sparrow, pauses. "Is the 'Eight' you are referring to William Yawn? A negro."

"I don't know his real name. But yeah, he's black as can be, man. That's why he's called Eightball."

"He lives here?"

"We wish he still did. But he's on the run now. He's a really cool cat. It's not fair. They framed him for that Black Panther stuff, man."

Marley nods. He is aware of the charges against Yawn. He turns back to Kevin Martin and repeats his question.

"Yes, sir," says Martin, "Jig and Bunny. They were in the Pillow Room all night. That's, you know, what they told me, anyway."

Marley stares at Martin. Stovepipe. Kevin. Ken Doll.

Martin sees this. "Well, okay, if Jig and Bunny gave you a different statement last night, it's probably because they were..." Martin smirks at Marley. "... out of sorts, you know what I mean, man?"

Marley hears this as he again examines Martin's apparel: a carefully curated collection specifically targeting an unspecific style. He decides that the only thing separating this getup from a costume is the slightly deeper investment in the man's handlebar mustache.

"How long have you been living here in The Motel?"

Martin rocks his head. "Ah, you know, hard to say. Been coming and going."

Sparrow frowns and looks at Ken Doll. "What do you mean? You barely just got here, man." He turns to the deputies. "He just got here. Like, not even two months ago. Me, me, I've been living here since I was sixteen!" Sparrow's proud face indicates that, whatever his scant age now, he considers it to be much older than sixteen.

Simian Suspension

There is something cautious and simian in the way Sheriff Conneley measures his suspension on the hollow floor of the strange little room he has entered. Deputy Arnold climbs up the metal step and packs in behind the sheriff. Sparrow is just a foot ahead of these two. They're all packed in under the low ceiling. Sparrow said he thought Jig and Bunny might be in their "cubbyhole," and this indeed seems to be the case. As Marley leans his head through the doorway, he can see the couple lying in a cushioned alcove in front of a black-and-white television that does its best to broadcast colorful cartoons.

Jig and Bunny raise their heads in slack-jawed surprise at the crowd suddenly inside their cubbyhole with them.

This would be the moment to get the most revealing statements from this young couple. If the sheriff had not rejoined them and insisted on taking the lead again, this is exactly what Deputy Marley would be doing right now. Instead, Jig and Bunny are given precious minutes to prepare their response, as the sheriff remains more fascinated with this structure than with the murder investigation. He touches the laminated wood of the countertop, then the edge of the tiny kitchenette sink that has obviously not seen water in years. His knees bend in slight squats as he discovers he can make the whole cubbyhole move. There is indeed a curious texture in the way the "travel" has been so thoroughly removed from this once travel trailer—something outstanding in the way the metal camper has become organically absorbed into the deep interior of The Motel.

Marley climbs up the step and into the trailer. He stands packed behind Sparrow and Arnold and the sheriff. Jig and

Bunny do not try to get up from the bed alcove at the end of the trailer; there would be no place for them to stand. The sheriff places his palm on an upper cabinet as he begins to ask Jig and Bunny questions. Marley lowers his head to peer under the sheriff's arm. He needs to see the couple's faces as they respond.

"Okay, man. Sheriff," says Jig, "Bunny and me, we were in the Pillow Room last night, okay? But so what? Is that a crime?"

"We're not investigating you two," Marley interrupts. He wants this to be clear—but he is speaking from under the sheriff's armpit. "We just want to know what you heard or saw last night."

Bunny, who has quietly pulled the bedding up to her nose, looks relieved. "It was just Breeze and Forward in there," she offers. "They took some burritos in there and shut the door."

"Yeah, Maldito Burrito burritos, man," says Jig. "We saw the bag. Has that Mexican man on it with the moustache."

Bunny giggles. "We wanted some of those burritos so bad."

"So bad! But Forward and Breeze, they wouldn't share, man."

"They probably only had two," says Bunny.

"They still should've shared, man."

"Easy for you to say, Jig," Sparrow interjects. "You're all about sharing because you never have anything to share, man."

"I do too; you borrowed my bike, man. Don't you remember?"

"Alright, alright, kids," says the sheriff, nodding and seeming done here. "This Forward fella—he was the only one in there, in that bedroom with the girl, is what you're saying."

"Yeah. I mean, until later, when he ran out."

Marley pushes his low head forward. "He ran out of the bedroom?"

"Yeah, he was freaked out."

"Freaked out. Uh-huh," the sheriff summarizes. He tries to turn around, but Marley is right behind him.

"Some furniture in the bedroom is broken," says Marley.

"Do either of you know when that happened?"

Bunny sits up. "Yeah, we heard it."

Jig looks at Bunny, then at Marley, as much as possible. "Oh yeah, I remember now too. They were screaming, man. And breaking things."

"Let me get this straight—write this down, Arnold." The sheriff's arm is raised above his head, his palm pressed against the low ceiling. "You're saying you two heard the Forward fella and the Breeze girl in that bedroom having a fight?"

"A fight? I don't know about that, man," says Jig.

"Yeah, no" Bunny agrees, nodding off the misunderstanding. "You can't really tell when people are in a fight … you know what I mean?"

"Fair enough," says the sheriff with a chuckle. He begins to back up, such that Marley must also back up. "The two were all alone in that room together, in there breaking furniture and screaming," he turns to leave, "but who's to say if they were in a fight? … You two have a lovely day now, you hear?" The sheriff, and consequently Marley, back out the door of the trailer.

Higher Than The Treetops

Middle of the night, high in the sequoia. No moon, but the tiny lights from the many stars, the pinholes in the celestial blanket separating Earth from white Heaven, are brighter—brighter than they can be when they share the sky with the moon.

Forward is rested now. Wide awake. He will sleep no more.

He rolls up to the edge of the nest, sets his elbows on the little platform—the lip, the flange of sticks where he once stood naked and was scrubbed by an angel, the place high above a hell where gargoyles howled Hendrix—and lowers his chin onto his forearms. He wears a poncho, a cotton poncho. It's a little small. Well, maybe it's a little small; Forward doesn't really know his poncho size.

The lunch box and the thermos rest by the bed, on the flange of sticks. More neatly than he left them.

He opens the thermos. It has been refilled with tea. And in the lunch box is another peanut butter sandwich and a cookie. But it's carrots this time instead of celery. He eats the cookie first. Then the sandwich. He shuts the lunch box and fills the Flintstones thermos cup with tea. He takes sips, his elbow on the stick platform, the flange. He looks out from the treetop. He looks up at the stars, far below at the town of Ashton, outward toward the forested mountainscape. The breeze is softer now, gentle; it hardly makes a sound. He drinks his tea with the Flintstones, wonders why he ever expected Heaven would be higher than the treetops … and then, despite another of his expectations, he falls back asleep.

Valentine From God

Deputy David Marley parks his patrol car under the late neon light. The light from a big, bright sign. A big, bright sign on a tall, fat post. Big, bright, tall, fat … and pretty pink. Busy and blinking. Seeming to change. But really just repeating itself. Flagrantly repeating itself. Flagrantly pink, flagrantly repeating itself. Flagrantly pink and repeating itself. It's a Valentine from our Roman god, the swirling glass tube excreted from the tip of his calligraphic pen. He wants to tell the world about the shakes and hamburgers in the diner below, but some of his words stumble through dim flickers, dither, even pause… It's late, and part of God's message is nodding off.

Marley takes off his badge. Sets it on the seat beside him. Then his belt, the whole package of gun and cuffs. Sets it on the seat beside him. The pink light on his hood, on the dash, on the windshield, and in his eyes… As it flickers, does it change everywhere at the same time? Or are his eyes just too slow to see where it starts and where it ends?

He pauses, then unbuttons his shirt.

The cool night breeze greets Marley as he opens the car door. It peeks up the little sleeves of his cotton V-neck, wiggles into the low collar, hunts for tiny tickle passages to belly button lint, softly forested nape, and other giggly places where it maybe can —

Marley stands up, straightens his pants, and tucks his T-shirt in, then bends over and picks up the things on his car seat. He carries them around to the back of his car and opens the trunk. Sets the items inside.

It's Cupid on the sign above. Marley can see this better from out here. The diner is named Cupid's. That's Cupid up there. Cupid the cherub archer, custodian of love affairs. Naked, but always in some Egyptian pose that keeps his own position on the love line a mystery. Who does Cupid love?

Marley's chest spasms, but not much. And probably just once. Nothing that could be seen from the outside. Not recognizable as a laugh, not even with medical equipment. Just an inefficient pause, a frivolous flirt with some passing irony. Cupid is up there on the sign. It's sort of his sign—Cupid's sign. And yet Cupid is the only one in the dark. He's the only one merely painted on —painted on by the persistent shadow of his own tube when it used to shine, compressed into the cold and dark that a star becomes once its radiance can no longer hold back the universe. Cupid's tube is burned out.

But the angel baby can still be seen by the light of the rest of his message. His flexed bow, though it too is a dark tube, shoots an arrow of pink light that arcs across the sign to lodge in a glowing hamburger—a glowing hamburger embedded in a pulpy heart. It does this repeatedly. Poor Cupid; his eyes don't have the relief of seeing where his arrow lands, so the chubby cherub just keeps shooting more.

Marley closes the trunk and walks across the parking lot. There's a strip of gravel where the pavement is being replaced. He crosses the gravel strip and opens the diner door unharmed.

" 'Boo Boo'? As in a child's injury?" Marley asks, finding himself seated in a booth. He doesn't remember his steps from the door—only his reason for being here, his need to talk with the woman now before him. He has important questions to ask her, but he starts with this one.

"No, Deputy," says the waitress, glancing down at the name tag in question, then at the place where the deputy's name tag would be, if he were wearing his shirt. "As in the conscience of Yogi Bear." She rolls her eyes, maybe resetting their conversation to the minimum required. "I'll be back to take your order. I got toast up."

Marley watches the orb of coffee as it accelerates away from his booth. His folded hands have turned into upward-facing palms under the menu laid across them, and he looks around the empty diner—toward the counter, toward the jukebox, toward the restrooms, back toward the jukebox—somehow urgently needing to discover whether waitress Boo Boo really has toast up.

Marley very much needs to talk with this woman. But she probably doesn't need to talk with him. So, he must have the right approach. And he is aware of his persona—the intensity of his *schwein-blau* eyes, how they can melt a person into a puddle. Not a warm, gregarious puddle, ready to share information, but a puddle beaded up on itself, trembling in its tightly drawn meniscus and wishing for him to go away. Marley is aware of what others see when they see him. He is aware of his mutilated head.

He shifts now in his booth to turn his back toward the waitress and the restaurant. He looks through the glass at Cupid before him, then lowers his eyes to the menu.

"Do you know what you want?"

Marley turns, startled, not expecting her back so soon. "A Reuben, please," he responds, with no memory of choosing this from the menu.

The waitress lowers her pen for a quick sword fight with the pad, then she accelerates away.

Marley turns back to his skyward palms. He lowers the menu onto the table.

"Here you go, enjoy," says the waitress, setting the sandwich onto the table in front of him and turning to leave.

Marley is startled once again. It seems that the sandwich must have already been prepared and waiting when he walked in. Maybe it was in her apron. But it's also possible that it was prepared in precisely the typical amount of time. He has been awake fifty hours ... fifty hours of frost and rage forming deep in his back room, blurring even his understanding of time and space.

"Miss? Please. Please." He sees her stop. "Could I ask you just a couple of questions? It's very important."

Waitress Boo Boo was walking away. Then she stopped. She turns now, considering this request. She pulls a pack of cigarettes and a lighter out of her apron. "About Breeze, you mean."

"Yes."

"Why ask me?"

"You live in The Motel. Where she lived."

"Me and about two hundred others."

Marley watches the waitress's face, the mistrust as she turns again away from him. "Wait," he says, "please don't go."

She turns back.

He nods toward the counter, the stool close to the cash register. "She used to sit up there. You two seemed like friends."

One of the waitress's eyes almost close. Not the other. "You've been watching us?"

Marley nods.

"How come we never saw you back? What are you, some kind of stalker?"

"Do you know of anybody who would have wanted to harm Sarah—Breeze?"

"Seems like the sheriff already has the suspect he wants." Her response is very quick, aggressive.

"Yes. He does."

The mistrust on the waitress's face begins to melt. "But you don't?" she says without inflexion.

"I'm investigating the murder."

The waitress puts the cigarettes and lighter back into her apron and slides into the other side of the booth. She examines his forehead, a cringe forming from her frown. "So, what happened to your face?"

"Vietnam."

"You were hit with a shovel or something?"

"Rifle butt."

Boo Boo nods, seeming to find the description plausible. "Rifle butt. Alright. And how about that?" She points with her lips. "Your tooth. Also the rifle butt?"

One of Marley's front teeth is much more than chipped; half of it is broken off. He knows his broken tooth has distracted many, but Boo Boo is the very first person to ever ask about it. "No," he says. "A toilet hit it."

"A toilet hit your tooth?" The waitress laughs. "I'll let you put it that way, if you want."

Marley feels a spasm in his chest. Short, then gone. He knows that his phrasing is in fact more accurate than what the waitress thinks she understands; she is not prepared to accept that it could be the toilet that was in motion. He wonders for a moment how close he comes to lying by not correcting her on this. Then he just listens to her laughter.

"And, um..." She finally gestures with her lips toward the large discolored blotch, scarred and hairless, on the top of his head.

"Napalm."

"What?" She cringes. "Like friendly fire?"

The blue cone at the base of the torch in each of his eyes softens, representing a laugh that cannot be released by other means. "I'll let you put it that way, if you want."

"Sort of an oxymoron." The waitress aligns her eyes with his. "Like 'military intelligence.'" She shifts her gaze back to the top of his head. "Do you, ahm, think your hair will ever grow back?"

"It would have by now, if it was going to."

"I like..." Her mouth becomes small and boxy for a moment, revealing her simultaneous curiosity and disgust. "... I like how you don't try to comb your hair over it." She blows smoke through her nose as she laughs. Her eyes shift back to his, and her face turns sad. "No, Deputy; I don't know anybody who would have wanted to hurt Breeze. Least of all Forward."

Marley hadn't noticed the waitress lighting the cigarette. "Do you know how long Forward has been living at The Motel?"

"Probably about six weeks." Boo Boo squishes her cigarette butt into the ashtray. She somehow smoked the whole thing with uncanny quickness. She glances toward his car in the parking lot—specifically toward the trunk, where he put his shirt, badge, and gun belt. "All the deputies come in here, but I haven't seen you before. How long have *you* been in town?"

Marley pauses. "About six weeks."

"Both six weeks. Hmm, a synchronicity. Maybe you and Forward came here for the same reason."

Marley pauses again. He is deliriously tired and questions what he is hearing. The synchronicities, coincidences he has experienced with Forward are so much deeper than the waitress could possibly know. "What do you mean, miss?" he asks.

"Oh, back to 'miss.' " She grins. "Thought you were a pig I could dig."

"Pig? Dig...?"

Boo Boo laughs. She is sort of awful and sort of lovely. "A 'pig' is a cop, and 'dig' means 'like.' But you already know that."

Marley nods. He processes the coincidence of their arrivals further. He knows he hasn't seen Walker since Vietnam. He knows he came to Ashton because he was worried about his sister. He came when he heard of the secret plans of his former employer to attack The Motel in Ashton California—where his little sister lived.

It seemed the flagship commune of the counterculture movement was turning out to be too harmonious for comfort for some special interest groups, and so they were planning on bringing it down. His former employer intends to break The Motel's harmony. Send it out of tune. Make an example of it. Marley didn't know Walker was also there. He didn't know Walker had been seeing his sister. He turns toward the waitress. "Just because we came to town at the same time, you think there could be a common reason?"

As she scans his face, unafraid, Boo Boo the waitress seems to somehow intuit that this sheriff's deputy and Forward the hippie are not strangers. "I mean just what I said." She slides out of the booth. "I'll bring you some berry pie. We have lemon too, but it's from yesterday."

Marley watches the woman go, then looks down at the plate

missing a sandwich he cannot recall eating.

PRESENCE

Pink Octopus

It is moments before David Marley will awaken in a Viet Cong pigpen to find a man trying to lick his forehead. Major Marley is unconscious. But to suppose that in this state he has no perspective, no point of view, no awareness, no recollection, would be incorrect. In this tempest between conscious states, while snow glitter is still suspended in his little globe, he is also not quite dreaming. The events he is experiencing on the inside of the eyeholes of his face have indeed happened. As he recollects them here in his meta-conscious state, they're just strung together with a strange efficiency, a weird proximity lacking intermissions or buffers, an uncanny groupiness similar to the way fish behave when they're strung together on the same stringer.

Marley sits in a chair, uncomfortably, in the Pink Octopus, a coffee shop in the Haight. All kinds of attic crap hang from the ceiling and walls, none of it utilitarian, or even decorative—just a curio explosion freeze-framed in midair. Dirty wallflowers from Goodwill, they're here now, stupidly suspended to form a reefy habitat for pink plastic octopi of various sizes, styles, and constructions. The spineless fish are everywhere, some of them dirty, most of them plastic, all of them pink.

This table in the corner is David's usual spot—the usual spot where he sits uncomfortably. He's in the corner, behind the fish tank. This is where his little sister sits him: in the corner, behind the fish tank.

74

The fish tank doesn't hold any water, and David can see through it. He can see his sister on the other side as she incrementally declines going to high school so that she can serve the beatniks—"hipsters," as they're called now. Hippies, flower children, beautiful people. They dress like Tarzan, wear their hair like Jane, and smell like Cheetah. The hygiene of an enlightened society. They've rejected hygiene, traditional responsibility, and attachment to material objects ... all so they can focus on brotherly love. Their mission is brotherly love. They're all about brotherly love. But none of that brotherly love reaches David in his spot behind the fish tank.

The bottom of the tank is lined with plastic rubble: three-wheeled cars, dog-chewed soldiers, a Barbie amputee with a haircut. The kind of stuff that Goodwill shovels into a dumpster. At the center of the tank, above the rubble, a pink octopus is suspended in an action pose. Compared to the soldiers, the octopus is disproportionately large; David has to look around the octopus to see his sister on the other side. The action-pose octopus is right on the other side of the glass, right in front of his head. The size and orientation of the octopus indicate that it wants to attach itself to his face, line its beaked butthole up with the partition between his nostrils, and clamp on. It's a pink mask that wants to attach itself to his face to keep him from watching his sister serve dirty hippies on the other side of the dry tank of Goodwill rubble.

One of the hippies has called Marley's sister over to his table now. Something's cold. Well, not cold ... but it could be, you know, a little warmer, man. Marley stirs in his chair, moves his face around on his side of the fish tank; he wants to move the octopus aside, so he can hate the hippie properly. But the invertebrate is protected by glass.

"No, Davey, it's not trying to clamp itself onto your face. That's just how the octopus looks when it's swimming away from you. You see that? Even the toy octopus doesn't want to be around you."

David hears these statements in his sister's voice. She's the only one in his head who refers to him in the second person.

"Sarah?" David stands up to call over the tank. He wants to know if his sister has a break coming up, if she'd be able to take a quick walk outside maybe. There's a dress he saw in a store window down the street … or something like that. He has something he has to tell her. He will be leaving to work in Saigon for a while. "Sarah?" he calls again.

She walks by carrying two plates of fries, and rolls her eyes without flinching, without responding. Her name is Breeze now.

David passes his eyes over his table, the fish tank, then leaves a deck of money beside his untouched pastrami. He exits the Pink Octopus, somehow stepping right out onto the trampled brown grass of the Golden Gate Park pan handle. The hippie from the Pink Octopus, the hippie with the cool plate, is already out there. With Sarah.

David walks stiffly through the crowd of dirty kids. Fifteen or twenty thousand of them, assembled like horny walruses on a sea rock. Fifteen thousand, maybe twenty, sweating and smiling all over each other—a pretentious community of kids with their tongues and fingers all over the frosting of love, and no regard for the baked cake that has always held everything up. And awful music. Loud, awful music. David knows the name of the band; he has encountered it before in other places where he has spied on his sister.

The hippies are moving. They call it "dancing." Too lazy to coordinate any of the motions, too lazy to cooperate in any respectful way with a partner, too lazy to add any kind of discipline to their art. Too lazy and doped up to add discipline to anything they do. Here in the rookery—a Be-In, they call it— they fondle each other and even copulate right in the open, right amongst each other, just as the walruses do.

"Sarah!"

David knows this is a mistake. Already, the hippies are turning to look. Already, Breeze is observing her friends observe her brother. Already, Breeze's hand is falling from the hair of the cool-plate hippie. Already, the hippie is releasing his clutch on the ass of Breeze.

David backs out of the Be-In. He ignores the circus around him. His eyes, too dejected for tears, are sewed onto his little sister. He seems to stand in one place as the whole Be-In moves like a giant river around him, carrying his sister further and further away from him. The banks and the shore and the trees and the sky, San Francisco, they all get sucked up and taken with it, everything moving downstream and far away.

Then, rushing in to override the feeling of shattered glass in his heart, comes a tropical breeze. It climbs over the gunnels of the Jeep in which he is suddenly a passenger. Below, a tarmac becomes road. Beside him, a man without uniform describes the experimental program Marley has been called here to take over. Behind him, everything has paused.

After an unmetered drive through suburb and jungle, the flat windshield of the Jeep suddenly melts into a sequence of interior windows showing thin prisoners being subjected to chemical experimentation and torture. One is crying inconsolably. One is screaming and smashing his fists on the glass. One is babbling without commas or periods. One is bleeding through cuts from a straight razor he holds in his hand. As if moving between the habitats in a natural history museum, Marley is ushered along the row of windows by the man without uniform. On the man's face is a signature of pride in the advances being made here toward the weaponization of high-grade hallucinogenic drugs.

"We have a rage-out mixture that makes PCP look like a third cup of coffee," says the man as they get back in the Jeep. The man cranks the wide, weatherproof steering wheel around a turn, showing little concern for the road repair workers, who drop their tools to scatter. "A perfect assassination is a suicide. And we can already do that, pretty much. But," he winks, "it's not always easy to get the drug into the target. Usually need a man on the inside who's close. But then you got the concern of that asset getting left behind. Brings you back to thinking that really what you want to design in the drug is more a murder-suicide," he explains.

The Jeep has parked. They are in the city.

"Here," the man nods at a three-story building, "here we're trying a whole different approach." They pass through a bicycle repair shop to reach a locked door in the back. The man presses a button on the wall. A buzzer releases the lock. "As you know, the reason for this program isn't really our enemies abroad, but our enemies at home." He winks. "We gotta get those communist longhairs under control, right Major? That anti-war crap they're doing is costing our sponsors a lot of money!"

The man continues to speak as he leads Marley up a narrow staircase. "Sure, we got all the VC prisoners we want that we test whatever we want on. Hell, already we can get them to cut up their cellmate and then swallow the razorblade." He laughs, stops at the middle of the flight of stairs, turns and winks. "But that still doesn't tell us how to control the beatniks back home. They're a different subject all together. Drugs affect them differently, Major. Seems they meet a different animal spirit than our prisoners in a cage do."

The man continues up the stairs. "We need hippies. But experimenting on them back home gets tricky—I'm sure you heard about the scandal with the Johns in Frisco." He laughs. "So now we just find the hippies back home and draft them. Bring them over here for the tests. Smart thing about this operation here is we don't even need to put them in a cage. Just supply the drugs and free-love pussy, and they'll walk right on in here on their own. Voluntarily." At the top of the stairs, the man finally smiles. "Here in Vietnam, we got our hippies from home performing the drug experiments on themselves, Major. Can't get more scientific than that." He rings a desk bell, even though the man he intends to call is already hobbling this way. "Now we just sit back and watch through the glass."

"Sorry, *désolé*." The thin man says this as he leads the two men around a mop bucket and down a hall. The man without uniform informs Major Marley that this man leading them, currently around a splotch of vomit on the floor, is Mr. Phong. They climb another flight of stairs. Mr. Phong looks at the giant watch on his arm. "Shoo, whisper." He holds a finger to his mouth, then turns to take a tray of tea from a teenage girl in the lobby of the brothel they have entered. He inserts napkins between the saucers and the cups and offers the tea to his guests.

"Oh, thanks. Maybe later," the man without uniform responds, then turns toward Marley. "Phong here's been running the house. I'll let him give you the tour and catch up with you later." The man without uniform winks, then moves to follow the young girl with the tea tray down the service hall.

Closed inside the dark closet with Mr. Phong, Major Marley holds his teacup. The closet is small and narrow with a pane of glass on each side, one of which is currently covered by a curtain. Marley's eyes haven't adjusted, and he can't see well through the one-way mirror. But he can hear.

"When you poow out?" Giggle, giggle. "Tell me when you poow out."

"I can't tell you things like that, man. But you can bite my ear."

"I want. Tell me. When you poow out?" Giggle, giggle.

Marley can now see the shadowy figures on the bed.

"Tell me when you poow out," she repeats. "Or no more." Giggle. "No more."

"I don't think I'm pulling out for a while. Don't worry. I'll be back next week."

"No. No next week. Next week, period."

"Period? Sweetie, I'm a soldier; you think I haven't already earned my red wings?"

" 'Red wing'?"

"Yeah, man, red wings. You never heard of that?" The young man laughs and pulls his head away from the pillow, away from the head of the bed, away from the wall mirror above the head of the bed, away from the teacup and napkined saucer just feet away in the spy closet on the other side of the one-way wall mirror.

Slurp slurp slurp. "Next week, Sweetie." *Slurp slurp slurp.*

The woman moans. She slaps her head against the pillow.

"Next week." *Slurp slurp slurp.*

Moan moan moan.

"Next week, be ready. We'll get so high and twisted up, we'll make this sheet look like a barber pole."

Giggle, moan, slurp.

Major Marley feels warm, moist tea on the napkin under his thumb.

"This one finish," whispers Mr. Phong as he very quietly pulls a curtain down over the window. *"Fini."* He slowly moves the cloth to cover every inch of the window. He points to the curtain, explains what he's doing and why. He's proud to include these details, proud to whisper the careful steps required to control backlighting. And then he begins to raise the curtain on the other side of the narrow closet.

As if on cue, a slow rhythm begins that seems to involve the whole building. *Ree ruur, ree ruur, ree ruur...* Back and forth. And the sound—*pat, pat, pat*—of a headboard as it gently kisses the wall. The momentum of the bed on the other side of the curtain seems to be under precise control, the headboard never missing the wall, yet never more than gently tapping it.

Ree ruur, ree ruur, ree ruur, pat pat pat... Periodic and slow.

Milky light from the room inserts its soft tentacles through the glass and helps Mr. Phong open the closet curtain.

Ree ruur, ree ruur, ree ruur, pat pat pat...

Major Marley is becoming lost, and without having found a place to set down his damp saucer. The two bodies on the other side of the glass form a single organism that floats over the pillows less than a yard away, appendages sweeping the glass as delicately as the headboard kisses the wall, as it pulses in an opening-and-closing manner.

"Slow man." Mr. Phong laughs in a whisper. "He real slow."

Major Marley doesn't hear Mr. Phong; Marley's on the other side of the glass now, pulled through the mirror by the tentacles of the sexing couple. His eyes are transfixed by the soft center of mass, where the animal's two opposite colors twist into disorienting contrasts that hide the boundary between the animal and its environment and suggest that even this camouflage can be further hidden, if needed, in a sudden cloud of ink. The animal's tentacles collect the major, draw him in. The four legs move in coordination, opening slowly and then rapidly closing in a manner that propels the tangled body forward, forward a moment, before it is drawn back toward the headboard again by an unseen current.

More warm tea spills into Major Marley's saucer, and he is drawn further in, collected by the tentacles, mesmerized by the to-and-fro, gathered into the animal's hem, coming ever—

Gunfire.

Something is wrong.

The animal is disturbed.

Scared.

Maybe angry.

The soft rhythm is lost. Everything is tinted now in black ink. The creature's mood has instantly changed. The central sphincter of the black-and-yellow beast compresses in a pulse, then flies open to reveal a tongue and giant white teeth!

Major Marley screams, shrieks as he passes through the eyeholes of his own face to leave this recollected reality—and enter an even more absurd one staged in a Viet Cong pigpen.

Finally Mourning

There must be a point to this. A reason for everything. Through diligent observation; careful study; experience in love, life, and war; and a prominent history with psychedelic drugs, Forward has developed an understanding that everything that he experiences around him is—in its most fundamental, quintessential, nitty-gritty sense—part of his own movie, man.

But of all the parallel worlds, resplendent in their permutations, his movie presently has him in this one. This one is a world carrying a recent past with sharp edges. Every thought now, every feeling, sits in broken glass. This one is a world Forward would like to move quickly through, forward, forward, forward. On to the next.

But he can't. He is trapped high in the nest of a very tall tree. He couldn't climb down even if he thought he should. Looking down terrifies him, paralyzes him. Worse than simply falling from the sky, he would first be battered by the branches. Looking down through the tree, he imagines a pebble falling down the core of a Peruvian rain stick. Until someone comes to help, Forward will remain right here, his movie stalled. Stalled following a tragic scene he would like to outrun. The scene where he woke, after having passed out from the mind-exploding drug, to find the young girl in the bed next to him dead. Strangled.

Forward is quite sure he would have never wished Breeze harm ... in his right mind. He is also quite sure that when she died, he was not in his right mind.

His ability to maintain the view that reality is an illusion, part of his movie, has been contingent on his ability to keep the present always moving forward, forward, forward. Always three steps ahead of even the closest past. At the base of his philosophy is the belief that history can only find you in the places you both know about. Move forward.

But he can't. He is trapped, without the room to even pace. The initial distraction and disorientation of finding himself perched high in the sky has worn off, and the peanuts under him have turned to glass shards. This part of his movie seems to be all about holding him down for a minute. Maybe to acknowledge his pain. Maybe there is something tremendously important he is supposed to see. Perhaps something awful he is supposed to discover about himself. If everything is his movie, could his movie allow scenes that include him strangling a girl with cute crooked teeth? A girl who regarded him with doe eyes as a counterculture mentor? A girl he most eagerly mentored on free love?

In another instance of his movie getting stalled, he was a prisoner of war, and the punishment for not adequately parsing the present was simply that his physical body would be ripped in two and thereby become two components of himself, one nut apiece, creating a new sense of sharing himself with two locations.

Everything happens for a reason ... including his lengthening stay in this strange predicament, confined to a high tree nest at the center of an expanded sky. This present threatens to dismember him not in space, but rather in time. A rip, and then two components, one nut apiece, living from then on at two separate locations on the timeline.

Now that Forward is finally mourning, the gargoyles are

more compelling than ever.

Silence In The Pigpen

The air in the pigpen is dank. The rainwater makes many sounds as it drips through the many gaps in the frond roof. These tiny sounds surely come from close by. But bigger sounds—sounds of distant airplanes and explosions—shake the earth and ether with less accountability.

"Well, if he ain't a pervert, then what was he doing coming out of that closet?"

"Well, ya know, Eight," says Edison, "just because he was in the closet doesn't make him a pervert. Don't ya forget the real purpose of the house, now."

"Shit, Ed. Phong and the house ain't really ever been about testing drugs," says Yawn. He turns toward Marley. "Testing whatever kinda shit they want on a bunch of 'G. I. Don't Know Joe's. Just so they can use it on us back home." He turns back. "Nah, all the brass really wants is a sex show. And Phong was giving it to them. Showing them all the cock and pussy they could ever want to see." Yawn and the other privates laugh. "They be back in their officer barrack, feel that gospel pipe go on between their legs, dick getting so hard a cat can't scratch it. Then they call over their driver. Gotta go check see how those drug weapons coming along."

As the privates laugh, they look toward the major.

"I don't think the officers just dropped by the house whenever," says Edison. "They had to call ahead first, so Phong could get the right show set up for them."

"Hell, yeah. Phong can't be having just any old 'G. I. Don't Know' show going on when the top brass come by." Yawn laughs. "Most of those young boys come in from the field, and they either drop their yogurt soon as they brush up against a girly leg, or Phong's syrup come down on them and they get all quiet and big-eyed, thinking about all the people they been shooting at out there in the paddies—people they don't even know. People they been killing. Phong ain't gonna send top brass into the closet with a box of tissues to go watch that kind of amateur shit."

"Nah," says Walker, shaking his head, "he's not a pervert, man. Look at him. At least he's not into the kinky sex-show shit we've been putting on for the other officers." The three privates look at the major. Walker squints. "Man, I think he's even a virgin."

Edison and Yawn quieten, pause. They observe the major more closely.

Yawn nods agreement.

"Huh," says Edison, coming to nod with Yawn. "But doesn't he seem a little old for that kind of nonsense? Ya'd think he'd have been at least curious by now or something."

"Boy real serious, hmh?" Yawn raises an eyebrow at Marley. "Wasn't looking at no titty through that glass at all, no, umh umh." Yawn's brow lowers as he leans forward to see the major better. "Or maybe he's still on that side of the big V because he's still sorting his own shit out. Discovering hisself and all that." Yawn leans forward further toward Marley, eyeing him closely as he continues to speak about Marley in the third person. "Maybe instead of titty, the major here was watching my orca ass up there in the glass."

The privates laugh.

"Watching it do its tricks. Thinking he's at SeaWorld or some shit."

"Nah, Eight," says Edison. "He wasn't there for SeaWorld, either. I took a long look at Phong's book. I think the major was brought in to be Phong's new boss."

The others stop, listen.

"Somebody got tired of seeing the program run more like an amusement park than a weapons lab." Edison looks toward Marley. "The major's here to fix that."

"Man," Walker says, now looking accusingly at Marley. "He's probably not going to need us around anymore. When we get back to Saigon, I mean."

"You mean *if*. *If* we get back," says Yawn. "You forgetting the enemy's got us chained up together in a pen with a pig."

"Oh, we'll make it back. You know that, Eight."

"You! You'll make it back! Heh! Sure know that. They could drop a nuclear bomb on us right here and now, and you come riding out of the mushroom cloud on a surfboard. Doing some hang-ten shit."

Edison is laughing too hard to speak. His nod indicates that he is in full agreement with Yawn's assessment of Forward's magical ability.

Forward grins. "Surfing serendipity, man. There's a way out of anything. You just got to feel it, channel it, let it happen. Hear the harmony and follow it."

"Surf the serendipity, hoo! Well, not even the most double-O-seven lucky motha can surf the serendipity like you do, Faw."

Walker's palms fan outward across the pigpen. "This is our movie. We're here for a reason, man. If you're worried," he laughs, turns toward Marley, and raises a chained ankle, "just stay close to me."

"Saya," says Edison. His face seems concerned. "If the major fixes it all up and gets back to using unwitting GI's, well, I guess they might finally get some real test results."

"Without us getting our crazy circus in to mess up the whole statistics."

"The show would be over without you stars." Edison laughs.

"You practically have your names on the marquee."

"Hoo-hoo! *Orca Eight!*"

"*Fucker Forward!*"

" 'Fuck-er Forward'?" Edison shakes his head. "Got to come up with something better than that."

"Hey, man, when are you going to climb up on the marquee with us, Ed?" asks Walker.

Ed smiles. "Happily married, thank you."

"Well, man, if you're never going to let yourself get into the yuck show with us, Phong should have stopped wasting a window on you. Can't have his guests watching you and Izzy play checkers."

Edison looks offended. "We do other stuff too, ya know."

"Tell me about the book," Marley says, his voice softer than previously.

The privates have been slow to notice that the major now looks worried. Very worried.

"The book you mentioned."

Edison turns toward the major. "You mean Phong's book?"

"Yes."

"Well, I don't know whether it's really a book. Sort of a calendar, or a planner, or a register or something. Whatever you call it, he wrote down which officers were coming, which day, their background, which show he's planning for them to watch —"

"Hoo! Yeah, bet old Phong had to be real careful figuring out which brass goes with which show. Can't have Colonel Sanders being eyed over by my angry black asshole up on the glass."

"And I'm guessing the colonel doesn't want to watch me play checkers, either."

"Or watch some kid drop his buckshot before he even gets his underwear off."

"Which leaves me." Forward laughs. "I'm the star, man!" He turns to Yawn. "I'm on top of you, my friend. On the marquee, I mean, man."

"Yeah, only as long as it's the chicken colonel coming. Then you the top star. But a whole lot of other guests don't want to watch you and Viro turning the space-time inside out, neither. With that nasty barber pole shit you two do. Uhm uhm."

"Show must go on, man. We give them what they want to see. Same as you and Claire with your octopus buttholes pushed up against the glass. You tell me which is grosser."

"THIS IS ABSURD!" Marley yells in frustration.

The men are suddenly quiet. They turn and look at Marley as though this is the first thing he has said that they respect, find helpful. As if they have been pulling him to this point.

This confuses the major.

The younger privates then look toward Edison.

Edison slowly nods, turns toward Marley, and speaks. "Yes, it is absurd, Major. That's why we're here."

Marley is further confused by this concession … or maybe it's a confession. Thankfully, it seems Edison will describe more, and so Marley is satisfied for now just to listen.

"*Absurd* means a few different things. At base, *ab-surdus* means 'out of tune.' And 'out of tune,' well, doesn't that sure describe the situation we get into all over the world?" Despite the fact that he sits on the ground, Edison's torso is professorial. He seems to pace behind a podium. "*Absurd* is certainly the situation right here, right now, wouldn't you say?" He laughs. "Well, I guess you just did say that."

The younger privates nod in a coherent manner that almost

inducts Marley into nodding too. In any case, all three now listen to Edison with straight backs.

"The Pythagorean Brotherhood created the word *katharsis* to mean 'a method for bringing things back into tune.' Things like the human body ... or the whole world. They viewed disease literally as the body out of tune—the body *ab surdus*. That could be a cell, the human body, or the whole planet. The Pythagoreans also created the word *harmony*. So, you can think of it this way: when things get absurd, a catharsis is needed to bring things back into harmony."

Edison observes Marley. "I think what the major has noticed is that even in our little local situation right here," he raises an ankle, "there's something definitely out of tune. And unless we want to chop some feet off, we're going to have to find a way to work together as a musical chord to bring back harmony. We are the katharsis, gentlemen. We need our one plus one plus one plus one to be more than four." Edison raises his palms skyward. "We need to think outside the box." His forearms lower into a choo-choo steam chug. "We need to let loose our zeppelins."

The other two privates are attentive, nodding. Marley is also attentive, almost nodding.

Edison pinches the corner of his mouth, tilts his head, then his index finger comes out. "But we probably don't have long before they read through Phong's book and discover what they caught: an intel officer. Probably already have. Maybe this strange way they have us chained together is already part of their interrogation. Get us working against each other. Maybe they think that a good way to break our solidarity is to force it on us. Gentlemen, we need to let our harmony happen!"

There is silence in the pigpen.

Washing The Riviera

Deputy David Marley sits at his desk—and not in the way one expects of a uniformed law enforcement officer. Uniformed law enforcement officers are aware that when they sit at an office desk, they look sort of … well, goofy. Like a reinforced receptionist or something. And so, they bring their feet up onto the desk corner. They hold the phone receiver with just an ear to their shoulder. They overstretch the phone cord. They speak loudly into the receiver and tap their pencils on the desk. They leave stale, half-eaten sandwiches around, and they push others to bring them coffee.

But Deputy Marley, despite the fact that his gun belt has landed in this stenographic setting, doesn't participate in this culture of compensation. His feet are planted on the floor, one alongside the other under the desk. Deputy Marley sits as a receptionist would sit, and he speaks quietly into the telephone. In fact, on this occasion, he has even waited until the others in the room went to lunch before placing his call.

"Miss Virginia Walker?"

"Abel. I'm Abel now. Walker's my maiden name."

Because of the unremarkable way he sits in his chair, Deputy Marley easily makes a note (Mrs. Abel) on a notepad on his desk. "Mrs. Abel, this is Deputy Marley with the sheriff's office of Ashton, California."

"Yes, I think I already talked with your office. How can I help you?"

"Thank you, ma'am. I just wanted to check a few things. Would that be okay?"

"Yes, that'd be fine."

"It'll be quick. Did you state that your brother is 'dangerous'?"

"Yes, he certainly is."

Marley is silent. He leaves the question still shining on Mrs. Abel.

"We had a falling out."

"..."

"A few years ago. He came to visit. I made the mistake of allowing him to take my young son out for the day. I haven't allowed my brother around my family since."

" 'Mistake'? Did Henry do something to your son?"

Mrs. Abel is silent for a second. "Yes, Deputy, he did."

"..."

"Nothing sexual or violent," she adds. "Just inappropriate."

There's silence on the phone again before Mrs. Abel explains, "My brother gave my son LSD, Deputy."

"LSD?"

"Ernest was only twelve then!" Mrs. Able finds that some of her anger has since softened into amusement; she almost laughs. "They washed my car ... the Riviera, Deputy."

"Henry and your son washed your car?"

"The Riviera."

"What was—"

"Seven times! Seven times, Deputy."

"Did—"

"I loaned Henry the Riviera because I didn't want him taking Ernest on the motorcycle. And did they go to the amusement park? No. Did they go to a baseball game? No. Did they go feed the ducks at the lake? No."

"When did—"

"They went to the car wash. The two of them. They climbed up under the back window and went through the car wash seven times, Deputy!"

"Did—"

"Seven times!"

"Di—"

"Is that even sane?"

"Yes. Or no, I mean."

"Who does that?"

"Thank you, Mrs. Abel."

Constructing Reality

Like life, reality begins at conception.

Among the living pine needles, hoisted up on this platform afloat in a cotton sky, and towering over the tiny lumber town far, far below, Forward is uncomfortable. One of his Indian-style folded legs is asleep. He pulls the leg out from under him and then sits differently, sort of on his knees and leaning to one side, his back straight and his arms up. The posture of a '50s bathing suit model on a beach towel. Not a more comfortable position, just a different position. Since the telescope arrived this morning, Forward has been looking through it, aiming it through the half sphere of solid angles that can be viewed from this high nest on the cliff of Quarter Horse. Then, for hours, focusing it intensely on the town along the river below.

The telescope must have arrived while he was asleep. On closer inspection, he discovered that it is really some kind of nature-photography camera. He is pretty sure that the squirrel girl is the only other person in this tree, so she must have brought it to him. But she comes only when he is asleep, and so he has still not completely met her. She seems to be avoiding him. The legs of the telescope's inverted tripod are tied to branches above the nest. Forward operates the telescope as one would a submarine periscope.

Ashton looks very different from up here. One of the things Forward can do from this new viewpoint is decide that the town below is so different, it is not really Ashton. A New Ashton. A New Ashton that does not include his own history in it.

In his first pass, Forward spent forty-five minutes tracing the Coulot River, from its most northern visible point, where it rounds the mountain, all the way through to its asymptotic exit on the southern horizon. He has seen logs floating in the river. He has seen laundry hanging near the banks. He has come to know which bridge is busiest. He saw a fisherman.

It was only during his second pass over the river that he sensed the asymmetry, and only in the third that he became consciously aware of it: the riverbanks at the south end of town hold more industrial buildings than do those on the north end. Once an internal voice could remark on the asymmetry, it became loudly apparent. *There are industrial buildings on the south end, but not on the north.* Others in Forward's position might take a moment to wonder how this wasn't more immediately apparent to them. But that is not a thought Forward has, because his conception of reality is different than most. For him, consciousness is primary, and the material world is an epiphenomenon—not the other way around, as is implicitly assumed in the Western sciences and religions. In his careful observation of this New Ashton, he is co-creating its parameters. He is making the movie by watching it.

Of course, Forward understands that his conscious center, his entity, his *self,* is just an eddy in a big river of consciousness manifesting not only this river town, but the whole universe as well. When, on the second pass of his telescope, industrial buildings began populating the southern end of town, it was not Forward deciding these buildings should be part of the movie; the buildings unfortunately appeared out of some sort of alignment with a reality he is trying to leave behind. Forward wants to change the movie.

In this new construction of Ashton, new pieces of the river and town appear in the telescope. Once seen, they do not disappear. And once seen multiple times, they develop explanations for their own existence—explanations securing them a stable role in the movie, the reality he co-creates with the collective consciousness. The objects seen reify their own reasons for being, their own logic. All those industrial buildings are on the south end of town because that's the downstream side. Forward's telescope climbs up from the riverbanks to find further confirmation: yes, all of the town's industrial buildings are indeed on the downstream side of town.

The reification of the riverside industrial buildings and a general understanding of flow prompts Forward's telescope to examine the relationship between these buildings and the river. He sees evidence that some of the buildings pour their waste into the river. It is clear now why the buildings have appeared where they do. As sure as every camper also pisses, it must have made much sense for the early planners of the town to have the biggest pissers camp downstream.

Forward pauses, offended for a moment by the behavior of the town he is creating. After all, the downstream side of Ashton is the upstream side of some other town. Man, to be fair to everybody, shouldn't it be the law or something that a town be required to camp its pissers on its own upstream side? What Forward is most certain about is that he wishes such laws existed for whatever towns are upstream of the New Ashton he is co-creating. It would instill such confidence in the New Ashtonites, once he has created them, to see their upstream neighbors drink from their own downstream side. Not a draconian law at all, he decides. No one is saying they can't pollute the river. They just have to drink the same water they send to the towns downstream.

Forward has deliberately set the telescope to its highest magnification level. He is creating the town from small pieces, assembling first the river, assigning even its invisible segments to a reality of continuity and slowly falling water. Then his telescope climbs the riverbank and begins to assemble the town. With his first discovery of a traffic light, he decides there must be a few more and creates these. There is no going back from what he creates. Once a traffic light has been imagined, it can't be removed; he can only create more. But even that has its limitations. An Ashton overpopulated with traffic lights would interfere with the reality attempting to assemble itself in neighboring towns, and Forward has decided that to create a world of good neighbors, the goings-on of towns should be coordinated. Their laws should be coordinated. Forward wants New Ashton's upstream neighbors, as a matter of law, to drink from their own downstream. Simply not putting piss in the river to begin with is a much cheaper alternative to trying to suck the piss back out later. In the good new world Forward wants to co-create, it's simply neighborly for towns to recognize this.

He is tracing Main Street when suddenly he sees Jesus. Jesus's giant hands are together in prayer, the nose on his downturned face nearly touching his mirrored thumbs in a compassionate and moreover just hugely sad expression. The religion Forward was raised with stopped making sense to him long ago, and yet there are elements of Jesus he has not been able to shake. Even the animal guides he conjures have carried traits of the man ... the son of God.

Forward suddenly gasps. The letters have been in view the whole time. But he wasn't looking at them—not at first. Once he realized Jesus was incomplete, the marquee cutting him off at the shoulders, he discovered that Jesus and his praying hands sit atop a church billboard, very tall and big.

But the words make no sense.

... Until they do. With a chill, Forward realizes that the words on the church sign do not have to do with Jesus. They do not have to do with New Ashton. Forward realizes that the words on the church sign of Jesus have to do with himself. They are a warning. To the girl in this tree. The marquee below the praying head and hands of the only son of God reads:

COULD BE A KILLER

UP THERE

BEWARE

Square Virgin

Major Marley is staring at the white sow sleeping in the corner of the pen. More accurately, his eyes are pointed in the direction of the pig to make his face less visible to the other men. He is unsettled, maybe scared.

He turns toward Private Edison. "You are sure they took Phong's book?"

"Yup. Saw them load it up into the truck. That, and some other stuff too."

Marley's breath is short. "In the book, there's a note that I'm intel?"

"Well," Edison qualifies, "some of it was in Vietnamese, and I don't read Vietnamese very well, and Phong was anyway quite a chicken-scratcher. But it wasn't hard to spot: the English words, 'coming. new program manger. philosophy Yale.'" Edison chuckles. "I'm pretty sure he meant 'manager' and not 'manger.'"

Marley pauses. "You said they took other stuff too?"

"Yep." Edison's lower lip closes over his upper lip as he nods. "I think they just took whatever looked important."

"What did you see them take?"

"Oh, papers, mostly." Edison recollects with a chuckle, "But I think I also saw a stapler, if you can believe it. They just piled all that in with Phong's syrup chest and loaded it into the truck with us."

"Syrup... The drugs, you mean?" asks Marley.

"Sure. Phong mixes up little cough syrup bottles."

"Yes, I know. Which drugs?"

"Oh my, who knows what all kinds of terrifying stuff he had in that chest. I guess you know more about that. You being the new program *manger*." Eight and Forward laugh. "Anyway, whichever syrup Phong was giving us, I'm sure he wasn't giving us the angry stuff. He had the show to think about and all."

Marley, who before today had never once shrieked, is not accustomed to fear; it's not in his personality type. But suspecting now that he will undergo interrogation by adversaries now in possession of a chest of weapons-grade experimental drugs, a new expression appears on his face.

The privates notice.

"Man. Man, oh, man. Look at him. He's scared," says Walker.

All pause. Edison leans over to see better. "Wow, you're sure right about that. My god, look at his shoulders! It's all over him. Pretty extreme." Edison turns then, confused. "There's something else. Forward, what are we missing about the major?"

"Oh, that's pretty easy, man. Look at his face."

The three privates look at the major's face.

"Not only is he a virgin, but he's also a square. That's what he's scared about."

"He's scared about being a square?"

"Yeah, man. I know it seems pretty weird—if he's supposed

to be the boss of the program—but I don't think the major really knows anything about drugs. He's a double virgin, man."

"Shee-it," says Yawn. His laugh sounds taunting and concerned. "Bet right now those gookas be backed up into their hut, thumbing through that chest of syrup bottles, trying to guess which one they should use to pop open this here bag of classified information. Probably won't even know how to dose him—give it to him like it was beer or something."

The privates are now less boisterous as they observe the listing major. Maybe they finally appreciate the consequence of their own chained connection to him. Maybe they are even concerned for the safety of the national security secrets held behind the major's rifle-butted forehead. Marley watches the privates silently, desperately, beggingly.

"Hell, those gookas ain't getting nothing. Major here's a patriot. Red, white, and blue, through and through."

"I don't know, Eight." Walker shakes his head with skepticism.

Edison leans toward Marley. "Saya, Major, that true? You never tried any drugs?"

In response to Edison's question, Marley's face gives a quick sideways shiver while his eyes remain still.

"Ooh. Okay." Edison combs his hair with his fingers. "Then how about when you get, say, really, really drunk? How do you get then?"

Another shiver.

"Ah. I see. Never been drunk, either." Edison backs up to the pen rails. "Ah, geez."

Walker leans in next. "Hey, man, Major, you're worried about the syrup, right? You don't know what it will do to you … if it will be like a truth serum or something."

Marley's mouth is a tight upside-down U, his eyebrows close together. He nods vertically.

"Damn, man." Forward frowns. Not the answer he evidently wanted to hear. "If we only had some of that syrup right now, we could at least take the initiative." He chuckles with the other privates as he looks at the major. "Send you through the multiverse to some place the enemy won't be able to find you, sir."

Sharp Edges

The sun is back. Quality of light: midmorning. It's a little overcast up here, barely below outer space. High cirrus clouds demand something from the sunlight; they tax and tangle the rays, then pass the mixed-up light down to catch like dryer lint in the needles of the trees. The fluffy light that hangs about is drawn from a palette of participation. Because, without the atmosphere, the sun's eight-minute-long rays would simply skewer the earth and hold it there to scorch like a campfire marshmallow. Planet Earth is alive.

… Forward has to go.

Number two.

Right now.

He has managed number one, bringing his pelvis to the nest edge, torso in backward counterbalance, fluttering his tinkle stream. But number two … number two is different.

Unfurling the stairs of his passage to Heaven, to descend back to Earth for a crap—this doesn't feel right. Or at least this is what Forward tells himself as he peeks over the nest edge, terrified … still completely terrified. The fear of falling is so basic in Forward that it remains impervious to his enlightenment. It is hard to tell himself that everything is an illusion, part of the movie he co-creates with the cosmic consciousness, when that movie could include him falling down through the tree—*baba baba baba ba*—like a pebble down the core of a rain stick.

Any descent—and certainly one from Heaven—is always scarier than the ascent. Forward is also pretty sure that in images he has seen or can imagine of escalators to Heaven, a downward escalator is never in view. Most importantly, he does not want to return to Earth—at least, not the Earth he last stood on.

Maybe he could call out—"Help!" or "Hey, man!" or something —and hope that his scrubbing-angel-turned-sandwich-provider will come to his assistance. But this doesn't feel right, either. He imagines his dopey little call poking through the tree breeze, picking its way through the branches, searching everywhere for her, almost in despair, and finally arriving in sniffles at her squirrel hole … where she would set down her peanut butter knife and come scampering up through the tree to hear the man who thought he went to Heaven explain his new need more completely.

No. He doesn't want to do that. He's not going to call on Squirrel Girl for assistance. He's going to have to figure this out on his own.

Anyway, she likely wouldn't come even if he called her. She thinks he's a murderer. That's why she's been avoiding him. Maybe she even gave him the telescope so he could discover this for himself—discover that he is a murderer.

It's an important consideration that Forward doesn't really consider; the edges of it are too sharp. Forward himself doesn't know. He doesn't know if he killed Breeze.

He remembers the burritos they ate together, the sex … and then the discovery that the tabs they took were not at all what he thought he bought. Or perhaps the tabs were, in fact, what he bought, but the burritos were laced. But why? Wherever the ferocious drug came from, it sent them up, down, and sideways.

It brought the screaming sound of both gas and brake pedals pushed to the floor simultaneously. It rattled them both apart. She blacked out, then he blacked out. When he awoke, she was beside him in the bed ... his belt around her neck.

Forward does not know if he killed Breeze. But he does know he removed his belt from her neck. He remembers the effort it took, through his upset and jittering hands, to pull the belt back through the loops in his pants. He does not remember why he thought recovering his belt was important. He does remembers fleeing. Forward does not know if he killed Breeze, but he remembers behaving as though he did. These are the thoughts and memories he wants to erase with a new reality. These are the thoughts and memories that make him afraid to return to Earth.

PATRIOTISM

Edge Of The Scissors

Major Marley sits hugging his knees, silent, his despondent face pointed pigward. He knows now that he is not in command. And he has become thankful for that.

Banter among the privates has returned. It seems they have reinstated the loose, undirected approach to brainstorming about their situation. It seems they are releasing their zeppelins.

"Ed, you was in four?" asks Yawn.

"Yup, room four."

"And you were really doing that to Izzy?" asks Walker.

"Well … sure… Is that weird?"

"One by one, man?"

"One by one? Well, I wouldn't say that. A few … a few at a time, say."

"With the edge of the scissors?"

"Yeah," Edison responds. He looks a little defensive. "You know, to curl it. Like you do with the ribbon on a birthday present."

"Uhmn uhmn uhmn… I tell you, old Ed here seem like the churchgoer type. Think you got him all figured out. And then you find out what he do with a lady… Just plain kinky."

"Well, ya know," Edison protests, "the idea only came up because of you, Eight. I myself liked Isabelle's tuft the way it was. I wanted to dip it in shaving cream and shave with it. That's what my plan for the show was." Edison nods understandingly to himself. "But then the topic of you came up."

"Me? Don't pull me into the middle of your kinky shit, Ed…"

"Yes, you. Isabelle said she wished she was curly down there, like you, Eightball. So, I was just helping her fulfill her wish, see."

"So, man, when the VC busted in, you were curling Izzy's little hairs, and you had to pour the syrup where?"

"Right here," says Edison, pulling his belt buckle out and adding a hand gesture. "Straight down. I heard the commotion out there and, well, you know, I didn't know if it was the MPs or who, so—"

"So the syrup's still down there, man?"

"Yes." Edison rocks his hips vaguely.

"So … so, where exactly, Ed? It soak up near the waistband?"

"Oh, no, ha. Betcha that'd be a lot easier. I pulled my belt all the way out, sort of like…" Edison pulls his belt all the way out, making sure to include the waistband of his underwear. "It went straight down."

Eight and Forward frown.

"Well, not straight down exactly, but it feels like…" Edison rocks his hips again. "… feels like it's mostly settled down sort of…"

"Sort of in the crotch of your underwear, man."

"Yes, in the crotch region. I think that's fair to say. Yeah, it's mostly down in the crotch."

"So, you got a whole little Phong bottle—like, six doses, or something—soiled up in the saddle of your undershorts. That what you saying, Ed?"

"You betcha."

"Well, there you go, man. We're set."

"We got syrup for the major, after all."

"We got syrup for you, Major. You can relax now."

The new compassion the privates are showing to the major seems fueled by the scared and suddenly boyish face he wears. Or maybe the privates were sent here to protect secrets in the major's head. Maybe the privates are just drafted hippies, finally considering how it would be to experience your very first psychedelic trip in shackles and with the Viet Cong as your trip-sitter. In a makeshift laboratory. Dosed by adversaries who will, with military curiosity, pull out and administer bottles of weapons-grade drugs from a chest they seized in a gun battle earlier this day. Any outrage the privates feel over the major's involvement in a program experimenting on unwitting "G. I. Don't Knows" might be mild by comparison.

The three privates demonstrate to the major that the reality they are experiencing is different than his. Everything in this pen is just as it should be. In their reality, everything happens for a reason. They make this statement always true by allowing the reason to be forever elusive. The privates that the major desperately depends on are sure there's a reason they are together in this pigpen. And they accept that they may never know what this reason is. They claim it is not something they know, but something they feel. They admit that they are also agents of the Pythagorean Brotherhood, here to save and ultimately recruit the major. They may also have demonstrated to the major that he can easily jump to conclusions in his wish to believe now that these three privates are really heroes here to save him from betraying his country.

In any case, whatever patriotic concerns the privates have over the national security crisis unfolding in their pigpen, they are not directly expressed. Rather, their newfound sympathy for the major has them trying to understand his perspective. For a hyper-patriotic square virgin like him, how is the world constructed, and what can be done about it?

The privates agreed that a simpler situation for all of them right now would be if that rifle butt had come down just a little harder on the major's forehead. They agreed that because of the high value of the major, they are now probably all awaiting the arrival of fanged interrogators.

The privates also agreed that even in their swims in the relative shallows of Phong's drug chest, his syrup is absolutely motherfucking mind-bending, extremely potent. They agreed that even if the captors somehow know how to select only the milder cocktails, and even if they know how to administer an appropriate dose, there is absolutely no way the major is going to be able to keep his shit together if any of that syrup winds up inside of him ... unless they have some control over how this happens.

Edison then suggested that there is more than one way to skin a cat. Then he apologized, explaining that he never really liked that saying; he loves cats. What he meant to say, he explained, is that there's more than one way to keep a secret. One way is to not let it out. But if you can't stop that, another way is to bury it in disinformation. It's all about the signal-to-noise ratio, he explained.

Yawn then suggested that such an unsatisfactory signal-to-noise ratio would be real easy for them to install in the major—if only they had some of that monster syrup right now to stick in his square ass. With their guidance and coaching, it would probably be no problem at all to launch him into an orbit where even the fanged interrogators can't reach him.

That's when Edison admitted to the other privates that, well, you know, technically, they do sort of have some of Phong's syrup, right here in the pigpen with them. He further admitted that he's been tripping on it a little bit this whole time. He granted that on account of his Scandinavian heritage, it has probably not been easy for the others to notice. But now, he said, lifting a knee and pointing toward his own perineum, he wants the others in his pen to consider that the skin down there is very thin; probably only the skin of the eyelid is thinner.

It takes the prisoners some effort to get the underwear off of Private Edison. One piece comes down a pant leg and onto the chain. But the more significant part—the part with the crotch—

is pulled up through the top of his pants, and it takes force to rip it from its classic waistband. Forward stretches the cotton cloth and tries to gain reference from the natural curvature it once possessed, while also contemplating the action of gravitational forces on viscous flow through pubic media. He considers how Ed has been sitting, as well as other factors.

"Here, man, this part right here. Feel it here. See, man? This is the part he should suck on, right here." Forward indicates the intended spot on the underwear with his finger and raises his face toward the major.

Major Marley then impresses the men. While the others were busy freeing the underwear, there was evidently plenty of time for Marley to make his decision on whether he wanted to take part in this plan. He now needs neither pause nor instructions, but slides over and immediately stuffs the crotch of the underwear into his mouth.

"How long you think he should seep, Faw?"

"I don't know, man. It's kind of hard to dose like this."

Forward does some thought calculations—how much syrup went down, how much may have soaked in, how much is being sucked out, first trip, hmm, not the best environment, man, hmm, so let's see … yeah … yeah … oh, yeah. Yeah. That should be plenty, man."

"Okay, Major, you done; spit out the undies."

The Light Of Jesus

It's the first time Deputy Marley has ever used his flashers, and this doesn't seem to be a very significant transition for him. He's responding to the call and, well, he's not driving slowly, but there's also nothing frantic or even excited about his priority on the street. Deputy Marley drives through Ashton, elbow casually out the car window and turn signals considerately appointed as he pulls into the parking lot of the Soul Shepherd Presbyterian Church.

"Pastor Bindie has him, trapped or something like that," said the sheriff on the telephone. He had reached Marley at the station. "Get over there; race over there. You're on duty—go get him. Who? Well, the Sign Vandal, dammit. My wife goes to that church. Now get over there and arrest that punk!"

The sheriff doesn't usually send Marley on calls, and Marley hasn't followed the history of Sign Vandal attacks in Ashton. The sheriff must explain that someone has been climbing up onto the tallest signs in town and editing the content. Particularly susceptible have been the signs of the Soul Shepherd Presbytarian Church and the Big Pine Drive-In Movie Theatre. Only the sign at Cupid's Diner is taller than either of these two. But the letters on Cupid's aren't removeable. In any case, no other signs in town come close in size. These three stand like oversized dolls in an undersized playland. The sheriff's office is pretty confident that it's the same perpetrator doing all the vandalism because some of the letters taken from one sign appear later on the other. Seems the sign vandal has been collecting letters and may now be capable of spelling anything!

Marley pulls into the church parking lot, under the tall sign, alongside the pastor, who is waving wildly at him.

"I got him, I got him, Deputy, he's up there, he can't get down, I got him, I took his ladder, he can't get down, I—"

"Please step aside, Pastor. So I can open my car door."

Pastor Bindie's expression makes Marley nervous, maybe a little disgusted. This kind of zeal has been reported in combat. The GI who keeps the Bible beside his cot, always a sober and neglected expression on his face ... until he gets out in the field, and then *ratatatatatata* he mows down anything alive, pumping extra bullets into the dead, the Bible-weary face suddenly and unfamiliarly alive in a cloud of flying shell casings. Right now, Pastor Bindie looks like that. He's got the Vandal. Hasn't shot him, but he took his ladder.

The church sign isn't lit. Even the pastor doesn't know who he's caught. But there's a shadow up on the catwalk—"See up there? Right there, he's sitting right there. Right up there, Deputy. He's caught up there, the Sign Vandal, I took his ladder, he can't get down, the Sign Vandal's right up there, Deputy. We got him!"

Marley has a flashlight, and if this doesn't reach, he can use the spotlight of his patrol car. He turns on his flashlight and hears a voice.

"Good evening, Deputy. Or is it morning yet?" The voice comes from above, from the little catwalk under the sign. An old man's voice. "I have a technical question—about laws and stuff."

Plenty of Marley's flashlight beam reaches up there, enough to reflect off a pair of enormous glasses as well as lighting up the adjacent gray hair ... somehow combining to return to Marley an image of a kid looking down from a bunk bed.

"See, I'm done up here, and I want to come down, but the pastor took away my ladder. Bindie took my ladder, Deputy. So, my question is, if I come down anyway, right now, as best I can without my ladder—here I come, just scooting off right now—and if I hurt myself, who's liable?"

"Fray!" yells the pastor.

Marley's flashlight suddenly turns—into the pastor's face. The turn is as unexpected as the little spasm in Marley's chest. To see all that gung ho so quickly melted, now dripping down into the pastor's collar.

And the show continues: some legs dangling off the catwalk, and a "No, wait, please, hold on, here's the ladder, just stay right there," as the pastor stumbles to return the ladder to the sign. Marley reaches through his car window; the spotlight pivots, and the sign above is suddenly illuminated. The upper half of the sign is an image of Jesus praying. The lower part reads:

KILLER NOT UP THERE

AFTER ALL

SORRY

Marley faces Pastor Bindie. He's sure he doesn't have to ask, but he does so anyway, pointing his flashlight at the pastor's face so he can carefully watch the response: "This message is not from your church?" he asks.

The pastor's expression builds into outrage, anger, hatred. Marley turns from him before the pastor can form his words, knowing that his phrasing of the question was a deliberate piece of mischief. He was trying to see if he could himself incite that spasm again in his chest. And he thinks he may have almost done so. "Have you been editing this sign, Mr. Fray?" he asks. The Sign Vandal's name is Mr. Fray; he is down on the ground now.

"Yay-us, I certainly did. Honestly, I didn't think anyone would mind." Fray's glasses are really spectacular—massive, thick, and obviously homemade. "I mean, considering there was only gibberish up there before."

Marley could learn mischief from this old man. Fray quickly has the pastor unsettled, blowing his top.

"Why the middle of the night, then, huh, Fray?" asks Bindie. "If you honestly think nobody would mind, then why you out here in the middle of the night? Huh? Explain that."

Fray grins, his eyes inscrutable behind the homemade goggles. He feigns a bullet to the chest. Then he lifts a finger and discovers he has not really been shot after all.

" 'Our guiding light'? Really, Bindie?" Fray smiles. "Bet you made that one up yourself."

"!#!!!!!"
Pastor Bindie's screaming sentences lose their letters.

"You know you're the only tall billboard in town that's *not* lit up, right? What kind of 'guiding light' is that?" There is something underwater and sharklike in the way the old man nudges the exploding pastor to the surface and feeds him to the birds.

"!#!!!!!"

"Okay, alright; I can see maybe keeping a sign like that *inside* your church, but—"

"!#!!!!!"

"You sure it's up to you to tell the whole town who their savior is?"

"!#!!!!!"

"Seems a little presumptuous, if you ask me."

"!#!!!!!"

"Sure, but did you even ask Jesus?"

"!#!#!#!#!#!#!#!#!#????"

"Why? Why did I have to use *your* sign? Well, because," says Mr. Fray, "I want it to be big enough to be seen from above." He waves his arm upward to show where his audience is located.

"!#!#!#!#!#!#!#!#????"

"Do I think someone's looking down at us with a telescope, or some kind of *malarkey* like that? Oh yes, Pastor. I'm sure of it. I'm using your sign for very important messages. Not malarkey. Not malarkey at all."

"!#!#!#POOR WHITE BALANCE!#!#!#!#!#NOT TOO BRIGHT AT SUNSET!#!#!#!#BIT BLURRY WINDY NIGHTS!#!#!STILL UNDEREXPOSED#!#!#!#!#!#!#!#!#!#!#!#!#!#!!!!!" Marley listens as Bindie counterattacks by citing phrases that have evidently previously appeared on his church sign—*malarkey* phrases, phrases the pastor is evidently attributing to the Sign Vandal, phrases he is evidently blaming on old man Fray.

All this commotion, Marley notices as he looks up, is taking place right under Jesus, his giant hands praying for all of this to stop. Marley feels in his chest the pulse, the spasm. He makes no attempt whatsoever to stop it, nor the argument between these men in front of him. A small, mischievous grin forms on the deputy's face as he looks on.

Möbius Trip

The effects of the drug are starting to kick in.

Major Marley is there every step of the way. Things in the pigpen begin to move … things that shouldn't move. Marley tackles and arrests the aberrations. The central post supporting the roof of the barn begins a slow and deliberate hula dance. Marley focuses on the post, shuttles away the distortions, and takes a mental snapshot of the post as it should be. He stores the snapshot for future reference. Twitches here and there on the floor suggest insects. Marley is unable to locate the insects. He restores the floor to its natural condition. Private Yawn's skin suddenly becomes very dark, even darker than black— some kind of indigo. Marley reminds himself that he is already familiar with Private Yawn's natural color; he restores the black man's hue. The stability of the other items in the pen is now shaking loose, and Marley's eyes become very busy disciplining all these things. But he must stop for a moment to regard the sow inflating uncontrollably in her corner. He stops her, completely stops her, reduces her from puffer fish back to pig. But then, realizing she needs to breathe, he allows her this freedom. He mentally records a short sequence of her natural respiration process for future reference.

"Hoo, looks like Ed's undies already starting to curl up with the major over there."

Edison gives a compassionate grin. "Going to be quite a ride."

Forward looks over too. "Oh, man," he giggles, "I think we gave him a rocket dose."

Major Marley's eyes become wider and wilder. They jump rapidly as they attempt to discipline all the objects coming loose around him. His body is motionless—just small trembles caused by the recoil of his eyes moving around so forcefully. His pupils are as big as his eye sockets. He doesn't speak.

"He's trying to control it, man. He's got to stop that, or he'll have a real bad trip. I mean, we don't want him to have a bad trip, right?"

Edison and Yawn nod, sort of. And then the men try to tell Marley this, but they're not sure how much he can hear through such wild eyes.

"Major? Hey, man?" Walker begins to gather chain and scoot toward Marley. He is chained to the major's foot, so there is already little separation between them. But he scoots over with the indication that they can become much closer.

It is busy inside Marley's head. Little fires … and there's no time right now to assess all the damage. Because of the incoming encroachment. Marley's ambi-ocular sharpshooter eyebrows are very busy; his eyes open and close as they take turns reading the parallax of the approaching object. Still approaching... It's through the perimeter... Unstopped... The parallax running off scale...

It's Private Walker's face, becoming ridiculously large in the crosshairs.

Major David Marley is not the type of man to divert his eyes from another man's stare, nor is he the type to abandon his personal airspace when someone flies into it. But he has never had anyone come at him this way, this close. The private is approaching, close, closer, a casual steadiness without pause. He's not stopping at any customary distance. He doesn't slow at the space between ranchers feuding across a barbed wire fence; he doesn't pause at the interval of gossiping Inuits in a crowded igloo; he doesn't halt at the customary one-camel-snout separation between furious Bedouins; he's not even satisfied with the butterfly gap between lovers' eyelashes. The private comes so close that he looks not into the major's eyes, but rather through them—as he would the lenses of a View-Master, say. As if what he seeks to see are slides projected on the inner back wall of the major's skull.

"Yeah, man … come look at this." Forward lifts a cupped hand from his temple as he calls back to the others. "He's trying to control it."

"Hoo!" Yawn comes forward, chains scooting along with him. "Boy backed up in there, sliding furniture around."

Maybe Edison is even placing himself next in line. They want to look through the View-Master too.

But Marley gives in. He flinches. His arm flails upward defensively, and he turns his head away. He's panting, and his eyes move again back to the sow sleeping in the corner.

"Major, imagine if you were to try to hug a tornado." Edison is up close. "You think you could grapple it down, fold it up, and stuff *it* into the cellar?"

"You got to let go, Major. Let it go. Saw a bad trip like that one time. Boy clenched down on hisself, holding everything back. Everybody telling him, 'Don't hold back, don't hold back; just got to go with it.'" The other privates nod as they listen. "This boy, nah, he had to hold it ahwull back."

"That's that kid who popped, right?" asks Walker.

"Sure was," Yawn answers, watching Marley. "See, a trip like that can last a long time, and the boy, he finally popped, I heard tell. Turned hisself inside out. Popped and just disappeared. Held everything back until he just couldn't hold it no more. Finally sat down on that toilet seat, and the boy just popped. Explosion pushed the water down the pipe, good as if he flushed. Boy turned inside out and went with it, sliding down the pipe on his own slippery insides." Yawn shakes his head again. "Heard that before he went down, he looked like a giant octopus with its tentacles flapping all over the place. Trying to grab onto something. Only managed to get a hold of that flush lever and pull some more of that blue water down on hisself."

Though his eyes have not moved, Marley's ears have shifted.

He is listening very, very carefully.

"But he came back, right?" Edison, looking at Marley, asks Yawn.

Marley's wild eyes turn from the pig and recommission the ambi-ocular sharpshooter eyebrows. They anxiously await Yawn's answer.

"Ah yeuh, he came back, alright. Gave birth to his own self. Head popped out of his own butthole, and he rolled outside-out again, flopped down wet on the bathroom floor."

"My. Sounds like a pretty bad trip."

"Hoo! Damned sure. Don't know really how it was for him, though. But the boy was sure different from then on. Went around saying something about how he was just one side, a Möbius strip—'Hey, everybody, look at me! I'm a Möbius strip, I'm a Möbius strip!'—and grinning all the time. Boy wound up kind of spooky, if you ask me."

"Möbius trip! A Möbius trip, man." Forward laughs.

"Hoo hoo, that's right! Boy had a Möbius trip."

Edison laughs too.

Marley is silent and almost motionless. But his eyes dart apprehensively, aggressively, between the various objects in the pigpen, his eye-rays lifting each object while he compares its documents with those he has on file.

Although his wild eyes make him look like he is stationed behind barricaded windows, pistols positioned in the broken-out panes, Marley has retreated further into his enclave. He has retreated from the rain and auditory stimuli. Muffled sounds wander in to find him in the back of his bullet-riddled hotel, but he barely greets them. He hears them—hears them clear enough, despite even the muffling. But listening to them makes the sounds mix confusingly with the technicolor explosions, the underwater fireworks, the lava landscapes, all that awkward light.

Marley cannot hide from his own head. At least, he cannot hide from his own head from inside his own head. The carnival ride quickly finds him in there and nudges him back to the surface, back to the light, dribbling him skyward on its dorsal fin as it humps the sea surface. In his sinusoidal dives and dips at the interface between air and water, Marley comes to understand that he is sewing the sky onto the sea. He understands now. So much of the world is ripped apart, and he is here to mend it.

During all of this, Major Marley knows that he has never collected such important intel—all of it deep and game-changing, explosions of revelation and insight coming one after another. Information of the deepest kind. This reconnaissance mission he is on is tremendous. And he feels increasingly overwhelmed trying to log it all.

Luckily, Private Yawn is ready to help out. He understands the problem, this battlefield cross talk between commo lines, the pressure to record it all for later analyses, all that very, very important intel coming in so fast from so, so many channels and directions. He sees a way that the major can get some relief, though. Yawn assures the major that he doesn't really have to try to record everything himself, because all auditory as well as some visual channels are already being reliably and completely captured, by the data-recording device Yawn has beside him now. He has an earlobe of the device raised and is speaking into it: the date, the location, the circumstances, and a few final personal messages that should be passed to his family members in the event of the worst outcome. He then elaborates further on the dire situation their landing party has encountered on this planet.

Forward interrupts with a question for Yawn: "Hey, man. Wouldn't your ... your pigtaphone—is that what you called it?" He giggles. "Doesn't the pig need to speak English?"

Private Yawn, speaking softly into the ear of the pigtaphone, documents that Private Walker has submitted a suggestion, or perhaps a concern, that an important language limitation of the landing party's pigtaphone may have been overlooked. Private Yawn identifies and codes the item as an engineering question, then states that he can personally provide the response. He returns to his usual dialect. "Don't matter, Faw. Don't matter if the pig speaks English. I mean, I'd … I'd even guess…" Yawn looks tenderly at the pig. "… I'd even guess she don't. Maybe some Vietnamese. Anyway, don't matter. See, Faw, you don't understand the advanced tech-nology of this here…" He slaps the sow. "… this here recording device." He turns back toward Forward. "This unit is capturing evrathing! Every little sound—the raindrops on the roof, the shells falling way out there, the sounds of us talking and breathing, the little pitter-patter of the hooves of that auburn ant walking around on the ground down there, the whole bit. Pigtaphone picking it all up. See, the major don't have to worry about remembering jack." Yawn wraps an arm around the pig's jowls and grins admiringly. "This unit got state-a-the-art tech-nology. Millions of years of R and D. Can't do no betta than this, baby." He shakes the sow's jowls. "Nooo, uh umh."

The major's giant pupils have turned to better capture the light from the direction of the pig and the private. The private continues, "See, Faw, the pigtaphone don't need to understand English or nothing. It's just a device for recording sounds—those little vibrations in the air that run up into your ears, shaking the tiny hairs inside around and making you say you heard something. You got the sounds of each one of those water drops falling on the roof, and each one of those bombs falling on villages out there, and each one of those little sounds is different from the others. Ain't really no two sounds alike, when you think about it. Each one got its own individual squeal. I mean, even each one of those raindrops—they sound kind of the same to you or me, but to this pigtaphone here…" Slap. "… each one com-pletely different. Pigtaphone, she slows it all down, so she can hear each one of those drops individually, hammering down just as loud as one of those shells out there. Listening in slow motion, hearing each drop, one after the other. Some overlap, but no two of them raindrops ever start at exactly the same time, and no two ever end at the same time neither. Each one dis-tinct, a whole little adventure of sounds wrapped up on itself, just waiting for a pigtaphone like her to write it all down."

"So ... so, say, tell us more about the technology, Eight. How does this, uhr, pigtaphone work?"

Yawn lifts a pig ear and appends to the minutes that the previous question was submitted by one Private Edison. He lets the ear drop and returns to his usual dialect. "Like I was saying, Ed, every one of those little sounds is a u-nique vi-bration, coming through the air. Coming through the air and banging against the bacon of this pig right here. And that bacon's got so many cells, so many millions and billions of cells—so many cells that no two different sounds ever budge the bacon quite the same way. Don't you worry," Eight sets his arm on the pig, "we getting it all down in the meat right here."

"Yeah, maybe, man. But how do you ... how do you get it back out?" Walker wants to know.

"Oh, say, that's a good question. How do you get the sounds back out of the pig, Eight?"

Yawn rubs his forehead. "Aw, hoo, get it back out... Yeuh, wull, that's a technical question. Anyway, we ain't going to be able to get it back out right here, right now." Yawn looks toward Marley. "Nooo. Uhm umh." He turns back to the privates. "For that, we need the juicer ... the juicer up on the mothership." Eight points upward.

Forward and Edison look upward acceptingly.

Marley looks upward too.

"Drop this pig in. Let that juicer count through all them millions and billions of cells, and we just wait on the other side for the LP to come out." Yawn smiles with confidence. "Hell, later we'll be able to lay the record of this here POW shit down on the turntable whenever we want. Sit down some day with the grandkiddies and some cognac."

The privates laugh.

"Let them hear all about how we fought for our country."

"How we're real patriots, man."

"Hoo! Patriots, that's what we be."

Moment In The Morning

There's a moment in the morning—maybe many moments, maybe a whole flock of them—when Forward rises in the tree, the tree the sky calls Sequitur ... and the sky and the breeze and the forest and the trees and the whole world with Sequitur is one.

There's a moment in the morning—maybe many moments, maybe a whole school of them—when Forward swims safely below the bridge of the troll, the troll of specification who has not yet opened his eyes to recall yesterday.

There's a moment in the morning—maybe many moments, maybe a whole bouquet of them—when everything Forward loves, has loved, and will love still giggles in the pillow, and the timeline teases a lofted feather above its orangutan lips.

But then comes the knock. The knock of day. The knock of a fisted tape measure on the Airstream shell of sleep. Bass notes from the weight of the measure's uncoiled seconds fall under the dingy tin crackle of the flopping segment of linear history that the measure has come here to talk about. Lips turn, the feather falls, and Night and Day bolt in, up into the sheets to lay claim to the pillow. The fluffy down explodes into the morning of the material world.

And so Forward is awakening, and he must meet the clown.

The big shoes descend from the sky, the striped britches, the big-button suspenders, and a painted ping-pong ball for a nose. The clown lands to bend over with his helium balloon bouquet ... which means the real spectacle never completely arrives on earth; it comes close, but never lands. The colorful morula is not of this world, and it would eagerly rise and escape it, if not for the weight of the clown. The clown has the tethers, a fist cinched around the many worldlines, and the fist loosens only to make a controlled offer: one. Forward can have one. He can pull one down from the clown's bouquet, choose one particular worldline. One reality. It's a brutal collapse of the wave function. The big shoes lift and ride away again under the magnificent bubbles, and Forward is left below, sleepy finger hooked on a worldline tethered to merely one monochromatic bubble of a noble gas.

As Forward awakens this morning, the squirrel girl is on the flange, reaching down into the nest to pull peanuts from his bed. She rakes one onto the flange. Removes its shell. Lips off the brown skin. Holding the nut with a thumb and finger from each hand, she nibbles off the nipple. The peanut falls into halves in her hand. She lowers her head and eats one of the halves. Then the other. She reaches into the bed and pulls up another.

Forward has not directly seen her, but he heard her speak once with a man, a visitor, a supplier. From their conversation, he learned that the girl's name is Sky, the man's name is Sherpa, and the tree is called Sequitur. When the visitor left, Forward saw the man's big backpack and the long blonde hair cascading over it, just as he cleared the skirt of the tree and before he walked off the edge of the promontory. This Sherpa is also almost certainly the same Sherpa he knows from The Motel. The earthy Sherpa always off in the mountains or doing other earthy things Forward has wanted to know more about. In avoidance of opening his eyes, Forward considers this further. This morning, he feels warm rays on his skin. They reach through the swaying filter of conifer needles. He loves this warm light as he lies facing flatly skyward in the nest and floats between the sleeping and waking worlds.

A girlish giggle. "Not your poncho size, I guess."

It's not the strangest lucid dream Forward has had in this tree. He keeps his eyes closed, listening.

The giggling continues.

There is also nibbling. A constant nibbling.

And crunching.

Crunching and nibbling.

Forward lies on his back in the nest, absorbing the sunlight that arrives on his body as galloping patterns associated with the specific arrangement of the collection of pine needles that rock above him.

Crunching.

Nibbling.

Poncho size…? These words roil up to the surface of his consciousness. Forward becomes aware that he just heard a comment about poncho size. The voice seemed exterior to him, and yet very close by. Forward wakes enough to recall that in this world, this worldline, he himself is wearing a poncho; it is the only thing he is wearing. What was initially his gown to meet God turned out, in the lit sobriety of day, to be a poncho. He can feel it on his skin now. Its texture announces to his consciousness the dimensions of his own body in this lit world, the full surface he aims at the sun. The direct sun rays almost reach his heart through the oversized craw of the poncho. His legs feel the warm light. His whole lower half feels the warm light.

Naked. He is naked. Or his lower half is. With this realization, coherent electrical patterns assemble in Forward's neocortex: The coincidence of him hearing somebody—a girl's voice, giggling—saying something about a poncho … about the poncho size. And his own accreting realization that he himself is wearing a poncho … a poncho that is an incorrect size.

Forward can no longer control the world he is landing in. That was done when he selected this balloon from the clown. As he awakens, he is now simply completing the worldline he chose. The wave is collapsing, and Forward's eyes begin to let in light.

The nest edge and flange take their place as a shadow line he can use to build a horizon. A zenith is established as the brightest spot overhead. The coalescing world now has two dimensions, and a third becomes defined by the unique vector pointing at the nose of the freckled and redheaded young girl who rests, chin on flange, staring down at Forward in the nest. There is something very bassinetal about this awakening.

"Oh, man! Man, man!" Forward jumps into a sit. "Sorry, man!" He pulls the poncho down over his knees ... or maybe he pulls his knees into the poncho. While he knows that a shirt always gets tucked down into pants rather than pants ever being pulled up over the shirt, Forward does not know which way the action should go for a poncho. In this worldline, this reality—or, in fact, in any of the worldlines or realities he has so far participated in —there has not been very much direction with ponchos.

As Forward springs into a sit, the girl lifts her chin off the flange and steps backward. She doesn't look backward—she just steps backward, her squirrel feet somehow finding a branch behind her. She reaches forward to collect the peanuts she left on the flange. She descends onto her haunches, disappearing to Forward. From the hull of the nest, he can no longer see her. He must come to the edge of the flange to look over and see where she went.

He sees then that she didn't sink far. She's right there, perched on a branch, using her lap to sort her peanuts. And maybe give him time to cover himself better with the poncho.

"Uhm ... hey, man."

The girl giggles. This makes flutter a piece of peanut skin that is stuck to her lip.

"I'm not a man," she says as she looks up at him.

124

Uncle Sam Wants You

Major Marley looks down at himself on Earth from a porthole of the mothership implanted into his hallucination by the privates shackled to his ankles. He sees that the other members of the landing party have noticed he's missing. They're snooping around his landed data collection unit, poking it, asking questions. One wants to shake it, but another says not to do that. Yawn (Eightball, Eight) asks Walker (Forward, Faw) to take a look. In a moment, Walker's eyes appear in the ship's portholes. Marley backs to the center of his saucer. The eyes are massive chocolate kaleidoscopes with billions and billions of individual flecks that swirl around in a galaxy of milky black pupils, each unfathomably intricate.

This is beautiful and very interesting but Marley dodges his head around the distraction. He must keep an eye on the pigtaphone at all times. The success of this mission requires protection of the data stored in the pigtaphone.

"How he going to do, Faw?" asks Yawn. "When they start pulling his fingernails off and shit?"

Walker looks over at Marley. "Whoa, man. He's pretty out there."

Yawn's head tilts as he looks toward the major. "Heard the gookas even slide a glass rod down your cock hole, then go smacking it all to splinters and shit."

"You know, you don't need to go scaring him. That much," says Edison. "I betcha he's dealing with plenty already."

"He's pretty focused on the pig, man."

"Hoo! Found his spirit animal."

"And his pigtaphone."

"One-stop shopping. Say, Major, you hearing any of this?"

Edison asks.

"Of course he's hearing us. He's hearing everything—even some things not making any sound. Don't you remember your first trip, man?"

"And your first trip probably didn't involve weapons-grade hallucinogens," Edison adds. "How you think he'll hold up? Will they get anything out of him?"

"Hell, no. Major here's a pay-triot! Red, white, and blue pay-triot. They ain't getting nothing out of this boy. He's one of those oyster fish. More they try to pry into him, the more he just pucker down. They can go ahead torture him; boy likes that shit."

Walker and Edison have turned toward Marley. They look like they want to agree with Yawn, but there's something on the major's face. It's a subtle, slightly helpless expression that begs for sympathy as it crawls out and finds the territory so cold and unfamiliar.

"He ain't one of those boys with conflicted allegiance and shit," Yawn continues, "and he also ain't going to wet all over hisself when they come at him with those jumper cables. Like I said, the major's a rockfish. They be out there trying their tricks, and he be inside just listening, hearing them scratch around the outside of that big oyster shell of his." All the privates are observing the major. "Even if the gookas get some kind of ... I don't know—industrial drill, or auger, or some shit like that, and they manage to drill through ... well, they just going to find the major got another shell inside of that one. Whole set of Russian dolls. Ain't no torture can get jack out of this rockfish, no um umh. He's a pay-triot!"

"Hmm." Edison looks concerned. "But do we really know what *kind* of patriot he is?"

"What kind? What kind you think, Ed? Of course he's an *American* patriot."

"You know that's not what Ed means, man." Walker turns toward Edison. "Not sure. He doesn't really open up, man. But I don't think he's one of those blind patriots. I think he could be the same kind of patriot we are: a real patriot, man."

"You mean a patriot of the whole planet?" asks Edison.

"Sure, man," says Walker, looking unsure. "Well, maybe he hasn't completely figured that out yet … but sure."

"If he's a real patriot," Yawn has not yet accepted Walker's thesis, "then how come he don't seem like the type to question authority?"

"Right now, he's questioning physics, Eight." Edison's hands fold thoughtfully. "Don't forget that a real patriot questions authority. *And* submits to it."

"Submit? Why's that necessary?"

"To get anything done. Think about it, Eight. What happens when there are too many cooks in the kitchen?" Edison's eyes move to Marley. "Like when you go to the dentist."

"Man, the *dentist*?"

"Yes. When you go to the dentist, you submit to his authority." Edison smiles. Somehow, he has laced his fingers comfortably behind his head. All privates now watch the major. "Already, when he sits you down in the chair and you let him strap that bib on you, you're submitting to his authority. Even when you see the needle." The men exchange conferring glances. They look at Marley. "Or when you hear those drilling sounds in your head—*gzirrrrrrrrrrr*—and every cell in your body wants to change its mind about the visit, you still stay there. Because you've decided in advance that you will submit to his authority. You've decided to repress those feelings that come up along the way."

"Alright. But suppose you sitting in there in the bib, and the dentist come into the room smoking a cigar and carrying a pair a greasy garage pliers?"

"Yes. That's what I mean. In that case, it's reasonable to get up and hand the dentist his bib back. It's finding that balance: submitting to authority while still keeping your eye on it."

"And being ready to take that bib off if you have to, man."

"And being ready to take the bib off, that's right." Edison scoots closer to the silent major. "The problem is really the reward system; it knows how to manipulate people, make them ignore their own good sense. Maybe that dentist with the garage pliers learns tricks to keep a man in the chair longer."

"Like what kind? What kind of tricks, Ed?" Walker and Yawn watch Ed watch Marley.

"Like... Well, I don't know." Edison's expression is creative. "Maybe he pipes in music that starts squealing like a pig when the patient tries to pull off the bib and run out."

"Or he could just have some sexy nurse around, man."

"Hoo, yeuh, that'd work! Try to reach up and pull off that bibby while you looking up at some lowng-legged lady looking down at you. Waiting to see what kind of man she's got in her chair."

Ed laughs. "Sure, yes, that's better than the piped in pig sounds."

"And what about, what about an Uncle Sam poster? Be a lot cheaper for that dentist just to get an Uncle Sam poster. That's what he needs. Shit's already been worked out. Sam be up there in front of you while you sitting in that chair, that knotty old finger of his looking like it's a mile closer to you than the whole rest of him—'Uncle Sam Wants You!' " Yawn scoots toward Marley. "Uncle Sam wants *you!*"

"... To stay in the chair and have your teeth pulled out with greasy pliers, man."

"By a doctor smoking a cigar. Hee-hoo!" Eight bends his index finger in a better imitation and tries this time to extend it more aggressively toward the major: "Uncle Sam! He wants you!" He cocks his finger again. "You! You, the pussy bear over there trying to pull your bibby off. Uncle Sam wants you! You, pussy bear, you!"

Private Edison is scratching his head. The clean symmetric sweeps—the reverse motion of a hand collecting poker chips—are, as always, respectful of the preexisting arrangement of his hair. "We are, of course, talking about the Eisenmonster."

Hearing this, the privates nod. The major twitches.

"Or, more correctly, the reward system that the monster utilizes to capture resources."

"Yeuh."

"Yeah, man."

"The Reward System. We're talking about the Reward System."

"Yeuh."

"Yeah."

"The Reward System. The Eisenmonster's reward system."

"Yeah, man."

"Yeuh."

Edison's scratching fingers seem to have found the spot on his scalp that corresponds to the spot at the top of a dog's tail —the spot that will, when scratched with sincerity, make a dog stop what it's doing, constrict its eyes, extend its neck, and take soft and delicate licks at nothing. He is quite admirably masking the effects of the drugs that passed through his perineum. With a post-scratch shake, he finally responds, "The same strangely long arm is used to separate men from their natural inhibitions. Uncle Sam is promising to stretch your arm out like his, pull your trigger finger so far away from you that you won't feel responsible for what it does. This is a primary weapon of the Eisenmonster. Creating this separation, I mean.

"That's why the Eisenmonster's so keen on technology; technology is great for creating the separation. A man is naturally equipped with a set of inhibitions that are just about appropriate for the damage he'd normally be able to inflict if he were just using his own tooth and claw. Look at the difference between rabbits and wolves. Wolves are able to inflict serious damage on one another, they're able to kill one another—and that's why they have a whole suite of inhibitions, like cowering and spittle-licking and throat-showing, a whole language of communication they can use to avoid senselessly killing each other." Edison smirks. "While rabbits, well, I don't know for sure, but I'd guess they don't have many inhibitions at all. Because they don't need them. I mean, even if they get real real angry with one another, what can they really do about it?"

"So, you saying you send a 'G.I. Don't Know Joe' out into the field to go kill somebody—somebody he don't even know—but this time, he gotta do it with just what he got from God. Can't use no technology, not even karate or some shit like that. Got to do it like an animal."

Eight is thoughtful. "So, I suppose come some point he be down chewing on a throat … or jabbing his finger in an eye socket … and he just, well, he just get sick of it. Just stop. Shit, I guess by the time you go trying a man's head on your hand like it was a bowling ball, you probably figured you already won. Ain't no need to keep going."

"So, man, if we didn't have all this technology, we'd probably get disgusted long before we finished killing anyone. And stop."

"Yes, exactly. From the Eisenmonster's side, technology is pretty useful at separating a man from his own best decisions. Separates a man from his natural inhibitions, his conscience, his own good sense. Technology moves faster than regret. It's technology that has stretched Uncle Sam's arm out like that."

"And a soldier winds up with those long arms too," says Walker.

"The monster makes sure of it. By the time the soldier pulls back on the trigger, his finger and the consequences might as well be around the block. *Plink!* A man falls facedown in the rice field. Where was the space for our natural inhibitions to step in and give us any advice? Where was the disgust?"

"You saying evolution, or whatever supposed to kick in at times like that, don't have enough space? No time—just *plink*, and there he go, somebody you don't even know, facedown in the paddies … all because of you."

"Yup. Maybe Uncle Sam wants you … but to be a real patriot, you have to decide if you want him back." Edison shrugs. "Otherwise, it's not really a relationship, is it?"

Marley remains quiet, but he is clearly listening closely. The others see this.

"So, Ed. Man, how about the weapons program the major's over here to take over? The program to cook up a bunch of drug weapons to use back home on the counterculture? Does that make him a patriot?"

"Hoo, shit, maybe that right there proves he's part of the Eisenmonster."

Edison's face sinks into thought. He holds somehow the face of a pacer. When finally he raises his eyes, he looks at Walker, at Yawn. He nods compassionately, and his eyes land on Marley.

"Earth needs him. For what's coming. The big war. Brothers, this man is a real patriot. He's just a little out of tune." Edison returns his gaze to the other privates. "Yes, he's absurd. And now we know. Gentlemen, we're not just here to help this man get through interrogation. We're here to help him hear harmony."

Movie Tickets

There's a place that David Marley goes in his candy-apple-red Karmann Ghia that is so unspecified, he knows he can't be intercepted. It happens after he descends from his apartment, after he passes his empty carport, after he walks down the block to his rented garage, after he lifts the big wooden door, after he removes and folds the tarp, after he opens the car's thin metal door, and then immediately when he lowers his head to climb inside.

The price he pays for the garage is unjustifiable, considering that a carport already comes with his apartment, and that he takes his car out of the garage only a couple times a week. Or perhaps this means he's getting a good deal; he's not sure. He's more sure about the paint: candy apple red. It's a ridiculous color for him. But it wasn't his choice to repaint the car this color. It wasn't even his choice to buy this car. Anyway, the interior is still the original color, off-white, so this is the color Marley sees from the inside. He sees the dash, and the glove box where Sarah used to place her bare feet. He sees the road map that remains in the passenger door caddy. Since years. It sits like a library card calling forth sounds from a tin engine that were so different when she was in the car: "Go right! No, go left. No, hold on, hur hur hur, the map's upside—Shake! Shake, Davey! Vanilla shake! Right there! Davey, pull off!" He hears her constantly.

Their mother died, leaving her savings not with her husband, but with her fourteen-year-old son. Before the son reached fifteen, he had removed the abusive father from the household. The son, David, raised his infant sister after that, forgoing his own adolescence to bring her into hers. And when he received a scholarship to Yale, she made popcorn. They sat on the couch together, curriculum on the coffee table, and Sarah threw popcorn at the syllabus until it was decided that Davey would study philosophy.

The remembrance, her voice in his head, the feeling of her inside this car. He has never felt bitter over his sacrifices for her. He simply misses so much feeling so needed.

Old man Fray sits comfortably on an old truck tire alongside the mountain road, six miles outside of town. The red Karmann Ghia chirps into a lower gear … again … each time sliding out a cute growl. Then the wheels find the shoulder of the road, and in a moment Marley sits in his little go-kart, hand on his window crank while he waits for the dust to pass.

Mr. Fray gathers his sweater and walks toward the car.

Marley rolls down his window and leans out. "Do you need a ride into—?" Then he retracts his question back into the car; Fray is already opening the passenger door. Next, he is inside. Marley feels a spasm in his chest. He puts the car in gear and pulls off the shoulder.

"I bet it's probably happened, during an earthquake maybe, that some blind cave ant was suddenly exposed to solar zenith," says the old man, looking out through his glasses and the passenger window. "Even if it doesn't have eyes, maybe there's something loud about the light that the ant isn't used to." Fray smiles. "Say, how would that sound? The noise of sunlight, I mean?" With his feet, Fray finds the thermos rolling around on the passenger floor. It's up in his lap now. He opens the thermos, sniffs, peers inside.

Marley glances over at his passenger several times, but he does not find eye contact. "Can I ask how you wound up alongside the road?"

"I was riding on top of a truck of logs." Fray turns to gaze at Marley now through his thick eyewear. "The driver, Pete Sorenson's boy, he made me get down. It's the third time they caught me on that curve." Fray smiles again. "I guess because when they go around that curve, they can see me up there in their mirrors."

"You were sitting on the logs?"

"Logs? Hwoh, no!" Fray's glasses make a gesture toward the size of his own lap. "Just one log. Horseback, see." He closes the thermos and returns it to the floor.

"This is the third time you have been caught riding on top of a log truck?"

"On that curve, yup."

Marley looks over with curiosity. "Why do you do that—ride the logs?"

"A wake," says Fray without hesitation. Now he is operating the camera around his neck, pointing it—as best he can through the close window glass—upward at the passing tree canopy. The low perspective of this little car seems to amuse him.

Marley waits until Fray seems less distracted, then asks, " 'Awake'? What do you mean by that?"

Fray turns, lifts his camera. "I'm the funeral photographer. Don't all the long-time residents around here deserve a wake?"

Marley stirs.

Fray laughs. "Well, after they die, anyway."

"Trees aren't people," says Marley.

Fray's lower lip stiffens as he nods roundly, showing incomplete agreement. "I choose a tree that's older than I am, see—I'm telling you how I do it—and I hold vigil all the way through."

"What do you mean by 'vigil'?"

"I mean, first I hide in the forest, with my camera, you know. I choose a tree and take pictures when they cut it down. And then I follow it from there. Until it gets nailed down as a pool deck, or what have you." He laughs. "From death to resting place. Isn't that how a wake works?"

Marley is fascinated. "You actually go through the mill?"

"Good question. I can see you're a paying-attention kind of young man."

David Marley does not think he's that young. But that doesn't really matter. He listens.

"The Company doesn't let me come inside anymore. But there are fellas in there who take pictures for me. They also tell me which load of lumber I have to climb up on coming out the other side."

"Hold on... Workers inside the mill—workers who work for the Ashton Lumber Company—take pictures for you, I'm guessing of the log you were riding, as it gets milled?"

"Correct."

"Why do they help you?"

Fray laughs. "Not so much about helping me. They want their pictures to be in *The Movie*. Whole town does. I get hundreds of photos a year, from millions of people. No exaggeration." Fray grins.

Marley is pretty sure the math is off there. Or the problem could be the syntax ambiguity in the statement. Anyway, he ignores this. "*The Movie*? What's that?"

"This is my stop here," says Fray, pointing at the lumber mill. "Got to go find my log. Thanks. Here, take these. Movie tickets. Come find out for yourself." The old man hands Marley two photographs—photo proofs, maybe—and climbs out of the car.

Marilyn Monroe

Torrential rain pounds the frond-thatched rooftop. Major Marley reminds himself that it has been raining for maybe an hour, or a month, that it was raining when he … when he ingested the drug. It must have been. And he thinks … he's pretty sure … he thinks it was raining right before he closed his eyes … right before he closed his eyes just now. Or whenever that was. It is not likely raining any harder now, right now. Or whenever it is. There is so much to hear. He needs a reference library for his auditory environment. He can't wait to juice the pig.

Major Marley hopes he won't tell the enemy his secrets. He wants to be a patriot. He doesn't want to pop inside out and flush down a toilet.

And so, he listens closely to the spectral characteristics of the raindrops, how they collide with the roof. Each collision has its own infinity of sound wrapped up in it. Yes, he's almost sure it does. If he listens closely, long enough, he might discover each of the little splashes to be irreproducible, entirely individual, described in detail only with an infinite number of parameters.

And the sounds of the storm are changing, non-ergodic … and still infinite. The spectrum reddens, the energy in the heavier sounds rising. Marley is sure of this. Rising rising rising, rising into an almost perpetual thunder. There are other sounds too. From the men: a "Say, Major, you might want to see this." A "No, man, we should let him be." And some mention of toilets, many toilets—top-of-the-line American Standard toilets, hijacked toilets, toilets so curiously arriving here in this pig barn with them. Toilets that Walker insists were headed to the new officer's club now under construction. But Marley is ignoring this; he first needs to create a proper reference of the background rain before he can admit these new sounds.

It's a half hour later—or maybe a week, or five seconds—when a new sound becomes more compelling than that of the rain. It's the mention of Marilyn Monroe.

"I mean, that one where she's lying sort of … sort of sideways … but on her back … sort of sideways below the waist, but on her back up top. You know what I mean?" asks Edison.

Other voices agree that they do, yes, the two *do* look alike. Marley opens his eyes, differently, to find the men staring at the pig in the corner. As well as at him.

Under normal circumstances, this would be a consideration Marley would immediately dismiss. But right now, his eyes are open wider than usual—or differently, at least—and he regards the Chester White sow lying on her side, bottom legs curled and stacked in an impish hurdler pose, long eyelashes lowered, with a full smile so extended to the corners of her mouth that it looks like the Joker's grin. Yes … yes … even Marley can see it. The pig in the corner *does* look like Marilyn Monroe.

"And see, that ain't no accident, neither," says Yawn. "Part of the convenient design. When you know the enemy's coming, and you got to be quick and dump all your body intel into the pigtaphone before—"

" 'Body intel,' man?"

"Hell yeah. You think only pig meat can record intel? A soldier's a mammal too, and his meat's going to be full of secrets."

"Right on." Forward laughs. "I get it. You're saying the major needs to dump his body intel into the pigtaphone before they start interrogating him."

"Damn right. And judging by that truck of toilets that just got here, the gookas already got something going on. So the major's gotta be quick about it. Plug into that pigtaphone and download as many ways he can." Yawn widens his look to include Marley. "I'm talking kissy skin contact, and any way he can find wet enough to conduct electricity. Whatever he got to do to download. Quick."

Sherpa

Sherpa is tall, lanky, and blond—very blond. It's a blond announced in many dimensions. His scraggly beard appears as dandelions in the third-season discovery of his face. Viking locks extend down his back like a hemp lifeline attempting to rescue his butt. In the pocket of his lower back, a few strawberry curlies hide from the thunderbird on the other side—the thunderbird with brows studded in warm, staring nipples and a whirly goatee that disappears into the shadows of his inner thighs.

This hairy experiment is displayed with few secrets at the moment, because Sherpa has just removed all of his clothes. He scoots over in the nest and sets them in Forward's lap. "Really, man, you can have them."

"You kidding me, man?"

"They're yours."

"… But these are … these are your *clothes*, man."

"They're just clothes; I got more down there." Sherpa points a thumb over his shoulder. Because he now lies on his back in the nest, the thumb indicates a downward direction, through the bedding and peanuts, through the sticks and branches of Sequitur, grazing the promontory, descending the cliff face of Quarter Horse, and landing on a purple patch of a motel complex in the mountain river town of Ashton below.

"I can really have these?"

"Yeah, man. They're yours."

"Far out!" Forward slides his fingers into the fabric in his lap, tossing it up into the air like gold coins from a treasure chest. They both laugh. "But are you sure, man? You got all this quilting and patches … and your friends have written you things."

"It's okay, man; now my friends have written *you* things. Besides, Sky told me to. She wants her poncho back."

Forward smiles, then grins. He finally accepts the gift. Squatting forward, he pulls the poncho off his head in one sweep, then rolls back to work the raggedy jeans up his legs. Next, he pulls on the blouse, then sits up to admire himself as best as he can within the smallness of the nest. "... So, man ... now you're naked. You going to wear the poncho?"

"No, that's Sky's."

"What's Sky's?"

The squirrel girl suddenly appears on the flange with Sherpa's deflated backpack; she has been down at the lower nest, unloading the supplies Sherpa brought. But it takes her only a second to see what's going on here. She smiles big at the poncho, kneels down, and plucks it out of the nest. Pulling it up onto the flange, she stands up, turns the poncho right side out, then holds it in her teeth while she removes the backpack. She hooks a shoulder strap of the pack on a branch beside the bundled rope ladder. She is preparing to change into the poncho.

Forward rocks forward in the nest. He tries to be discreet, but there's no sly way of bringing his chin to rest on the flange.

Sherpa does about the same—sort of an awkward change of position that leaves his head about where Forward's is. As Sky begins to change into her poncho, the men look like two carp at the feeding end of a pond.

On the flange, Sky turns to face the afternoon sun, her back to the nest. She takes the poncho from her mouth and squeezes it between her knees. The billowy blouse comes up and off in one gusty gesture. She drops the blouse beside her on the flange. Rays bend at her edges and braid over her bare back. A downy light crawls with messages over her shoulders and under her arms. There's a splendorous glow to her red hair.

But Forward doesn't see that. He's looking at the sweater tied around her waist, watching the sweater.

Sky wears dirty Dickies. They're stained all over and fraying where they've been scissored off at the knee. The Dickies also begin to descend. The motion of Sky's elbows indicates hands busy with fasteners; the frayed threads at her knees jostle and drop in increments like a collapsing jungle canopy; her glowing elbows push downward, and the Dickies fall.

But Forward doesn't see this. He's looking at the sweater, watching the sweater. She wears it around her waist like a woolly mud flap. And even as she sends the Dickies away, the swollen yarn of the now inflated poncho swallows every clue. The Mexican drapes have been lowered. Show over.

Sky, her recovered poncho now splendidly refracting the backlit orange light, places her hands on her hips, turns on the flange, and faces the carp in their pond. "They call me..." Her head cocks, and her neck stiffens. "... Taquita!" She makes some mariachi music sounds with her mouth as she incrementally gallops to the end of the branch, then squirrel-jumps into the air. She and her poncho have gone up the tree to tend to the cameras.

"She's flirting with me, man."

"Who?"

"Sky."

"Oh. Hmm."

Forward grins, turns his head toward Sherpa. Sherpa looks back. Their faces are closer together than they would be if the nest were bigger. "See how she always keeps a sweater around her waist?" Forward says with a sleezy, whisperish laugh, ribbing Sherpa. "You ever seen her ass, man?"

Sherpa nods. "Her ass? Yeah, sure."

"She always keep it covered up like that?"

"Covered up? Maybe. She thinks it's too big."

Forward lifts with intrigue. "Too big?"

"…"

"What else, man? Tell me more about it. Her ass, man."

"…"

"She's got a tiny waist. How big could her butt be?"

"…"

"Oh—the peanuts, man! I bet that's why her ass is so big."

"…"

The two have been passing a joint between them as they lie in the nest together. Forward is presently in the phase of the high where he thinks he gets it. He *gets* it, man. "It's quantum physics. The uncollapsed potential. Her ass is perfect—all meaty and magically shaped." His hands knead the air. "It's *perfect*, man."

Sherpa's face shows disapproval.

"And you know why? You know why, man?" Forward's eyes are slightly crossed as he studies the joint tip. "Because I haven't seen it. Her ass is still uncollapsed, man. That's why it can be perfect. When it's only your imagination collapsing the potential, you can create anything you want, perfect things. Perfect things, man!" Forward, his grin willfully grimy, rocks over and hands the joint to Sherpa.

Sherpa comes up onto a shoulder. The joint burns in his hand as he carefully regards Forward lying beside him. He finally finds his words: "It wasn't you, Forward."

Sherpa's message tries to reach Forward, but Forward pretends that he didn't hear it, or that he did, but didn't understand it. In any case, whatever Sherpa just said is simply not as interesting as the uncollapsed potential of Sky's unseen butt. Forward's voice is higher now, the words tumbling out faster, his body stiffer and more separated from Sherpa than it was a moment ago.

"You didn't do it, man," Sherpa tries again.

Forward's face visibly shakes away Sherpa's words and gives a tin laugh. "She's flirting with me, man. I'm probably going to get to see it. Her ass, man."

"Pops, Granddad, he has proof."

Forward has somehow retreated deep into the peanuts below them. "I'm going to collapse her perfect ass, man." His tin laughs become muffled.

Sherpa points down to the town. "Did you see the new message he wrote to Sky?

"Can't help it if *you* want something with her. She's flirting with *me*, man."

Sherpa leans into Forward's face. "Come back to Earth, Forward. You didn't do it."

Come back to Earth, Forward. You didn't do it. You didn't do it.

"And Sky's a child."

You didn't do it. Come back to Earth, Forward. You didn't do it.

Forward snaps back from his internal distraction over the words reverberating almost silently inside him. "Sixteen, man. Old enough to bleed, old enough to breed." His grin is desperately sleazy now. "Don't be a square. Free love, man."

"Free?" Sherpa sits up. His face is backlit as he looks directly into Forward's eyes, his voice deeper: "It wouldn't be 'free' for her."

Come back to Earth, Forward. You didn't do it. You didn't do it.

Sherpa's words cycle a limbic and skeletal resonance in Forward that builds a wave that grows exponentially. It suddenly shatters the celestial reality Forward has been hiding in. He falls back to Earth.

He stops. Stops talking, for sure. But he also stops thinking ... at least with the mind he was just using. Sherpa makes so much sense. And as a result, Forward is left with a distasteful feeling of embarrassment—distasteful enough for him to blame Sherpa and maybe Sky in three different ways before accepting the logic and wisdom of this naked man beside him.

Instead of the fantasy butt filling his mind, Forward recalls now the freckles on the quirky little girl's cute face, the way she giggles, the way she scampers through the tree. Even after she stopped hiding from him, he couldn't see her. Now, he can. Now, Forward can imagine that the young girl who has been feeding him, caring for him, raking away his shit that must fall at the base of the tree... For the first time since arriving in Sequitur, Forward can imagine that this young girl still sleeps with stuffed animals.

The two men are silent as these thoughts flood through Forward. And then Forward suddenly sits up—all the way up. Because he wants to be a straighter man, a better man. Like Sherpa. A man who would not justify collapsing the innocence of a young girl. A man enlightened enough to detect when philosophies are erected for self-gratification. A man who can see when "free love" is not really free. A man who can tell when his primitive sexual urges have been summoned just for the desperate distraction they provide.

"Thank you," he says. "What you said. It makes sense." He relights the joint. "You're a guru, man."

Sherpa tells Forward that he is welcome.

Later, when they are lying again side by side, during a quiet moment, Sherpa turns his face to Forward's and says, "You know she's my little sister, right?"

IDENTITY

Right Shoes

Outside, offering only unadorned cement tables at which to stand, the dining area seems designed to be hosed down. Deputy Marley's eyes take inventory. He counts the eight circular tables that easily resemble tall birdbaths. His eyes locate a hose stored on the side of the glass restaurant. By his estimation from the size of the hose coil, the brass nozzle would indeed reach all eight birdbaths. The floor of the dining area is a slick, seamless cement —the kind one would find in a professional dog kennel. Pull the hooded trash cans aside, and the whole dining area could be hosed down in three minutes.

Sarah loved this kind of place. She loved the pimpled young employees in paper hats busily swimming around on their side of the glass; she loved seeing the food passed through the hole; she loved receiving it on tippy-toes with gleeful claps and giggles. She loved undressing her food from the layers and layers of cardboard and wax paper; she loved the squeak of the plastic straw as it slid through the lacerated X in the plastic top of the paper cup; she loved the foil packets of ketchup; she loved ripping the ends off the itty-bitty corrugated paper rafts and shaking out the salt or pepper. She loved finally collecting all that trash in tiny armfuls and feeding it to the tall, hooded trash cans she referred to as "hungry robots." David Marley loved the "nom nom nom" sound his little sister made as she did this.

He stands in the center of the outdoor dining area. His hands fall from his hips as Sheriff Conneley and Deputy Arnold bring their orders over to the table Marley happens to be standing closest to. He has ordered nothing, and yet he has selected the table at which the others will stand to eat their "fast food," as it's called.

"I don't have the right shoes, Sheriff. Can't even hope to keep up with him if I don't have the right shoes."

The sheriff considers his chili dog, then points it at his deputy. "You said he wasn't wearing any shoes."

"Not this time." A glint of admiration on Arnold's face. "He wasn't, Sheriff; he wasn't wearing anything!"

"Wasn't wearing anything?"

"That's right, Sheriff. Naked as a blue jay."

"So, what kind—"

"Buck naked."

"So, what kind—"

"Except for his backpack, I mean."

"So, what kind..." The sheriff takes slow, deep breaths around his chilidog. "... what kind of shoes do you need to keep up with a kid who's not wearing any shoes at all?" He takes a bite.

"Well, Sheriff, a lot of it's about ankle support. But you also got to—"

"Whad in the hrull is so goddamned hard abou' sthopping' and searchin' a kid on froot!" The sheriff is angry now.

"He's not just on foot, Sheriff. He's got ... I don't know ... hooves or something. He crossed Quail Creek, over by the curly bend, and I thought first he was going to, you know, just jump out to that middle rock. But he—"

"We're running out of time, Deputy. I got people breathing down my neck. They're already thinking we botched the murder case, and now we gotta make that up. They want The Motel gone, and we're going to get that done." The Sheriff raises his eyes late to scan for listeners.

He lowers his head again and speaks more softly. "We know The Motel's growing more than fancy tomatoes—growing it somewhere, even if we didn't find it at The Motel—and we know this Sherpa fella makes regular pack trips from The Motel up

147

into Quarter Horse. And when you put the two together... All I need you to do, Arnold, is either, aiyee—" The sheriff raises a chili digit off his dog. "—follow him up and find the marijuana garden, or beeyee—" A second chili digit raises. "—search his pack and catch him hauling a harvest down."

"I did search his pack, Sheriff. Twice already, like I told you. He didn't have any marijuana. He just had—"

"A whole lot of film rolls. Yeah, you told me already. Because he's a nature photographer or something. Now—"

"But like, a whole lot, Sheriff."

"Oh, stop it, Arnold." The sheriff spits a piece of onion from his teeth. "By the time you stop him, he's almost all the way back into town. He's already unloaded the goods. Can't you see when someone's pulling the wool over your eyes?"

Arnold's eyes get small as he reviews his humiliation.

"Now, what you're going to do..." The sheriff dips a finger into the paper liner of his cardboard basket to collect some brown droppings. "... you're going to climb up there—high up there—and wait for him. Just wait there. 'Longside the path. Just wait."

"But he stays up there for days sometimes, Sheriff."

"And that's what you're going to do. You just wait 'longside the path for him."

"What path, Sheriff?"

"What do you mean, 'what path'? The one that goes up the goddamned mountain!"

"He doesn't use a path, Sheriff. That's what I mean. He's got, I don't know, hooves or something. You can't—"

"You're wearing me out, Arnold. Now, you drive down to Franksville, to the Big Oscar's Sporting Goods. You go in there and get you those shoes, the ones you talked about, plus a canteen, a rain poncho, and whatever the goddamned hell else you need, and then you catch this beatnik with something!"

Arnold has not taken even one bite of his chili dog, while the Sheriff is already done with his. Retaining the same tone of impatience, the sheriff says he's got to get back to work and walks off, leaving Arnold with his trash.

Marley observes the hurt face of Arnold as he watches the sheriff climb into his patrol car and drive off. Marley observes Arnold's uneaten chili dog. Marley sees that he himself has not treated Arnold with much respect or consideration, and he decides that he can easily improve this. "Do you have... Deputy, do you have an idea, more or less, of how many film rolls he was carrying?"

Arnold turns toward Marley. "Yes, sir. More than four dozen—but not five."

Marley appears surprised, impressed.

This appears to embarrass Arnold. He looks down. "Well I made an estimate, I mean."

"Did he have a camera with him?"

"Yes, he did. Two of them."

Marley nods. "That's very interesting. Good work. Do you know what kinds of cameras they were?"

"Well, I've got a camera, but it's nothing like these. These were bigger and had real long lenses."

"Perhaps when you are in Franksville getting your shoes, you could visit a camera store and see if they have any cameras that look like the ones you saw."

Arnold nods. "Oh, yes, sir! That's a great idea. I'll do that."

Marley decides to wait while Arnold finishes his meal. He watches the young deputy's lips move as he nurses his straw. He watches him carefully fold back the wax paper as he eats his chili dog. He is amazed to see not one drop of chili fall into the paper liner of the tray.

"Where did you intercept him?" Marley asks.

"Right by the falls."

"Both times?"

"Yes, sir."

Marley smiles. Well, maybe it's a smile. Whatever it is may feel compassionate on his side. "You're spending your time there because you're trying to catch the litterers, aren't you?"

Arnold's eyes widen. "Well … well, I was kind of doing both, sir. Because—"

"As you should. It's okay, I won't tell the sheriff."

Arnold looks at Marley. "So … so, you remember seeing that too, right, sir? When we were up there? All that awful trash…"

Marley nods with his newly formed compassionate smile. He is truly interested to hear what more Arnold has to say about this, and this must be apparent to Arnold, who unloads, "All that trash up there. Remember? We were wading through it. All that trash, right on top of our falls, our beautiful falls. Who would do that? And how can you ever even really clean that up? I mean, a lot of it has gone over and downstream to who knows where. Folks are going to be finding that trash in the river for generations…"

Marley listens patiently, even with surprise and admiration as he hears the passion build in Arnold's voice. It becomes clear that Arnold's outrage over The Motel hippies littering in nature far outstrips anything he feels over what they could be growing. "And we know it's the hippies, because it's all hippie trash!" As Arnold goes on, it becomes clear that he is also outraged over the disparity in the punishments the hippies could face if they're caught growing marijuana versus dumping trash in the river. It becomes clear that Arnold sees the marijuana thing as sort of being their own business, and maybe even within their rights in a free country—whereas dumping trash in the river, that's everybody's business, and a whole, whole lot worse. It becomes clear that Marley must ultimately return to the patrol car and leave the young deputy alone before he will ever finish his chili dog.

Alien Recall

Forward is learning to see and shoot. Both background. *Click.* And foreground. *Click.* He follows the graceful eagle as it glides in the mountain air, carefully maintaining it at the center of his telescopic camera lens. His back is straight, his posture in the nest disciplined. *Click.* Forward is studying flight.

Before he can leave the nest, there is much he must learn, a maturity he must reach. He understands now the purpose for which he has been called into this tree, this tree called Sequitur. He understands the better man he is to become, the collective movie he is supposed to help build. He understands the crusade to which he has been called and the rigorous training ahead of him.

Precisely now, he is learning that even while maintaining a soaring eagle almost still in his viewfinder, there is a whole story told in the background through which it flies. The giant bird takes him first over lush old growth. *Click.* Sailing in circles over this still pristine forest before entering, in grades, the landscapes degraded by the greed of man. *Click.* Catching, finally, an afternoon thermal rising from a parched clear cut, the eagle leaves the mountain valley. This sequence has finished, and Forward's back relaxes.

He stands for a moment. His palms come together symmetrically high above his head. His arms, torso, and legs arch to the right side. Then to the left. His arms then reach down to the nest floor in front of his feet. His hands return to prayer position in front of him, and he wraps one leg around the other. He squats and holds this twisted, one-leg balance for several minutes, then switches to the other leg. He understands that these yoga movements Sky has been teaching him are needed to condition his body for the day to come—the day he will leave the nest.

When Forward unfolds his legs and sits again before the telescope, he holds the eyepiece first between his palms. He closes his eyes as his arms move in a stirring motion to select the next direction.

When Forward lowers his eye to the scope this time, the view is abruptly upsetting, a grappling hook thrown up from the swift boat of his past. If he could believe in random coincidence, he would quickly turn the scope to a different view. But he hears the voice of this tree, this mountain, this valley, this planet. They have turned his scope toward this point. There is something he needs to see, even if it must remind the soldier-monk he is becoming of the self-indulgent hippy he recently was.

Forward recalls the motorhome, of course. And the campground. He wishes now that he hadn't been so rude to the elderly couple. He recalls that in his hallucination, they looked like aliens. He recalls trying to threaten the aliens with a ratty little shit shovel. He recalls them not appearing threatened. Instead, cheerful, even cooperative. He recalls that they lifted the tarp from their minibike and explained they hadn't started it in a while. He recalls kicking and kicking and kicking and having to pause before kicking and kicking and kicking again. He recalls the couple laughing at him as they watched. He recalls them making fun of his appearance. Joking about his "hero's uniform". Joking that he is needed in the coming war. They said everything happens for a reason. He recalls that the aliens waved as he drove off on their tiny motorcycle.

Now they're sunning themselves, in reclined beach chairs and sunglasses, just beyond the awning of their RV. They are right at the center of the magnified circle Forward sees with one eye.

And they are also in the road. A car driving through the campground can't get by.

The driver doesn't honk. Forward watches this: the driver who doesn't honk.

The man gets out of his car, a long black luxury sedan. Dark suit, sunglasses. Hat. He walks up to the sunbathing couple. Their sky-tilted faces acknowledge him, and they stand up to slowly begin moving their reclined chairs. The man with the hat helps the woman move her chair, since her husband's busy with his. The man in the hat is then back in his car, and he pulls forward.

Forward watches the car, the black luxury sedan. It drives to the north end of the campground and parks beside a second car that is obviously a rental.

Meek Little Sound

It's the meek little sound of a boot, or maybe a tennis shoe. It tries to push the barn door open a little more, wants to provide more clearance around the truck, around the truckload of toilets. And even though the sound repeats it is lost among the more prevalent sounds of pig and chains. Though the sound of the little shoe is even loud compared to that of a raindrop, right now, there's a huge commotion in the barn because a pig is squealing. Squealing as though bacon slices are being removed from it, one by one. And there is also the sound of thrashing chains. The metallic sound of the chains resonates in the ceramic of the truckload of American Standard commodes that has recently been backed into the barn.

Some Viet Cong soldiers in their black pajamas enter the barn; they pass single file alongside the truck, then kind of—*bomp, bomp, bomp*—pile up as they reach the end of the toilets. There they stand, amazed at what they see in the pen before them. One of the prisoners is on top of a pig. The pig is on her back, struggling and squealing, desperate to turn over, her violently writhing ham wishing very much to escape the missionary posture being forced on her. The prisoner has his pants down, his shirt open and pulled up. He presses much skin against the pig. His wet mouth is open as his snout thrashingly battles hers.

Could the prisoner really be trying to fuck the pig? ... That way? Why's he trying to kiss her?

A critical pajama finally arrives from the back and barks an order. Several pajamas from the pile reanimate into men, and these men climb over the fence and remove the maniac from the sow. It takes three to hold him. The prisoner wears the uniform of a major and seems violently disinterested in anything but the pig—the pig that has backed into the far corner and now eyes

155

him suspiciously.

The boss pajama is older than the other pajamas; he has a different scarf, and a calm expression. He walks around the side of the pen, stops midway, and rests an elbow on the top rail as he inspects the prisoners. One of his men arrives to deliver a pet of sorts: a foreigner with dark, curly bangs and a leash around his neck. Probably a translator. The boss takes the leash and casually drapes it over the rail of the pigpen. It's clear his pet will not run away. He takes a cigarette out of his pocket and lights it. He wastes the first draw—pulls it into his mouth and out the side of his face. Same with the second. Only when the end of the cigarette is glowing red and he gets a full, hot draw does he pull the smoke into his lungs. He lets the smoke warm him for a moment, eyes on the prisoners, then tosses the cloud out through his mouth and nostrils. He nods, and several more pajamas climb over the rail and into the pen. They stretch the chain out in a line, kick the feet of the prisoners into position, and attach one end of the chain to a post that supports the barn. The other end they attach to the back bumper of the truck.

But the symmetrical chain line they're trying to set up is immediately broken when they release the man in the major uniform. He lunges to the end of his ankle shackles, and from there he tries to swim the rest of the way to the pig. The other prisoners recover, holding wide-legged surfer stances, and watch the one on the ground carefully.

The boss barks orders at his men twice more to set and hold the shackled prisoners in the line that he has evidently envisioned as the starting point of his interrogation.

This is a complete failure. The problematic prisoner keeps pulling down the line when they release him. The boss is on his third cigarette—even the second one came out of the pack more clumsily than the first—when he forcefully crushes it against the rail. He nods to a soldier, who calls to another one, who then climbs up into the truck. The engine starts.

The three prisoners that have been preoccupied with getting pulled off their feet by the fourth start to look around. They're starting to better examine the sequential configuration of chain and legs and wonder about it. They see their new attachment to the post. They see their new attachment to the truck. Pensively, they lift one chained leg up, then the other. They start to draw horrible conclusions.

The black prisoner now speaks: "Hey, boss, you ain't thinking of trying any of that mid-evil shit with us...?"

Yawn's question receives no answer. Boss stares back with cold eyes. It seems the zeroth order of business in the interrogation is for the captives to fully understand their predicament. He walks to the exit. His entourage follows. Before he leaves, he nods to the truck.

Ka-poonk! The load of toilets makes a heavy chandelier sound as the truck goes into gear. The truck pulls forward.

Day-Glo Girdle Mannequin

The case against Henry Walker is strong. Marley silently tells Cupid this (the two have learned to ignore the late-night diner glass between them). Walker and the victim were alone together when she died. He and the victim were heard shouting and breaking furniture. Fibers from his macramé belt were found in her neck. As Marley runs through these facts with Cupid, there is no explicit admission that he has any personal experience with either Walker or the victim. But if Cupid is paying close attention, he will notice that the deputy will at least say the name of the suspect. But not the victim. He refers to the suspect as "Walker," but never to the victim as "Marley" … nor does he ever say "Sarah," or "Breeze." He only says "victim."

"What! You got Movie tickets?" Waitress Boo Boo stands with her coffee orb. "Who… How did you…?" Boo Boo is scanning Marley.

He sees her doing this. "A man named Fray gave them to me. Earlier today. I gave him a ride." Marley admits that he doesn't know what movie the tickets are for, or why the tickets are really photographs.

"Twenty-four," Boo Boo explains, lowering her coffee pot to the level of her customer's ignorance. "That's how many people each year get to see *The Movie*. Mr. Fray shows it only once a year, and his igloo has twenty-four chairs." She seems disgusted at the deputy's stroke of luck.

"Igloo?"

"*The Movie* wraps over you in a dome, and what you see depends on which direction you're looking."

Boo Boo goes to tend to another customer, but she soon returns. "You don't realize how special it is. Four generations of Fray's family have been taking pictures of these mountains.

Each year, Mr. Fray shows *The Movie* to twenty-four people. Only twenty-four people. They come out transformed."

"Transformed? Why, what's so special—"

"It's a movie about the environment, Deputy. How we've been changing it over the last hundred years. It's also a photo album of Ashton's history. But these are just the parts that can be described. There's always more. Revelations. That's what people who see it say. Each gets a revelation, and it depends on what part of the screen they were looking at. They come out transformed. You're so lucky. I'd die to see *The Movie!*"

Marley pauses, trying to understand. "A movie about the environment? You mean nature?" He slides the photographs/tickets across the table toward the standing waitress. "Why don't you take them? I'm not fond of movies."

Boo Boo's fingers come up like they will pounce on the two photos before her. But then she stops. Nods. "If Mr. Fray gave you the tickets, then you're supposed to see *The Movie*, Deputy."

Marley is now plenty confused about *The Movie*, the igloo—is that the name of the theater?—and the seemingly unnecessary exclusivity. "In any case, I don't need two tickets." He nods to the photos. "Why don't you take one?"

Waitress Boo Boo frowns, her face not friendly. "Not sure I need another deputy trying to ask me out on a date."

She stares at the photos for a moment, then quickly at him. "Especially such a dim-witted one. You're not a very smart pig, are you?" She slides the photos back to his side of the table. "All the movie tickets are different, and Mr. Fray gave you these specific ones for a reason. Look at them." She almost pushes his head down. "Nothing jumps out?"

Marley looks down at the photos. One is of Coulot Falls, the other of the town's trash dump. Location and time are printed at the bottom of each photo.

Marley continues looking at the photos while the waitress looks on. He feels a short spasm in his chest. No, he's not a very smart pig. He's not sure what he's supposed to see.

Boo Boo sees this and shakes her head, rotating with her coffee orb to leave. Over her shoulder, she gives the dumb pig a hint: "Day-Glo girdle mannequin... Nothing strange there?"

Marley is then alone with Cupid and the photos before him. And this is probably good, because it would be embarrassing if the waitress stood by to watch how long it takes him to put it together, even with her hint.

Sure, he sees that both photos show trash—one where trash is supposed to be, the other where it's not supposed to be. Sure, both trash piles have a discarded mannequin—maybe a girdle mannequin, fair enough. He feels a train of vibration in his chest as he hears a voice inside his head. It's his sister's voice. His sister's voice mocking his own: "Heyyy, wade a minit... ain't that there the same girdle mannequin in both pictures? Is that hippie paint? Don't that there Day-Glo girdle mannequin look just like it could be some hippie's throwed-away art project?"

Marley sees that the photo at the dump was taken a week before the photo at the falls. If it is indeed the same mannequin in each photo—and there are not likely to be two such customized and separately discarded girdle mannequins—then someone must have taken the mannequin from the town dump and re-dumped it at the falls.

More Than Four

Despite the humidity and stench in the barn, Major David Marley finally understands the blessed experience he has been given. A spiritual awakening has reached him. Everything preceding this moment—the parental role he adopted at fourteen to take care of his little sister after their mother died, his removal of their abusive father from the house, his aborted studies at Yale, his recruitment into dark intelligence, his deployment in this senseless war, and finally his arrival in this pigpen … all sewn together to blow his mind in precisely this way, right now. He is here to observe and log all of this tremendously important and fundamental intel swirling around him. He must carefully log *all* of it.

But right now, the others won't let him plug back into the pigtaphone. Marley must. But he must also choose his battles. For now, he has learned from his brothers in chains that he absolutely must stand calmly—just stand calmly with them. In a line. It's very important.

So that they don't repeat what just happened.

"Look at the tire tracks. That's got to be one meter, almost exactly." Yawn's voice is now accurate and mechanical. "And you know what that tells us? That tells us we got ourselves here a gamester. You watch—that boss be back here in five or some other precise-ass number of minutes, and he's going to ask his question again. If he doesn't like the answer, he's going to stomp his pajama ass out of the barn again like he did, and pull the truck forward another meter. One meter each time we don't answer his question." Yawn kicks at the chain. "See the slack? See the slack we got? That's how many questions we can get wrong." Yawn nods with admiration, and disgust. "Sure clever how they sewed all our feet into one predicament." He turns and straightens. "What I want you brothers to know—and I even mean you over there, you crazy motherfucker—is that we don't have much time to get it together. By 'get it together,' I mean our MTF: our More than Four. Can't come in at only three point one or some shit." Yawn lifts his ankle shackle. "That's exactly what the gookas want—thinking we'll show them, all on our own, our weakest link. We got to get our MTF together, my brothers!"

Yawn then sighs. He looks at Edison. Walker looks at Edison.

Escarpment

Deputy Arnold sits against the escarpment. His binoculars monitor the trailheads below; there are three. Trailheads are not where he expects to catch a glimpse of the vaulting Sherpa, but it is where the sheriff would expect him to look. Arnold can still hear the sheriff hollering about the cost of the boots and camp stuff, especially the canteen. The deputy did buy the very best one. The canteen. The sheriff only got angrier when Arnold explained that the reason why it was expensive is that it is avalanche-proof.

Arnold monitors not only the trailheads, but also the trails —at least the few parts of the trails that are visible through the treetops. He knows the sheriff would expect this too. But most importantly, the deputy also allows his field glasses to cast random motions over the whole landscape below. His surveying motions are not truly random, of course, but directed by a subtle logic he is only subconsciously aware of. To help enable this, his grip on the binoculars is loose and sensitive, ready to respond to any ethereal tug.

Deputy Arnold believes in such tugs. In all matters of religion or importance, it is the only way he has ever found anything that was hard to see. Of course, he understands that in the workaday drop of his house keys, he can expect the keys to be near his door mat; that's where he should look. But he has also learned that to uncover things more majestic and spiritual, his expectations must be humbler. Less knowing. He must relax his pesky mind and preconceptions. He must avoid being told where to look. He must let his eyes simply listen and be called.

And so soon the echoes of the ranting sheriff have faded. Deputy Arnold has forgotten the trailheads and the trails. Instead, his torso is loose and gyratory, his observing head a gimbal, its distant gaze in soft Brownian motion, his preconceptions religiously absent yet spiritually eager.

Arnold currently views with his left eye dominant. Usually, ocular dominance goes to his right. It is usually his right eye that decides what the two eyes look at. But not right now. Arnold has learned to see with his left eye in charge. This is a different kind of seeing, more of a gestalt view. It is perhaps less critical, less focused, but more holistic. Or at least his trained fish-eye gaze has allowed him to capture suddenly and simultaneously two distinct directions of interest. One is the flash of a backpack moving through a forest clearing below. It moves with such speed and grace that it could only be on the shoulders of Sherpa. The other, registering in his upper peripheral vision, is a rising trail of dust above a forest road on the opposing mountainside. Interestingly, when Arnold's right eye busts in to reclaim the wheelhouse, he finds his restored regular vision aimed, as the first priority, not at Sherpa, but at the dust snake.

Arnold knows much about dust snakes. As the only child of a single dad who worked a logging skidder, Arnold spent much time sitting on or in his dad's work truck and looking at forests. Motion is especially interesting to a young boy. Arnold learned about every piece of heavy equipment the Ashton Lumber Company owned and saw the powerful things these machines could do to trees. This included completely removing them from the forest, and thereby creating spectacular views. With these views, Arnold learned to identify vehicles and their drivers by the dust snake they stirred up as they drove up the mountain roads. Big trucks had a different snake than light trucks. Loaded trucks had a different snake than empty trucks. Even the same truck driven by a different man had a different snake signature. Snakes in the morning look different than snakes in the afternoon.

As a child, Arnold was celebrated for telling the men when the boss was driving up the mountain—or which wife was driving up, and whether her snake seemed angry. It is perhaps because he has had so much experience with dust snakes that this snake before him, and not Sherpa, is the first priority of his restored focus.

He does not recognize its signature. This is not a snake Arnold has seen before. It is distinctly careless and aggressive. Up the mountain, a light truck or van is being driven furiously, towing the dust snake high and wild behind it like a paper kite pulled by a racehorse.

The hollering of his sheriff returns in his head, and Arnold snaps back to Sherpa. Sherpa is already halfway across the clearing. His springs between the felled and discarded tree limbs are high and effortless, all energy in his landings recycled into forward motion. How can a man move like that?

In great excitement, Arnold pulls up his tent pegs. He begins to stuff things into his pack, but then abandons that and holds only his avalanche-proof canteen. He takes a big drink, then abandons it too. He must be as light as can be if he has any chance of catching Sherpa. He brings up the binoculars.

Arnold heads not down toward the place where he spotted Sherpa, nor toward some extrapolated point where Sherpa will be. He moves instead, at least for this first part, along a topographic contour of the escarpment, for Arnold knows he can never be fast enough to chase Sherpa. But he can move around the bend of the escarpment and then descend to intercept him. Like an eagle on a fish. He will need only one step for every three Sherpa must take.

Soon Arnold stands, binoculars fixed on a creek below, but bobbing in the waves of his excited breath. He figures Sherpa must cross the creek, and when he sees this, he will chart his line of interception and descend.

Sherpa appears. A sure-footed skip over several high rocks, and he has already crossed the creek and disappeared again into the forest.

Arnold drops his binoculars and leaps forward. Down the escarpment he goes, no path, his feet precise and fast, tapping the tops of rocks to keep his whole motion mostly in the air. With the best boots and gravity in his favor, he is able to vault like Sherpa. Deputy Arnold feels majestic, believing his eyes have listened and the contingencies of the world around him have sponsored exactly this beautiful moment.

Smoke. The new shoes are still a bit sticky, but with close attention, Arnold easily compensates. Smoke. His knees move together, waving right and left as he slaps the topsides of the moguls of the loose mountainside down which he skis in his good new boots. Smoke. Smoke! Smoke!!!

Deputy Arnold suddenly stops. A timber landing on the mountainside across the river is on fire.

Who Is Major Marley?

"Who eaze Majeur Marlee?"

The underwater poodle swims right up to the glass wall to ask this. Major Marley can see the sea mammal bobbing before him, waiting for a response.

Major Marley is, however, in no condition to provide one. He understands that the poodle is an extension of the sea monster behind it—the sea monster with the strange eyebrows. He does hear and understand the question. He just has a hard time retaining for very long the understanding that he is the one being addressed. His sense of self is essentially very provisional, evolving. And in any case, he is still engaged with an important task right now.

The task at hand is to reestablish electrical contact with the pigtaphone.

And that's what Marley is trying to accomplish. He has so much important intel to log. The world—whatever that is—and his location within it are so multifarious and baffling right now. Marley, whoever he is, is so happy to have this important task to pursue. The pigtaphone is the payload of this reconnaissance, the guiding star—a star he must not lose, or he will be absorbed into the storm of multiverses opening and closing on either side of his self-identity.

Major Marley understands that the pigtaphone wants this too. She is a receptacle. Marilyn wants Marley to drop his data into her. Although Marley is right now held forcibly upright by two guards, he will leap to the pig again as soon as he can. Now, while they restrain him, he is thinking only of being back on top of her—how maybe he should, as sea otters do, bite her snout this time to hold on … and only then should he run his tongue into her wet nostril. Not before.

The boss pajama asks again for Marley's military occupation.

Marley is consumed with the moment he feels coming very soon, when he will be back on top of Marilyn and unloading his data. He is consumed with consideration of better ways for obtaining electrical contact. The boss slaps Marley's face. This emphasizes to Marley that biting her nose should work, but he absolutely should not try to plug his tongue into her snapping mouth again. The boss slaps the prisoner again and seems both disgusted and amazed at the response. The prisoner has eyes only for the pig.

"Hey, boss man! Take a look at this."

It's Yawn. The captors turn to observe the prisoner.

Yawn raises his heel, toes on the ground, and his leg turns to a profile pose. "See that? See that thang there? See how big and thick it is?" Yawn speaks slowly so that the translator can follow. "What you're looking at there is the leg of a Bronnasaurus Rex. Hold that in your head a minute. Now look over there— look at the cotton-candy legs on these other boys." Yawn then nods at the truck. "Now Boss, you drive away with those toilets ... everybody knows it ain't going to be no dark-meat drumstick snapping off this bird. So, you be sure now and give me some points for vol-un-tary co-operation when I tell you this: you got more luck getting your answers out of that hog over there than you got getting it out of this burnt toast. Boy ain't really together anymore, if you know what I mean. Since you rifle-butted his brains in, the only thing he good for now is looking for land mines."

Ka-poonk! The toilets make a chandelier sound as the truck goes into gear. The truck pulls forward.

Ferrying Breeze

From Deputy Marley's perspective, waitress Boo Boo is suddenly three o'clock and overhead. Over multiple late nights in the last few weeks, he has seen her collection of colors come forward from behind his right ear as he sits in precisely this booth, gazing through the diner window at the giant Cupid high on his pole. But tonight, she immediately slides in ... into his booth. She sits across the table from him now.

She clenches a lighter underneath her elbow—the elbow that supports the forearm supporting the hand that holds up her unlit cigarette. It's clear that she has something to say. Instead of saying it, she turns to nod at the Cupid sign out front. "Did you know," she says with a laugh, "did you know his bulb burned out the same night *hers* did?"

She lifts her face to look at the deputy. Her eyes constrict, and her whole face pulls closer to her nose. "Maybe Cupid climbed off his pole to ferry Breeze into the next world." A tear rolls over the edge of her eyelid and streaks down her face. "I'm sorry, David. I'm so, so sorry. I didn't know. I didn't know who you were." A second tear falls. She laughs, her eyes and palms skyward. "I think I'm the only one in Ashton who's put it together."

Marley considers what he has heard. Then he asks, "Were you and Sarah close?"

Boo Boo's nostrils become small. She nods. "She was close with a lot of people ... but yes." She draws her cigarette and lighter toward her chest. "She was proud of you, you know?"

Marley stares back.

"I mean, she didn't want to be around you, because you're so straight and unplayful. But she was real, real proud of you. She said you're ... you're like, top of the class in anything you do."

Marley's hands find each other under the table. " 'Unplayful,' huh?"

Boo Boo nods, smiling. "She said she always felt so safe around you." The compassion in her laugh shouts into his face. She watches his breaths. "That's why she had to get the *hell* away from you! Swat you away, like a fly. Get away!"

Marley's head tilts back to avoid the swat the waitress demonstrates. His eyes have not left hers. His eyes are filled with tears he will, of course, not allow to fall. But he has less control over his chest; it spasms ... and again, this time welling up almost audibly into his throat.

"She said you were her dad, her brother, and her best friend. But not her adventure. That's why she just had to get the *hell* away from you!" Boo Boo swats at him again, slower this time, a shorter reach.

A triplet of tremors rise in Marley's chest, and he breaks his eyes away from Boo, understanding now that the giant brown saucers on the other side of her glasses are the only eyes in the universe that see his pain ... understanding now that waitress Boo Boo has the power to make him laugh and cry, even at the same time. Even if he is incapable of showing either.

Boo Boo slides an unlit cigarette back into the pack. As she stands to go tend to a customer, Marley feels the brush of her fingers and cigarette box on his shoulder. "I'll be back," she whispers.

PERFECT PITCH

Fake Eyes

This time when the boss comes back and asks, "Who eaze Majeur Marley?", he waves an arm to emphasize that all of the prisoners may contribute to the answer. He seems angry that this was not already implicitly understood—part of the clever design of this setup.

Yawn leans forward, his face showing amazement. "Well, look at that! Just noticing right now." He squints as he looks straight at the boss. "Faw, Ed, you boys seeing the brows on this gooka?"

"Wow, oh boy, that *is* something!"

"Man, how weird. It's like each one is a black dot."

"If his face was a domino, we'd get to turn it sideways when we lay it down."

"Double ones. It's a good stone, man."

"And how he supposed to keep the rain out of his eyes with those things?"

"No, man, they're fake eyes."

"What you mean, 'fake eyes'?"

"Yeah, like on a butterfly. An evolutionary adaptation, man."

"And how would having eyebrows like that be an adaptation, Forward?"

"... Huh? Yeah, I don't know, man. Maybe so his predators will think he's looking at them, even when he's really asleep."

"Hoo-hoo..."

"Heh-heh..."

The prisoners are laughing at something. Boss pajama throws down his cigarette, nods. The truck starts once again.

"Wait wait wait wait!" Forward yells. He steps forward, tremendously wanting to communicate something.

The boss pajama, Domino, listens.

"How about, man ... how about changing the game, so that we can also win a backward step? You're all stick and no carrot, man. Wait, wait, wait. Just wait. How about this: if we give you an answer to a question you didn't even ask, you pull the truck back a step? We just want a carrot, man."

Domino listens to his poodle. The reference to a carrot seems to translate poorly, but the boss understands. He straightens, then nods with powerful caution for the unrequested answer to proceed. He is demonstrating that an excellent interrogator will allow suggestions from the prisoner.

"Okay, so, man ... these toilets." Walker points up to the load on the flatbed. "Do you even know what you got here?" He grins. "Real special. Real special, man."

The poodle translates. Domino straightens.

"Man, just unpack one of the crates. You'll see what I mean."

The poodle translates, and Domino becomes very interested. He sends his men to do as the prisoner suggests: climb up onto the truck and unpack one of the crates.

Domino very soon discovers, however, that inside the crate, or even inside the toilet, there are no drugs, no cash, no arms or explosives. When he turns again to Walker, his expression shows that he does not understand why the prisoner has suggested that he unpack a toilet crate.

"Top of the line, man! See that toilet?"

"..."

"Do you even understand American toilets, man?"

Yawn steps forward helpfully to confirm that the partially unpacked toilet before them is indeed one of the best. "That ain't no regular shitter, boss; that there's a Cadillac crapper. You understanding that, Domino? What Faw here's trying to tell you?"

"..."

"Those toilets were headed to the officer's club, man," says Walker.

"Wait!" says Yawn. "Come back, Dom. Don't go starting that truck. What Faw's trying to tell you is that you can be damned sure the big brass is coming for their crappers."

"You took their toilets, man!"

"They coming for you!"

Confusion and impatience grow on the boss's face as he listens to the translation.

Ka-poonk! The truck goes into gear. It pulls forward.

The Falls

Deputy Marley parks in the lot of scenic Coulot Falls. He removes his shirt and carefully folds it. He removes his gun belt and sets it on his folded shirt. He takes the items to the rear of the car and puts them in the trunk. One can see, even from afar, that the deputy is now unarmed.

Of course, he could have arrived earlier and stashed a gun down at the meeting point. Beside the falls, where gunshots will not be heard and the river will carry a body far from where the trigger was pulled. Stash a gun.

This is exactly what Marley did. He is surprised that Baskin agreed to meet him like this. Baskin should know that Marley wants to kill him. For killing his sister.

Before Marley left the diner, Boo Boo explained that she never knew Breeze's real name. She explained that they don't use real names at The Motel, pausing for a moment to suggest that there are environmental activists at The Motel who need it this way. She explained that she never knew Breeze's real name, even though they were good friends. She explained that, well, of course, she did know Breeze's real name once she saw it in the paper. But she hadn't put everything together because she didn't know *his* name. He has no name tag, she explained, because he takes off his shirt in the parking lot before he comes in. Waitress Boo Boo explained to Deputy Marley that it's only because Munchie and Canoe saw him at the chili dog place, while he was wearing his shirt, that she found out. That he and Breeze have the same last name. Boo Boo then raised a palm to her chest and explained that that's when, "Oh my god!", she realized that she always knew. She explained that she shouldn't really have needed him to wear his shirt in the diner, because she already knew. She knew, but she didn't know she knew. Because, the waitress explained, raising her face to look squarely at David across the diner table, "Breeze had the most ferocious blue eyes in the whole world. Just like yours."

His last time at the diner, Boo explained all that. And right before he exited, she gave him a bag. A paper bag. The top of the bag was folded down tight, suggesting it should be opened later privately. She explained that this in the bag is the present he sent his sister for her birthday. She explained that Breeze really loved it, and that they played with it together a lot. When it wasn't busy. She pointed toward the counter, and specifically at the stool by the register, where Breeze sat. She explained that Breeze kept it here at the diner, right under the counter, because with all the sharing that goes on in The Motel, it would have quickly disappeared if she took it home. Boo Boo explained to David that the last time they played with the bright yellow tape recorder he sent his sister, they accidentally left it recording when they put it away under the counter. It recorded the conversation of two customers. Boo explained to David that he really needs to listen to it.

Marley played the tape right away, right there in his car in the diner parking lot.

On the first part of the tape, he could hear his sister. And Boo Boo. He sampled only single syllables as he fast-forwarded through to find the accidental conversation. One of two men was doing the talking.

Marley recognized the voice. The man. Tom Baskin. They had once worked together. Maybe better said, they once worked alongside each other. Marley had resigned. Baskin went darker. Blacker.

Baskin's voice is not very identifiable. He sounds like many men. But his cadence, the timing of his words, reveals the thick strategy under his spontaneous and casual sentences. And that carefully honed strategy is what identifies his voice.

At the falls, there is one car in the parking lot. Marley knows it is a rental car. He knows this without really knowing how he knows this. Baskin is already here.

Marley leaves his car and walks down the path to the falls. His left hand glides on the handrail as he descends several stairs. He is slow, observant. He arrives at the river and follows a second path over to the base of the falls.

He finds Baskin there.

The two men are almost behind the wall of falling water. The roar makes whatever Baskin is saying inextricable. Marley glances down to see that the rocks are still stacked over the gun he hid earlier. He comes to stand by his weapon as he observes Baskin trying to speak further.

Marley requested the meeting. There's no reason for Baskin to start the conversation. And yet this is what Baskin is trying to do. In increments, Baskin leans further forward in his pursuit of being heard over the roar of the waterfall.

Marley observes the man's crescent eyebrows, the friendly smile with its twisted glitch. As Marley watches Baskin's lips, he can tell that Baskin is now making a joke about him—about Marley getting captured by the enemy on his first day over there. Baskin will follow this with a statement, more seriously, of how he's really so, so glad his friend got out of that okay.

Got out okay...? Well... Baskin's nod will reference Marley's head scars, and there will then be a joke about that.

Baskin absolutely must bring up how weird it is. How things turned out and all. With the program. Baskin is suggesting now that Marley recall how, despite Baskin's seniority and fifteen years of experience, they gave the program to somebody else. Some young guy. Ha, they gave him a major's uniform! Probably the first uniform the kid had ever had. Baskin will then laugh about how the man who made that decision—that decision to hire the young guy over the older one with more experience—how that man has since been fired. Coming closer to Marley, Baskin is describing how not only did the young major get captured his first day over there directing the program, but on his first day back, he got the program defunded. Baskin will laugh. That young major made some enemies.

Baskin is too close to see the gun Marley now holds at his waist. Baskin does not seem concerned to look.

This is what bothers Marley, raises his awareness of the clarity required for the type of vengeance he's really after. He knows the operation Baskin works for. Even if the choice of victim was just a spontaneous element of the operation, they would have at least taken the time afterward to find out who they killed and who cared about her.

Somehow, Baskin doesn't know of Marley's relationship with the victim. His relationship with Walker? The Brotherhood...?

Marley is unsure of the reason for Baskin's extreme cluelessness. He is unsure of the reason for the cluster of coincidences. Most importantly, he is unsure of who sponsored his sister's murder. Marley comes to realize that even more than the assassin—or Baskin, who hired him—he wants the sponsor. And maybe the sponsor's sponsor. However long it takes, he will find whoever's at the top of this ladder. Marley will get reasons. Then revenge.

Baskin has come so close now that Marley can't see him anymore. At least not continuously. Baskin keeps leaning over to Marley's ear. His face is wet. He's grinning and telling Marley in shouts how he can understand how he must want back in. All that action going on at The Motel now. Important battlefield of the big war that's starting. Baskin is telling Marley that he knows that's why Marley has been hanging around town as a sheriff's deputy. Because he wants back in. Baskin, still grinning, gloating, is explaining that maybe he can put a word in for him. But god! Baskin laughs again over how bad Marley messed up in Nam.

Marley slides the gun into his pocket. He turns, ignoring

Baskin, and walks away from the falls.

Real Major

With the reverse motion of a claw collecting poker chips, Private Edison combs his hair. He appears thoughtful and concerned. "They'll be back in five minutes." He straightens. "They're just going to pluck legs off of us, and then drill into whatever's left of the major. Boys, it's time. I have to step in."

Walker and Yawn are quiet. They appear concerned for Edison.

"How can we help out, Ed?" asks Yawn.

"Help—yes, that'd be great," says Edison, returning from his thoughts. "Okay, could you get the major up and get him into, I don't know, sort of the splits? If we spread our legs, there's still enough slack for one of us to pull our ankles together and twist a knot in the chain. We can make it look like we've made me the only one safe from getting my legs pulled off when they pull the truck forward next time."

Walker nods, regarding Edison with admiration and sadness. "Has to be you?"

Edison looks at Marley, who is stretched on his stomach across the floor of the pen as far as he can reach toward the pig. He chuckles. "No choice now. Has to be me."

Walker and Yawn nod. They understand, and they get to work. Pulling the chain ends taut, they then work to pull Marley into the splits. The major remains violently disinterested in anything but the pig, but they get him into position even without his cooperation.

Edison gathers the slack in the chain and pulls his ankles together. He turns in place, twisting the chain onto itself, trying to make a kink or a knot of sorts.

He has to settle with whatever knot he's managed when the boss and his men return, entering alongside the truck of toilets. The boss resumes his position at the pen rail, a cigarette promptly lit in one hand, poodle leash in the other.

The boss is on his second puff when he notices what the prisoners have done. This interests him greatly. He has a man climb into the pen and inspect the knot in the chain at Edison's ankles. Soon, he has his man climb back out of the pen. Then he eyes Edison and laughs. He points to Edison. His poodle says, "Majeur Marley, ee eeze you!"

Edison looks resigned, irritated. "Well, I'm glad you didn't have to rip legs off my boys before you finally figured that out. Sure took you long enough."

The post-laughter face of boss pajama first displays his pride in the success of his chain design. This expression dissolves a bit as he listens to his poodle translate the prisoner's words. He shifts to tell Edison that he suspected this all along. "Young major, old private?" he says without his translator. "I don't believe."

Edison's Midwestern dialect is gone; he speaks now with ivy-league arrogance. "I'm sure you must know that when your men busted in on our whorehouse, we were all upstairs undressed. Under the circumstances, I can't say that I minded at all finding this private's uniform before finding my own." Edison nods toward Marley. "And that junkie there would put on a dress if that's what was left."

The boss looks very, very pleased. It seems that he was growing impatient with the absurdity in his pen, and he is proud now of the cleverness in his chain design. It seems his interrogation may finally begin.

Donuts

The deputy Marley observes the deputy Arnold arrive, donuts first, through the passenger door of the patrol car. Arnold has the box open, a hopeful smile. Even before turning to properly seat himself, he pulls the passenger door closed behind him.

"I don't eat donuts." Marley glances at Arnold. "But thanks." He drives the patrol car forward.

Deputy Arnold closes the donut box. He fastens his seat belt. If Deputy Marley doesn't eat donuts, then neither does Deputy Arnold. He sets the donut box in the back seat.

They return to the scene of yesterday's crime: one of the Lumber Company's timber landings, where logs are pulled out of the forest to be loaded onto trucks. Arson. Two D7s, a skidder, and a yarder. And an office trailer. Destroyed. In principle, people could have been inside the trailer, so this is much bigger than just vandalism. "Ecoterrorism!" the sheriff called it. A new and powerful term seems to have been handed to him recently. He repeated it several times.

Marley has not yet gotten out of the car, and so neither has Arnold. Hand still on the steering wheel, Marley looks forward through the windshield, out at the landing of cut trees and charred machines. A moment passes, and then Marley turns to get the box of donuts from the back seat. He opens the box, chooses a donut, holds it over his lap, and turns the box to Arnold.

Arnold sees Marley staring at him now, a strange expression of both accusation and gratitude. Arnold cautiously takes a donut from the box. He sees that Marley has taken a donut only to allow him to take one. This respectful consideration is confusing for Arnold. He tries to take a bite, but then lowers the donut again.

"You figured it out, didn't you, sir?"

Marley nods, the accusation receding now from his face, but the gratitude remaining. "Thank you."

On this matter, that is all that is said. The men need voice no further clarification. The sheriff had put Arnold in charge of finding the murder victim's next of kin. And Arnold reported no living relatives. Certainly not a brother working at their own sheriff's station. Marley would not be allowed to stay on the murder case if his relationship with the victim were known.

By birth and training, David Marley is not the type to feel sorry for himself, because he's not the type to feel himself. At fourteen, he became a father to his own sister. The head of the household. The maturity that demanded took a piece of his smooth, adolescent timeline and spliced it over the resulting discontinuities. With the whole reason for that erected responsibility suddenly gone now, the missing pieces of his own childhood roil up into his present. The compassion shown by Arnold triggers Marley to allow compassion for himself. The missing pieces of boy roil up to reveal the missing pieces of man.

Now, the sound of Arnold gets louder as he comes around to the open passenger door to get a new donut. This makes Marley aware that Arnold has been talking to him for several minutes. From outside the car, excited, pointing, moving back in front of the patrol car and pointing again from there to be sure Marley sees him. There's something very important Arnold wants to show him. That's why they're here.

"... they haven't used that old donkey in years ... and look there at that yarder; doesn't even have a cage; insurance won't cover ... that D7, there? Boy, if the Company ever had a lemon..."

Marley, still inside the car and holding his donut, puts together what Arnold is trying to describe. All the big machinery burned here was a bunch of old shit the Lumber Company wasn't using anymore.

"And who would tow an office up here? Geez, any paperwork

you need to do up here, you can do from a truck cab."

Marley comes to finally lower his donut and exit the car. He understands now Arnold's point, and it's a good one. It seems the Ashton Lumber Company was at least consulted during the design of this arson attack on themselves. They towed their broken and outdated machines up here to get burned, and they hauled up an office trailer only so that it can be claimed that people could have been killed in the fire. Ecoterrorism.

"We can't, sir. Even if the sheriff's telling us we have to, we can't arrest him. He didn't do it. I can't, I just won't!"

"What?" Marley finds himself beside Arnold and one of the torched D7s. He sets his donut down on the charred track of the machine. "No, he didn't do it. I know, Arnold."

"You do?" Arnold looks surprised. "But how, sir? I haven't even told you why. I mean, I tried to tell the sheriff, but he wouldn't listen. And I know, I know why it looks like he did it, but—"

"You're right. He's being framed."

"Exactly! That's what I was thinking too. But sir, how—"

"I had my own autopsy done."

"Huh? Your own what, sir? You mean for the..."

Marley turns toward Arnold. "Not many would have had access to the drug that was inside the victim."

"But it's The Motel, sir. They got LSD and all kinds of—"

"The drug is from an experimental weapons program, Arnold. Few could have gotten a hold of it. And in any case, Walker would have known better than to expect a good trip from it. I think somebody put the drug in the burritos or something else they ingested that night."

Arnold nods agreeably. He also looks confused. "Sir ... I don't understand what that has to do with Sherpa."

"Who?"

"Sherpa. Sherpa, sir. The sheriff says we got to arrest him for the arson, but he didn't do it. He didn't do it, sir."

"Sherpa? You mean the kid the sheriff has you chasing through the mountains on a fool's errand?"

"I'm not a fool, sir."

Marley looks back at him. "No. No, I don't believe you are. Tell me about Sherpa. Please."

Arnold's face now looks proud. He speaks quickly. "Okay, well I was following him, see. Following him just like the sheriff told me to do. He went up the mountain with his pack, and I knew he'd have to funnel through Snider Canyon on his way down, so I was camped out and watching for him. From a place up high, where I could just drop down on him real fast and catch him with whatever's in his pack, just like the sheriff wanted. And that was about to happen. I spotted him coming through, and I was running down to get him, like an eagle coming down on a trout. You know what I mean? But I didn't get to, because right before that happened, he changed direction. On account of the fire, sir. He saw it and—"

"Wait. You saw the fire?"

"Well, the smoke. It was across the canyon, but yeah, I saw the smoke. Sherpa did too, and that's why he changed his direction, to run toward it. Once he started up the other side of the canyon, oh, wow, no way I could keep up with him! He moves like a deer, sir. By the time I got to the landing, he had the whole fire put out and was already gone. Emptied three of the Company's fire extinguishers. He didn't start the fire, sir—he put it out."

Arnold then looks angry. "I wish now I hadn't ever even told the sheriff. Sheriff wants us to arrest him, and he wants to use my testimony. But just the part about me seeing him nearby when the fire started. Didn't even care about the empty fire extinguishers. Said it could have been Smokey Bear or anybody else who put the fire out. And, well, yeah, I didn't really see Sherpa put out the fire, but anyway, he couldn't have been the one to start the fire, because after I saw him down by the river, there's no way even he could have gotten up to the landing that fast. Not by the time I saw the smoke. I also told the sheriff about the dust snake I saw going up to the landing. Right before the fire started, and—"

" 'Dust snake'? What do you mean?"

"The dust snake, sir. Somebody driving up to the landing. I saw their snake right before the fire started."

"You mean you saw dust in the air? From somebody driving up the logging road?"

"Yes, sir. And that wasn't anybody from the Company, or probably even anybody from around here, I can tell you that. Probably somebody from the city. They were in a light truck or van. Anybody from around here would know they're tearing their suspension up driving that fast on a timber road."

"You can tell the kind of vehicle from the … the dust snake?"

"Pretty much, I mean, the particular snake depends on not just the vehicle, but the driver too, and other—"

"Would you be able to identify this dust snake if you saw it again?"

Arnold chuckles. "Oh, yeah. There's no mistaking a snake like that."

Marley nods, his face seeming surprised to show admiration for Arnold. "When you spotted Sherpa coming through the canyon, you radioed the sheriff to let him know?"

"Yes. I did. He told me to. And now I wish I hadn't. We can't arrest him. Sherpa didn't do it. He didn't start the fire, he—"

"How much time was there between when you radioed the

sheriff and when you saw the dust snake?"

"Oh, I know what you're thinking, sir, because I'm thinking the same thing. About twenty minutes. Plenty of time enough for the sheriff to make a call. And then, whoever he called would send their man zipping up here with a bunch of gas cans, right when Sherpa's in the area."

"Good work, Arnold."

Arnold is suddenly silent. He beams.

"You don't trust the sheriff, do you?" Marley asks.

"Well..." This is awkward for Arnold. "Not completely, sir. The Company's been putting pressure on him to take down the hippies at The Motel. And this is a timber town. Sir, for a while now, the Company's been spiking their own trees. When you look close, you see they're only spiking the twisted trees they can't get good lumber out of anyway. Those hippies are bringing a whole bunch of attention to the environment and the old growth that's being timbered. They're chaining themselves to trees and stopping operations. Everyone knows the Company wants the hippies gone. And the sheriff, well, he's gotta do what the Company wants, because this is a timber town, sir."

"So, the sheriff helped the Ashton Lumber Company set fire to their own equipment, so they can blame it on Sherpa and The Motel?"

"Yes, I think so, sir. They'd do that. But murder? Sir, they wouldn't do that. I know the people in this town. We don't have murderers. Murderers come from the city, sir."

"Do you think the Lumber Company set the fire?"

"Well, I think they were in on it. And the sheriff too. But they didn't set the fire. Nobody from the Company has a dust snake like that. I think they've just let somebody bigger take charge. Somebody capable of murder." Arnold wipes his face with the sleeve of his uniform. "Somebody from the city, sir."

Sorbonne

Boss Domino knows something about the now-properly-identified major. He lets this slip out because there's something Domino wants his ranking prisoner to know about him.

First, he paces slowly in front of them, his abbreviated eyebrows raising at times as he organizes his thoughts. "I wez noat uhways a soldier, deed you know?" he begins in a casual and confident tone that is entirely lost in translation through the poodle. "I wence wez a student of pheelo-sophee at zeh Sorbonne ... zeh Sorbonne in Paree, you knowe?" Domino watches closely. He looks like he'll be upset if there's no response.

"Oh, yes, the Sorbonne." Private Edison bobs his head. "The Sorbonne is a very good school." Edison's correct pronunciation of "Sorbonne" indicates that he is familiar with it and sufficiently impressed. But he continues anyway, flagrantly abusing the collegial invitation extended to forget the war for a moment and relate as gentlemen scholars: "Really? The Sorbonne, did you say? You attended the Sorbonne? And so far from home! Congratulations, I'm sure you're very proud. *Oh*, you'd like to tell us about it, brag a bit, perhaps. Yes, please do; I don't think any of us have other engagements, and your presence keeps our colleague off the swine in such an agreeable way. Philosophy? Oh, you *al*-most finished a thesis. Is that right? On what, did you say? ... Bacon? I'm sorry, meat processing? Oh, Francis—*that* Bacon, yes, the bastard son of Elizabeth, Queen of England and the Scots. Father an illustrious horse master. What, now? You say he invented the scientific method? Well, my, that's a pretty broad stroke, a dangerous generalization. I also studied philosophy, as I'm sure you've recently read, and I too didn't finish. But my reason for abandoning my studies was not war, as I guess yours was—am I right? Did you leave philosophy for war?—but rather, love. I left philosophy for love. I suppose it's just a natural switch triggered in a species when it senses its own overpopulation, but I've never been attracted to women. And I left Yale to move to San Francisco because I heard my romantic inclinations toward house pets would be better received there."

Domino's leashed translator parries the English words like high-speed ping-pong balls; he returns most of the sentences correctly, but he seems to also be rattling apart.

"Got to get your poodle a bowl of water, Dom," says Yawn. "And what was all that about Bacon? Thought he was a painter ... or something like that."

"That's a different Bacon, private," says Edison. "The Bacon our captor is referring to may have been a furtive prince, as well as a ghostwriter of Shakespearean plays, but his main accomplishment, as our captor suggests, is the invention of the scientific method."

Yawn grins encouragingly at the way Edison is speaking. "What you saying? He invented the pocket protector?"

Edison wears a slight grin back. "Yes, perhaps indirectly. But it is probably better to say that when those many generations of courageous spelunkers finally climbed in dank tatters from their unreasonable grotto, and brushing cobwebs and bat shit aside, stood blinking in the rose-pink light of the Age of Reason ... everyone looked over, and, well, it happened to be Francis on torch duty.

"To be the one holding the torch, on the first occasion that its light became entirely unnecessary, was of course a distinction. And as discoveries grow weary of clarifying their true parentage, claim for the modern scientific method fell to the house of Bacon, First Viscount St. Alban. So, when we say that Bacon invented the scientific method, we are really just making an expeditious association—similar to the convenient though ludicrous classification of chicken eggs as dairy products."

The poodle stands. He holds his own leash. He delivers a few more sentences to his master, then lowers his head, ashamed.

Edison then turns to discuss the early Greeks—specifically, the dynamic tension between the Apollonian and Dionysian tendencies (he clarifies that he means the Piaget interpretation), lateral analogies with the sympathetic/parasympathetic counteractions in biological organisms, and the prevalence of such dynamical tensions in the long history of man's attempt to find meaning and understand his place in the cosmos.

"However, 'counteraction' is not the right word," he admits. "Let me please retract that. This word has been so commonly applied to this context that, well, I must admit, I have tried steadily to refrain from using it. But its familiarity is a trap I find myself repeatedly falling into."

The poodle retrieves some words.

"For you see, *counteraction*... Let us deconstruct this word a moment—and I'm sure you already see the problem. This word suggests that the action on one side is canceled, eliminated, by the action on the other. In certain applications, the word is probably very appropriate; I may suggest the gravitational action on a block of mass, m, and the counteractive upward force of a solid tabletop, T. In this case, the two tendencies for action cancel out, and the result is *no* resultant action: stability. *Counteraction* is apparently a very appropriate word in describing the table's participation.

"But when this word, *counteraction*," Edison says now with a suggestion of disgust, "is applied to the aforementioned *dynamical* systems, it fails completely. It fails completely to capture the most important property of these systems. For previously, we were discussing systems possessing a property beyond that of merely the stagnation of a block, m, on a table, T. It is even fair to say, I think, that it is primarily the non-static, dynamic part of these systems that we were most interested in addressing with the misapplication of this word." Edison shifts in his ankle chain, as if customarily he would reach toward a podium to retrieve a glass of water. "The word *counteraction* suggests two opposing forces with opposing action tendencies that cancel out, thereby delivering *no* action to the system. But in the nature of complex dynamical systems, the opposing forces do not merely cancel one another out. Typically, these counteractions combine to create a new action in the system. The system evolves through these emergent phenomena that pop up in the complex negotiation of the parts. And the system gains a new behavior, which may be qualitatively unlike anything suggested by the individual action tendencies of its component parts."

Private Yawn suggests again that the poodle needs some water, and Edison understands that he should return to the investigative aspect of his thesis and wrap things up.

"Now your word, *enemies*, which you offer us from the depth of your observant study of the internal relationship developing in the U.S. between our military and general population, may, for the purpose of any sophisticated discussion, be as hollow and misleading as the word *counteraction*. For the American political and social system, which I believe we are discussing, is surely a complex dynamical system—very different than that of a block, *m*, in stagnant repose on a table, *T*. And to refer to opposed components in this system as being, ahem, 'enemies' is to suggest that the sides are 'counteractive'—and this is surely a dangerous and misleading abbreviation. America is not quite at war with itself, as you have asserted." Edison's palms turn upward creatively. "America is simply growing."

A man comes into the barn. He parks his heels together and stands straight-legged and blank-faced, waiting beside the toilets. Boss Domino notices the man. Domino appears ready for the interruption. He appears ready to change the format of the interrogation. He appears ready for something more violent. He walks over to the pen fence to receive his message.

"What's he doing, man?"

"Boss getting an important message, looks to me."

Domino returns to his prisoners. He pauses in thought a moment.

"Aiy ave juste received some news. I am towld Americans weel be arriving ... very soon." Domino steps back to the fence. "Zeh reason why I share zis wis you..." he says, his words launching from the casually crossed legs on which he stands, "... eeze because now we have very leettle time." He brings his face close to Edison's. "Let us speak zeh langu-age we bose know: zeh langu-age of logique. And as we see, *I* am in charge here; it eeze *I* who decide whatever happun to *you*."

Domino sucks on his cigarette. "I can use you een two ways ... and now I muste choose wheech one. I muste leave zis place right now. If I sink I weel get information frohm you, zehn I bring you wis. If I sink I weel noat get information from you, zehn I leave you here ... keel you, leave you here." Domino sucks on his cigarette again. "Maybe you can help me to decide whatever I muste do?"

The older prisoner nods his head, pinches his chin. "Oh, I see then. Okay, so you have a decision to make. I see. And it would help to know whether I plan on giving you information. Well, let me say, especially because of the alternative you have mentioned, I am more than willing; I'd be delighted, in fact, to provide answers to any questions you may have."

The poodle translates. The boss nods with satisfaction.

Edison continues: "I don't think I've shown any unwillingness so far ... or, well, the switch in uniforms, I guess. But maybe I can even demonstrate. If a sample of my newfound forthcomingness will help you choose, I'm eager to provide it. Please go ahead and ask me any question." Edison stands receptive, respectful.

Domino pulls on his cigarette, inhales, turns his wrist, and blows the smoke out from the glowing red tip. He will call the major's bluff, and there's no logic that can outsmart the question sequence he has planned.

"Whut eeze your militaire occupassion?"

"My military occupation? Well," says Edison, "I guess I work for the Agency. But I'm administered through Army Intelligence. I'm an expert on acid, you see—LSD—having had quite a bit of experience with it myself. That's the real reason I quit school, you know. So, they come to me and say they have a program in Saigon they want me to take over. And I say, 'Ha!' They sure didn't have to ask me twice!"

"Stoap!" Domino approaches Edison. "No mowah of zis boosheet. Who do you rually work for? Tell me *now*! If noat, I keel you, leave you here."

Edison's face changes. "Fair enough. For whom is my service? That's your question, right? Ok, I'll tell you. It would have been disrespectful of your intellect to give myself up too quickly. I'm sure you understand." He clears his throat and immediately begins: "Well, first of all, it's sort of like attending a Calvinist church because there's no Lutheran church in your neighborhood. As I think you've guessed, my affiliation with the intelligence service is secondary; it's not my primary affiliation. I attend this service simply because my primary church doesn't congregate very often."

Domino straightens. "Zhen whut eeze your primary affeeliation?"

Edison combs his hair with his fingers, the reverse motion of a hand collecting chips. "Pythagorean Brotherhood," he says neatly.

Domino blinks in irritation, then gains control over his eyelids. "Zeh Pysagorus Brozahoood—eet has not met since four hundred BC. How can zat be your affeeliation?"

"Oh, there's still a Brotherhood. It just doesn't congregate like it used to. And though it's called a 'Brotherhood,' they treat women as equals, by the way."

Domino nods at the ground. "And zeh Brozahoood, whut zay do now?" Some anger or ridicule seems lost in the poodle's reproduction of this.

Edison is happy to explain, but he bids that some background is first needed. "The Pythagoreans were the first—first in the West, at least—to unite science and spirituality. They understood that they are different metaphors describing the same thing, complementary languages for praising the mystery. To be complementary in this way, though, they must be used together. The ancient Brotherhood would be baffled to see how long it is taking the world to understand this last point."

"You are officially wis Intelligence, but really in zeh service of zeh Pysagorus Brozahoood—zeh Pysagorus Brozahoood zat has noat met since four hundred BC?" Domino turns and steps back. "Zen tell me what eaze zeh mission—zeh mission of zeh Brozahoood?"

"*Katharsis*," says Edison. He explains further, "The Pythagoreans created the term to mean a method for tuning something that's gone out of tune—something gone *ab surdus*. It was a central concept in Bacchism, Orphism, in the cult of the Delian Apollo, in Pythagorean medicine and science. Pythagoras replaced the soul-purging cure-alls of competing sects, through an elaborate hierarchy of *kathartic* techniques; he purified the very concept of purification, as it were."

Domino gives Edison a long stare that exaggerates a thin dew of sadness masking his soggy humiliation. "Zehn okay," he says. He turns and steps up and over the pen rails. With his back still turned, he pulls a cigarette out of his pajamas pocket, then lights it with an extra deep huddle of his head and neck. He straightens, blows out a short command with his smoke, and exits the barn.

Several men climb into the pen. They unshackle Edison.

Major David Marley's eyes suddenly fall from the pig, his fervent gaze now directed at Edison as the pajamas escort him up and out of the pen. Marley's face flickers an expression of blurry concern ... then he growls and bucks wildly. He desperately wants to follow Edison. But the pajamas clamp Marley's leg in Edison's empty shackle. They leave.

If Domino wanted to have the last word, then he shouldn't have left his poodle behind. With the poodle, Edison deposits further remarks on the discussion he was having with his colleague who so prematurely and rudely left. "Aside from treating women as equals to men, the Pythagoreans were also vegetarians," Edison's voice continues from outside the barn. "They shared all material items and held no personal property. Of course, they did have some silly taboos, like not eating beans..." Pajama voices goad the chatty prisoner to keep up. "... but when we consider the context, and the technical literature available to them to help explain such supernatural degassing, for example..." The voice becomes fainter as he is led away. "... reincarnationists, incidentally—staunch reincarnationists, I would say. This is especially important because..."

Marley, Walker, and Yawn hear Edison carry on as black pajamas lead him away. Twelve minutes later, as American flying machines are audibly approaching, they hear the sound of a single shot from a nearby pistol.

Fresh Batteries

Tonight, Deputy Marley sits right up at the counter next to the cash register. Right where his sister used to sit. He is without gun belt or badge, of course. In his V-neck undershirt, he sits, understanding now why Sarah used to sit here.

He understands this because it is busier tonight. And maybe because it is earlier. In any case, Boo Boo has plenty to do. Too much to do to talk. As he watches her buzz around, he becomes aware of the multiple tasks a waitress must perform simultaneously. It is impressive. She is everywhere, maybe stepping on each floorboard in the restaurant multiple times in a five-minute frame. Her motion is densest here by the cash register. These boards get stepped on by her the most. This is why Sarah sat here: to talk with her friend.

On the counter in front of Marley is a hot coffee in a ceramic cup. Boo Boo went by with a big tray for a table of four on one arm, a coffee for him in the other. She set it down as she flew by without pausing. But she had smiled at him from the coffee pot as she correctly guessed he would want a coffee, black, no sugar.

Beside the coffee cup in front of Marley is a paper bag. The one Boo Boo had given him. Inside is the tape recorder. Fresh batteries. A fresh cassette tape.

The floorboards behind the counter are indeed walked on most frequently by Boo Boo. The specific floorboards behind the cash register are stood on the most by her. Here at the cash register is the only place one could sit and hold at least an intermittent conversation with the waitress when it is this busy.

"Boo Boo?" he says.

She is ringing up a bill, too distracted to respond. She has rung up the bill and now is out on the floor again, drawing her notepad from her apron as she targets a table in wait.

"Boo Boo?" he calls again.

Now she stands at the kitchen window, back to him. She slides the ticket into the turn wheel, spins it 180 degrees, then spins herself the same. "Ah," she says and smiles. "Fresh batteries?" She takes the paper bag and sets it below the counter.

"Yes," Marley says. But she is already gone.

It seems that she already understands that he would like her to record those men if they come in again. Because "Wouldn't recognize them; it was just after my shift," says she in a pass toward the kitchen window. "That's why we put it down there." She turns the plates in her hands and forearm and nods at the shelf under the counter. She means the tape recorder. "Julie was on that day after me, but she never remembers her customers. Sorry." Boo Boo is gone again.

There are never the less related questions Marley would like to pose, but they will have to wait. He has a different question. Important. Something he heard on the tape.

"Did Sarah ever go by 'Gaia?' " he asks in a burst at the next opportunity.

"The earth goddess?" Boo Boo asks, distracted as she slides a precise collection of coins up from the register drawer. "No, Breeze never called herself that."

Earlier, Marley had shared the tape recording with Deputy Arnold. Not the part of the conversation between his sister and Boo Boo; even Marley has not listened to that. Just the conversation between the men that was accidently recorded by the accidently left-on tape recorder. Initially, Marley had had no intention of sharing the recording with anyone from the sheriff's station. Even though he felt he could trust Arnold, he didn't see what help Arnold could offer. The man doing the talking was Baskin; this Marley already knew. The other man was mostly just a few "okays" and "got its." Not much of a voice sample.

Marley could guess from the conversation that the second man was receiving orders from Baskin. The man has probably infiltrated The Motel. He could be any one of the large number of hippies living there. Baskin instructed the man to "hit Gaia" and "frame it on a Brother." And to "make sure there's sex, drugs, murder—the kind of things that will make folks reading about it terrified."

Marley had not intended to share the recording with Arnold. What changed his mind was Arnold's report of a piece of evidence he smartly put together regarding the illegally dumped trash up at the falls. When they chased Walker up the mountain, the night of the murder, Marley had asked Arnold to take a cast of a tire print on the shore of the river where the trash had been dumped. He did.

First, Arnold quickly discovered that the print was not in fact from Walker's tire-tread sandal, as Marley had supposed. Marley had been tracking Walker and understood even from the incomplete impressions he could find in the pine needles that whatever shoe Walker was wearing must have a recycled tire as its sole. The imprint on the bank of the river was simply the most complete print they'd found ... so he thought. It was too narrow to be from a truck ... so he thought.

"It's from the same kind of tire you have on your Karmann Ghia, sir," said Arnold. "VW stock." Arnold explained that he knew—in fact, maybe everyone knew—that Marley drove a Karmann Ghia. Because it's so little and weird-looking, it's hard to miss. He—in fact, maybe everyone—found the little car to not be what they'd expect Marley to drive. Then, what Arnold most wanted to report was that he thinks the tread could be from the same vehicle that made the dust snake he saw leading up to the Company's landing, right before the arson. "It's either a VW van or a VW pickup, sir." Arnold could also loosely constrain the vehicle's year of production.

Marley, a little astonished, complimented Arnold on his

work. Arnold deflected this, saying, "Well, there aren't many trucks or vans with such a light and narrow tire print. And the mattress and trash we saw up there wouldn't have fit in a car, sir."

So, Marley shared the tape. He played the tape for Arnold and asked if he recognized the younger man's voice.

Arnold's answer was prompt: "Oh, you already met him, sir. At The Motel."

"Who? How...?"

"Kevin Martin. Ken Doll."

Marley couldn't understand how Arnold could be so confident that he recognized the voice from such a small sample.

"I'm in the choir, sir," Arnold responded, his expression seeming satisfied that this was an explanation. "I've got perfect pitch."

Dragon Snot

There's more happening on the surface of the planet than Marley can expect to record. This has been true for a while, but not as true as it is in this moment. The camp—or farm, or whatever it is—is under attack. Explosions of all sizes are preceded by whistles and grunts of disturbed air, then screams and sounds of splintering wood, dirt clods raining from the sky. Yellow light tickles the barn through the stick walls, suggesting that already there's a lot of fire out there in the dark night.

The pajamas are frantic. One climbs in to start the truck while others deal with the three remaining prisoners. They use the tips of their rifles to point out their improvised plans: two of the prisoners are already chained to the truck, so let's see, these two can just climb right up, but the third prisoner... Well, that won't do; his foot is chained to the barn post... Among the pajamas, there's some confusion, probably about the key. It sounds like: "The key? Didn't you have the key? I thought *you* had the key? Where's the key...?" But then the pajamas find the key and finally unchain the pigfucker from the post. They pull him up onto the truck, run his hands through some crating, and shackle his arms tightly around the partially unpacked commode. The truck pulls out.

It's then that Marley realizes that the pajamas intend to leave the pig behind. Even as they shackled him onto the truck, his eyes remained on the white sow. But now the truck has pulled out of the barn.

The truck frantically speeds through the camp. Ceramic clatters in the crates as the truck swerves to avoid the chunks of its path that are evaporating in explosions. And in the rain of earth, there's also fire. Napalm comes down from the American gunship like dragon snot, spraying fiery slime over everything. As the truck punches out of the yellow cloud, its wheels are on fire, wild flames drips down the sides of the crates, and fire dances strangely in a puddle on the metal hood. Flames hop over the camp like crazed monkeys as the truck speeds toward the river.

The barn is burning. Marley's eyes are locked in the direction of his last sight of it, despite the motion of the truck and the aggressive convulsions in his torso. He's breaking crate, making splinters, shearing nails ... ripping out his ties to the truck bed.

All at once, as the truck reaches the middle of the bridge, the mangled crate releases the toilet—and Marley falls off the truck with it. Two ribs break as he lands, but he doesn't notice. He rolls off of his back, rights himself with the heavy fixture, and locates the direction of the camp. Running, immediately running, running down the bridge, toward the huts, toward the barn, toward the pigtaphone...

Another gunship suddenly appears overhead, completing the figure-eight assault. Marley's toilet takes fire. Rounds graze the ceramic; white flakes spring violently from the commode, but the premium bathroom fixture is still intact. The gunship makes another pass, sneezing a diabolical lunger of napalm. Everything becomes bright yellow. Patches of Marley and his toilet are on fire. The bridge is on fire. Everything is on fire.

Marley feels the splinters enter his wrists. He hears the heavy ceramic crash through the bridge rail. Suddenly, his load is strangely weightless. His hair is on fire, his uniform is on fire, the barn is on fire, the pig is on fire ... and suddenly, his toilet—though it too is on fire—weighs nothing.

Library

Deputy Marley pulls up in front of the Ashton Public Library. He parks and gets out of the patrol car.

A woman in her early sixties, probably not even a hundred pounds, wears a breezy polka-dot dress and flat-soled sandals and pushes a powerless lawn mower. She's out in the middle of the grass, right in the center of the big lawn. She hasn't made much progress.

Marley breaks into a skip to reach her, responding as if she were dropping groceries. Before he has thought it out, he has a hold of the T-bar mower handle—and has taken over mowing the lawn of the Ashton Public Library. The lady's smile is confusing and beautiful as she pulls the notepad out from under his arm; he can hold onto the mower better now.

His chest spasms once. It's a very big lawn.

Deputy Marley removes and neatly folds his shirt, placing it on the library steps. He mows the lawn. He pulls the mower over to the side of the building, into a shed. He replaces his shirt, tucks it in, and goes into the library.

He finds the librarian. She has her back to him and leans over the front side of her own desk. There's a quick sound, sort of "kwhooo-weh" … and again. Marley has heard the sound before, he's certain, but not often enough to immediately recognize it. The librarian turns, and he sees the canister, and two plates of fruit salad, each with a dome of whipped cream.

"Ma'am, I'm here to ask you a few—"

"Shhh!"

Marley looks around. He lowers his head and speaks more softly, "I—"

"Shhh!" The librarian picks up the two fruit salad bowls and motions with her face for him to follow her outside.

Marley takes another look around—a closer look than before. The library is empty. He follows the librarian.

He finds her outside on the steps, one plate in her lap, the other beside her on the right. He sits on her left. "I came here to ask you about—"

"Shhh!" She holds a finger to the pucker of her frosted lips. "Whisper." She places the second plate in his lap.

Marley holds, with both hands, the plate by the edges as he turns to look back into the library. He turns forward again and whispers, "Why do we need to be quiet?"

The librarian spears a frosty grape. Once it's in her mouth, she responds, "They're listening."

Marley leans over. "Who?"

"I don't know. Some spooky men."

"Why would they be listening?"

"They want to know what The Motel is reading. I wouldn't tell them. Try the fruit salad."

"Thank you, ma'am," Marley whispers, "but I don't eat between meals."

The librarian pauses a minute to try to understand the response. She laughs. "Then we can make it a meal. I've got more whipped cream."

Marley looks at the plate. He identifies grapes and cantaloupe. Already much whipped cream. "It looks good," he lies, "but it is not the kind of food I eat."

"Sure." The librarian laughs again. Seems when they are talking or laughing about the fruit salad, they do not need to whisper. "A strong lawn-mowing man like you must eat only seal meat."

Marley's chest: a triplet spasm.

She leans over to his ear. "There's two. Two men. They take turns." She licks cream from her lip. "They're here a lot. Sit pretending to read, in a chair where they can watch my checkout desk. I guess if I won't tell them what people are reading, they'll watch and get it for themselves."

Marley turns and scans the library interior yet a third time. "But they're not in there now."

"No, they're not." The librarian appears disappointed as she looks over at the untouched plate in Marley's lap. "That's what makes me think they bugged the place."

"Why spend so much effort to know what The Motel is reading?"

"I'm not sure, Deputy. How about you tell me?"

Marley looks down at his fruit salad. He is here to get answers, not provide them. Before Vietnam, he would have ignored her question and returned to his. But during his brief experience as a prisoner of war, he learned that sharing information can bring better returns. "The Motel is important in the countercultural movement," he says. "The anti-war message is taking hold and costing powerful war profiteers quite a bit of money."

The librarian laughs, and in no whisper—sort of a snort. "Oh, it's much bigger than that, Deputy."

Marley nods. It is clear he suspects she's right.

The librarian has finished her fruit salad. She sets down her plate and reaches over and picks up his. She grabs his fork and stabs a slice of cantaloupe. "It's not just here. This is going on everywhere." She rolls it in the cream, then brings it up to Marley's mouth like it's a little boat that wants in. "There's a new kind of world war starting. Eat your fruit salad, Deputy."

Marley declines. He takes the raised fork from her hand and

sets it back on the plate. "A new kind of war? What do you mean?"

"It's about controlling information. Isn't information the fundamental currency?"

Marley nods.

"Controlling information used to just mean controlling access. Back when they burned the Library of Alexandria, you could keep people from getting the information by just burning it." The librarian laughs with disgust. "When Alexandria burned, so did a whole lot of information that wasn't recorded elsewhere. Now, because of the printing press, there's usually so many copies that you can't control information by just burning a library."

"So, how do they control information now?" The "they" echoes off the end of his sentence and through the cold halls of his head. He has an incomplete feeling of having changed sides.

"Disinformation."

Marley nods.

"When you can no longer control information, you shift to controlling awareness."

"Awareness? What do you mean?"

"Information is not really the most fundamental currency. Not anymore. Awareness is."

Marley considers this.

"Think about my reference section." The librarian points backward. "All that information on the shelves in there can be had by anyone; just open the books." She takes his plate into her own lap. With his fork, she begins combing the frosty cream into a hill at the center of the plate. "Let's say there's some information in some of those books you know you can make a huge profit from, but only by keeping others from being aware of it."

Marley nods patiently; yes, let's say that. She has meanwhile raised the still speared cantaloupe canoe to her own mouth and bitten off the bow.

"If you can't burn all the books, how do you stop people from getting the information they contain?" She asks this with frosted lips, a cantaloupe piece parked in one cheek.

"..."

"If you can't burn the books, you can instead bring your own books—full of a bunch of incorrect information—and you slide them right in among the real books. The real information is still right there, but it's so mixed together with the lies that nobody knows what to believe. You haven't burned the information, you've just hidden it from awareness."

"So, this disinformation war you say is starting, it's really a war on awareness?"

"War on awareness." The librarian considers this. "War on Awareness!" She laughs. "I guess the acronym would be 'WOA!' That's good. We'll tell everybody you came up with that."

Marley knows that disinformation warfare is not new. But he also thinks the librarian's urgent concern could be accurate. Information is not the fundamental currency anymore; awareness is. With steadily increased access to information, those trying to hold control over it would shift to target awareness instead.

The librarian is cringing. She has his salad plate up to her nose. "My God. Now I know why you won't eat it. I'm so, so sorry, Deputy." She laughs. "I should have smelled it. Smells maybe a little sour." She continues to sniff but cannot make a decision.

"No, that's not it. I mean, I don't think the whipped cream is sour."

She looks over. "Well, how would you know?" She lifts the

plate up to his head for him to smell. He lowers his nose, she lowers the plate a bit, he lowers his nose to follow. They repeat this, then all at once she raises the plate into his face. He slides away, his tongue quickly out and cleaning his frosted muzzle. The librarian laughs like a hyena.

Deputy Marley's chest diesels. "It's good," he says. He takes the fork from her hand and spears a grape.

Bottom Of The River

David Marley came back into his body pretty promptly once it was underwater.

As Marley's burning legs entered the water, his flaming head still searched for the pig. The toilet was reluctant to enter the water with him. Its life-ring seat came crashing up into his chin. The lid came down on his head. Then, after the splash, everything stalled vertically due to air momentarily trapped in the ceramic.

After just seconds, the attitude of the toilet completely changed. It lost its reluctance to enter the water; suddenly, the toilet wished to explore the river's depths. This is when Marley's hallucination was renegotiated. Marley found himself to be not the guardian of a top-secret data-recording pig, but simply a man hugging a toilet at the bottom of a river.

TRUNKWARD

Ketchup

"No," says Sky, "uh-uh. I'm more liiiiike..." Her face is pensive. Her index finger comes up to her right dimple. "I'm more like the ketchup in the refrigerator."

" 'Ketchup in the refrigerator.' " Forward smiles, savoring the explanation. "You don't say." His accent sounds vaguely British. She likes him to play with her in this way. It is part of his training.

"I can see you down there," she says, very precisely adopting his version of a British accent. She glances down through the branches at him. "You asked me about my self-identity, did you not? You want to understand how I see myself, *n'est-ce pas*?" Sky lifts the back of her knees onto the next branch above. She lets her hair dangle. She muffles her own giggle as she hangs there a moment, tragic and soundless. Then she pulls herself upright. Her British accent reactivates: "First of all, sir, you absolutely must appreciate that I think of my essence as the ketchup, and not the container." Sometimes, Sky comes at him across the bed of peanuts, on her knuckles, her freckled elbows outward. Sometimes she comes to the nest before he is awake and pecks on him like a bird. She thinks she's frightening. "This may be a new container, but the ketchup has *always* been in the refrigerator!"

Forward regards Sky with awe. Sky is Earth. She is also the most wonderful little freak he will ever meet. "Are you trying once more to convince me you're as old as I?"

"... am. 'As I am.' On both counts, I'm afraid. Yes. First, I am correcting your grammar, and second, I am telling you that I am not as old as you—as you are; as you are old, maybe I should say. I am much, much older."

" 'Firstly' and 'secondly,' you mean, man. Now, do we agree that your current ketchup container is sixteen years ol—"

"Seventeen. When rounded."

"Fine. The ketchup container is seventeen."

"Oooh," says Sky suddenly, in the manner of a very superstitious Japanese lady. "Maybe *I* don't even know how old I am. I move through bodies."

Forwards effort toward the British accent wanes as he becomes completely involved in their playful nonsense. "Man, that's right. We always say 'the ketchup' is in the refrigerator. We don't mean the specific container. Ketchup is a collective concept, man." He laughs. "You're a collective concept, Sky."

"Sky is..." says Sky, in what Forward takes to be her usual voice. "Sky is age-old; Anita is, Anita is sixteen."

He laughs. "So, you're saying you mostly identify with your old ketchup?"

"No, Ward, I don't think that is what I was saying. Let's just say I identify with something bigger than my current container." Sky flips her hair, as if being coy with a "Ward" who is drying dishes beside her. "You need to stop seeing me as just..." Sky's inward hands uncurl fingers. "... the porn star I was when we met. That June is gone, Ward. Define me now not by my meat, but by what I do. My purpose. Our future." She adopts again a Japanese accent, male and monkish this time: "You will leave this tree not as the maggot you came, but as butterfly. Listen. Listen, maggot. Earth calling you. Big war coming."

Forward laughs, shakes his head, considers. "So, you..." He sits up and leans toward her, his face and gestures slow and friendly, like he's attempting to communicate with an alien. "You know how sometimes you get a peek into someone else's car when you pull up alongside them at a stoplight?"

The wrist of Sky's poncho sleeve raises to her lips, and her head bows. Her giggle knows where this is going.

His voice softens. "Sometimes you pull up alongside

somebody and they're singing. Sometimes you pull up alongside somebody and they're picking their nose. Sometimes you pull up alongside somebody and they're arguing with themself."

Sky grins.

"Well, you—you, man." Forward laughs. "Pull up alongside you, and I see a bunch of monkeys in the car throwing a beehive around!"

Sky laughs—laughs hard. Then she frowns. "I'm not a monkey. But you already know that, Ward."

Forward does know that. Forward does know that Sky is not a monkey. There is simply so much about her that is so busy with things he wants to understand. He has seen how she walks through the tree. He has seen how she squirrel-jumps. He has seen how Sequitur will never let her fall.

"What I mean is ... I'm just so happy you're in my movie, Sky. You make me proud of my species, man."

Sky smiles, grins. "I'm not a man." She squirrel-jumps.

Eight Thousand Calories

Earlier, the lumberjacks of Ashton were by far the toughest and meanest men around. And they were strong. A predictable consequence of sending men to spend twelve-hour days felling giant trees with axes and handsaws is that they developed combative expressions, jacked physiques, and eight-thousand-calorie-a-day appetites. The giant lumberjack sitting at the desk in this trailer office appears to have retained at least the latter from his forefathers.

Maybe a smile was forming on the man's face when Deputy Arnold climbed through the door, but that quickly vanished when Deputy Marley appeared behind Arnold.

"What do you fellas want? I got work to do." The man's head lowers as he continues writing on a paper on his desk.

"We're investigating the arson that occurred on your landing," says Marley.

"Ask your sheriff. He's already got everything we have to say."

"We have some further questions about the equipment that was burned."

The man ignores him and continues writing.

Marley steps over and pulls the paper out from underneath the man's pen. "We'd appreciate your cooperation."

The man retains for a brief moment his posture, face turned toward his pen, now suspended over the vanished page. An eruption is brewing.

As the giant man stands, his desk slides forward as if it were made of cardboard. He swings his arm like an axe, and the paper in Marley's hand becomes sawdust against the wall. The expression he presents to Marley indicates he might be next.

"I don't know who you are, Deputy. Maybe you came up from

the city and think you're a big shot. But if you think you can come in here and … and…" His fury only builds. "… and grab my paper…"

Arnold and Marley cringe sympathetically. Arnold leans in to whisper to Marley, "Could you go wait in the car, sir?"

Beer And Chablis

Herb and Carol sit in folding chairs beside their packed motorhome. They drink beer and Chablis and cast last gazes at the mountain face of Quarter Horse, at the forest, and at the Coulot River below.

"Hear that river? The mountain and trees?" Carol points with her wine bottle. "Mother Nature's calling us to stay longer, dear."

Herb takes a sip from his smaller bottle. "She's already had us stay a bunch of weeks longer than we expected. We never even made it to Yosemite."

"Yosemite schmozemite." Carol laughs. "Who knew we'd be needed here?"

Herb smiles. He nods as he scans the majestic scenery. "Seems just fine to me too, my love." He takes the last swig from his bottle, then fits it onto his middle finger. He moves his knee so Carol can see how the weight of the glass lowers the frequency of his finger's natural bounce. And then he turns back to the mountain, back to what his wife was talking about, and says, "Yup. Once you get out here in nature, she's not really all that hard to hear."

"Maybe in the city, we're just always just too busy to listen."

Herb sighs. "Anywho," he says as he cocks his arm and giant glass finger, "if we don't get home and pick up that incontinent little cat of ours, my sister's going to disown us." He throws the bottle in a high arc. It shatters in the road.

Carol laughs, sighs. "You're right." She stands, lifts the wine bottle to her mouth, and drains it. She arches her arm and throws her bottle into the road, too. It shatters. "At least we got our tipsy on for that long drive ahead."

"Yup. We're ready."

The two aliens fold their chairs, climb through the side door of their spaceship, and drive away.

Where Willard's Snake's Been

" 'Willard' means 'strong desire'?" Marley holds the steering wheel by the horn. He has pulled the patrol car off the road to better listen to Arnold.

"Yes, sir. In Old English."

Marley feels a single short spasm in his chest. He is intrigued. "How do you know that?"

"Oh, I read it in a book about baby names. From the library."

"Baby names. You have a baby coming?"

"Ah, nah." Arnold chuckles shyly. "Gotta first get a wife for that."

Marley feels a second spasm. "But you'll be ready?"

"Yes, sir."

Marley returns the car to the road.

"So, Willard told you that the Lumber Company wasn't behind the arson?"

"Oh, yeah, he made sure to be very clear. They didn't set the fire. They do want The Motel gone and all, and he told me that Sherpa's one of the hippies that's been chaining himself to trees, so the Company's plenty happy if they help frame him. But it wasn't their idea. He said the worse they've done on their own was spike their own trees. He also said it wasn't the sheriff's idea, either. He told me the sheriff told him the plan was set up by a man named Baskin who's working for our national security. He said Baskin told the sheriff cooperating would be patriotic."

"So, the sheriff tipped off the Lumber Company. But why? Are he and Willard friends?"

"Ah, nah. Not really. They grew up together, but I think the sheriff's plenty tired of the Willard family telling him what to do. The sheriff had to tip them off so he could get them to park an office trailer up there to get burned." Arnold laughs. "No way they would have needed a trailer like that on a landing like that. They just towed it up there so it could get burned like the sheriff asked. Like Baskin asked, I guess."

Marley nods, understanding. "Because if a dwelling is burned, the arsonists can be classified as ecoterrorists."

Arnold laughs angrily. "Baskin and those guys change the laws so they can charge a tree-hugger like they're a terrorist, and they make marijuana a Schedule I offense so they can send a hippie to prison just for growing a plant that exists anyway in nature. Meanwhile, if we ever catch whoever dumped all that trash up at the falls, all we can do is charge them a little littering fine."

Marley feels a chest spasm. Then he asks, "But why did Willard tell you all this? Are you close?"

"Close? Not especially. I was sort of friends with his son for a while. While we were in school. Sometimes I had dinner over at their house."

"That doesn't seem like a reason for him to give you the confession he did. Why would he tell you all that?"

"..."

"Why would he just give you all that, Arnold?"

"Ahmm. Well. I think he's a little scared of me, sir."

Three chest spasms in rapid succession. "Scared of you? Why would that giant man be scared of you?"

"Well, sir." Arnold looks uncomfortable. "I sometimes chat with his wife."

At this moment, Marley finds Arnold to be an unexpectedly brilliant storyteller.

"I mean, when I see her in the grocery store or something."

"…?"

"And, well, he knows I know some things about him. Some things he wouldn't want his wife to know."

Marley's torso turns receptively toward Arnold.

"About his dust snake."

"…"

"Sir, I know where Willard's snake's been."

Upside-Down Dog-Ears

David Marley pulls his Karmann Ghia off the highway and into the scenic rest stop. In the turn, his elbow secures the tall stack of library books riding in the passenger seat next to him. He parks and turns off the headlights.

At the Ashton Library, as Marley finished his fruit salad, he finally described to the librarian the reason he had come. He described that he was investigating the murder at The Motel. He would like to see any books the victim may have been reading. He would also like to read about Pythagoras of Samos and the Pythagorean Brotherhood.

The librarian smiled, her head tilting compassionately. She rose from the step. "On your first request, you know I'll only give that information to next of kin." She entered the library.

A moment later, she returned with a large stack of books. It seemed the section on Pythagoras must be shelved close by, and she simply scooped up the whole thing. But just in case, she somehow had time to sort the stack for his suggested reading. He has preserved the order, reading the stack from the top down by the vanity light of his Karmann Ghia over several trips to this scenic rest stop.

The Brotherhood existed a very long time ago. Marley has learned that Pythagoras of Samos formed the Brotherhood after he arrived in Croton in 530 BC. That's five hundred and thirty Bee Cee. Marley has spent a moment with this—a moment to imagine a world getting by without Jesus. At a time when faith and reason were not yet divided, the Pythagorean Brothers were both mystics and savants. They were the best mathematicians of the time, and they developed a theory of music and harmony that they used to understand their spiritual place and path in the cosmos. Their cult was communal and secretive. They dressed simply, treated men and women equally, and did not mistreat animals, nor eat them. They saw the world fundamentally as numbers—or more accurately, relationships. They showed that the most harmonious musical intervals could be expressed by simple ratios of the natural numbers. They found irrational numbers very upsetting.

The Pythagoreans were not just brothers and sisters; they were not just mathematicians and scientists, musicians, and spiritual practitioners; they were healers. Illness arrived when the body and spirit became discordant, out of tune: *ab surdus*. Everything the Pythagoreans developed and stood for was aimed at bringing or restoring harmony to the body, the world, the cosmos.

Marley has learned that the Pythagoreans conceptualized the world not in a pragmatic, point-wise consideration of locally observed parameters, nor even through a linear model capable of very accurately including slope—if perhaps also suggesting absurd asymptotes. The Pythagoreans were not focused on a mundane point, nor the local topography of their existence, but rather on the grand circle of life encompassing at the very least the whole planet and their present, past, and future lives on it— the grand circle of past, future and cause, effect in which their spiritual aim in each incarnation is to restore harmony within the grand *Circus Absurdus*. The Pythagoreans were healers of the whole planet.

Marley finished reading the books on Pythagoras of Samos and the Pythagorean Brotherhood. Several nights ago. There were only three. The six books below those three describe a different subject.

Three nights ago in this rest stop, when he reached the third book, it did immediately seem off topic. He then scanned the five books below that. Though one described the toxicity of pesticides, another the damages of dam building, and another the extinctions of species, all five books seemed to be about the environment and the harmful by-products of human activities.

He considered that these books could in fact be related, at least in the librarian's eyes, to the deeper theme of the Pythagoreans, and so he perused, skipping pages as he had not before. And that's when he saw it: the clear indication that these books were ones his sister had read. As he desperately hugged the six books, tears formed in his eyes, not falling as drops, but evaporating into a light fog reflecting the vanity light of his tiny car.

He had misunderstood the librarian's compassionate smile, as he thought she was refusing his request for the victim's book list. Somehow, she knew he was next of kin.

Marley had scolded his sister many times for dog-earing the pages in books. It seemed so disrespectful. She did not see it that way, but rather thought the dog-earing showed that somebody had really gotten into the book. A really cool book would have dog-ears. And maybe a broken spine.

Although his sister was not likely the only dog-earer to mark pages in an Ashton Library book, she was very likely the only one who dog-eared upside-down. The bottom corners. She said it was because she was left-handed.

Since discovering the left-handed dog-ears in the bottom half of his book stack, Marley has been up at this rest stop every night with the books, reading them again, sometimes just looking tenderly at their injuries.

Tonight, he's far from finished with either when a loud motorcycle pulls off the highway, up behind him in the scenic view turnout, then alongside his car window, *geerogugu grogugu grogugu grogugu*... Even while idling, the machine disturbs the peace. Then it shuts off.

The helmet suddenly looking down at him is shiny black. Marley can see a number eight in a circle over the ear. Although the helmet is open-faced, a tinted visor hides all but a large, gleaming set of teeth, with anything besides these bright and giant teeth fading into the inner shadows. The mouth, thus suspended in the manner of the Cheshire Cat, speaks: "So, you a deputy now? Hoo-hoo! Regular Barney Fife?"

Marley smiles, only in the incomplete way he can. His head tilts slightly. He has missed hearing this voice, its cadence and poetry, its humor and honesty. "Yawn," he whispers.

The suspended smile turns into a grin. "So, you do remember me! Okay, Peek, now listen up. Ground rules: first off, this hog ain't no kick start. I got a magic button, right here under my thumb—right here. See that? Just mash my thumb down on this button, and you gonna see me and hog here disappear, good as if someone called us away with a Ouija board. We got that?"

Marley's agreement is a deliriously round nod, his mouth almost smiling.

"And see how I snuggled up to your door?" Yawn continues. "Can't open your car door now. See that, Peek? Anyway, you and me both know I got more horse between my legs than you got packed into the candy ass of your weenie-bug here." He nods toward the rear of the car. Marley reflexively twists backward to acknowledge the rear mount of his little engine. "But in case you get any ideas, just remember this magic button; I got this magic button right here. And you don't want me disappearing because, in particular, I got something you want to hear about."

Slowly nodding, still smiling in his incomplete way, Marley brings both hands up and places them symmetrically on top of the steering wheel. He looks forward.

"..."

"..."

"..."

"So what? Where we stand, Peek? We agreed? What you doing in there, some kind of meditation?"

Marley looks up into the Cheshire mouth. A spasm in his chest ... and another... His torso is pistoning. He nearly chortles.

"I have no intention of trying to apprehend you, Eight. Ever."

The teeth disappear into the darkness. The helmet nods. "Hmm. Alright. Okay. We good then. That Black Panther shit about me ain't right, anyhow. They just trying to frame another Brother."

"..."

"Hey. Daymn. Hoo!" The suspended Cheshire grin returns above Marley's car window. "I get it, uh huh: you drinking in there, is what you doing!"

Marley's head turrets; his chest spasms. "True."

"Well, pass it on out then. Let's see the baby bottle you got in there."

Marley's chest spasms a record-breaking seventh time. He lifts the thermos over the half-mast glass of his car window. "Here. My baby bottle."

The helmet visor doesn't need to flip up; baby bottle slides under and right in where it needs to go.

Yawn "DJAHs" like John Wayne and hands the thermos back to Marley. He looks down through the Karmann Ghia glass sternly, starts to say something, then breaks into laughter. "You gotta warn a boy, Peek! Can't be passing him some kinda freak-ass hot toddy without first telling him it's a freak-ass hot toddy."

Marley wants Yawn to call him "David." His expression indicates this. "The hot toddy's one of a kind ... some very special liquor."

Yawn's helmet halts. "What you mean, 'very special'?"

"So special, there's only one bottle of it. Anywhere. Anywhere in the whole world."

"You mean 'special,' like 'laced-with-some-kind-of-shit special'? What kind of special you mean?"

"Irreplaceable. Only one."

"A home-brew batch?"

"So special that … that … this is the only bottle of it there will ever, ever be." Marley is looking forward again, his depth of field set more closely now on a whiskey bottle he has raised, a bottle he emptied into the tea thermos.

Yawn pulls off his helmet. The night is dark, and he is still Cheshire, but his head is obviously less protected now. His knuckles move toward Marley, closer, *toc toc* against the glass. "How about you roll all the way down, humn? Bottom part of you starting to look like you in a fish tank."

Marley rolls the window all the way down. His simultaneous sadness raises him in his seat, and he turns to look out and up and through the opened window, up at Yawn. "Rooibos and Wild Turkey." His chest spasms. "That's what we're drinking."

Yawn shakes his head, grinning, laughing. Then his head tilts, waiting for Marley's to follow. "Your sister." His lips tighten, his voice becomes soft. "She left that Turkey in the car, didn't she?"

Marley stops. His eyebrows arch, his chest—almost a convulsion. He turns and looks up at Yawn. "She *hid* it in my car!"

"Hoo! No shit?" Yawn laughs. "I had a sister did exactly that too. Wasn't no secret place in the house, so she hid her booze and weed in the family car." His Cheshire grin entrances Marley. "So, one day, a Sunday, Daddy's finishing up at church. And some of the folks leaving see he's got a flat. Right away, folks are rolling up the sleeves of their Sunday best to help the minister with his car trouble. Whole circle of parishioners help him dig into that trunk, pull up that spare, and … oh my … they find that shit stashed down in there—hoo! Daddy left God at church when he drove us home that Sunday." Eight is laughing. "I tried to tell him it wasn't me, but he whooped me even harder for trying to blame it on my sister."

Yawn sees Marley's expression. He watches, then nods incredulously. "Hold on. Hold on, Peek... You saying your sis stashed her booze under the spare wheel like that too? Both our sis's did exactly the same clever-ass thing?"

Marley nods, grins, some kind of pride seeming to light up his face.

Yawn leans back from his handlebars, roaring with laughter. Marley, chest pistoning, holds his steering wheel; he is inducted into the roar. His chest diesels, ignites. He feels the full-body spasms coming uncontrollably like a train of lifesaving sneezes that summon his sister deep inside him to upside-down dog-ear his deepest pages.

"Last place anybody expect a girl to hide her shit. Thinking she don't have the technical sense to get that wheel up."

"That's why your father blamed you!" Marley says this within his convulsions.

"Sure tell you! Nothing wilier than a teen-age girl!"

"She must have had to..." Marley twists the air with his right fingers.

"Yeah; she would have had to know how to unscrew the wingnut to get the wheel cover off."

"And she would have had to—" Marley's chest spasms interrupt his ability to speak.

"... screw it back down. Yup." Yawn's arms are folded, and he's smiling toward the trees. "You didn't expect your sis was such a mechanic. That's what this about."

Marley bobs excitedly; this is exactly what he meant. He nods at his windshield. "I've been driving around for years with her bottle of Turkey right under my nose, and I didn't even know."

"What? *Years?*"

"I only found it tonight because I ran over a piece of broken

Coke bottle. On the way up here." Marley passes the thermos back to Yawn.

Yawn sips. "DJAH!" He screws the lid back down and hands it back. "But hold on… What's this 'years' shit? You saying you ain't never had a flat in years?"

Marley nods. "First flat ever."

Yawn's look is incredulous. "You got Fred Flintstone wheels or some shit? How you never had a flat?"

Marley shrugs. "I'm careful."

" 'Care-fuwll'?" Yawn laughs. "How you mean, 'care-fuwll'? You driving around leaned over the steering wheel while you scanning the road for nails and thumbtacks?"

Marley nods. "Yes."

"… You serious?"

"Well, not while I'm busy with an intersection or something, but yeah, sure. When I'm just driving down the road, I'll look." Marley wants to call Yawn "Eight."

"Umh, umh, umh." Yawn laughs. "You something. You really something."

"…"

"Umh, umh, umh, Peek," says Yawn again as he smiles at Marley. "Alcohol seem to be the drug for you, no doubt. Now listen: Ed, he wants you to go see him. In Reno. I wrote his address on a taco bag inside that trash can right over there."

"Edison? He's…"

"Yeauh. He's alive just fine. Had to make his own arrangements getting out of Nam's all. He sure appreciates that medal you got for him." Yawn laughs. "All posthumous and shit."

Marley becomes calm, peaceful. He stares forward through the windshield of his little car as he absorbs this. Edison is alive.

Eight puts his hand through the car window and places it on David's shoulder. White eyes bleed through the black helmet visor. A school of sympathy swims to David.

Then Eight, Eightball, Yawn, he straps on his helmet, mashes his electric start button, and is pulled away by a Ouija board.

Blowing Up The Engine

"Imagine," says Sky to Forward as she walks backward through the tree foliage, branches sprouting where needed beneath her feet, "imagine you're a monkey who wants to know how an engine works." She sits back into a green chair that temporarily assembles from the needles and wood in the sky behind her. "You want to know what's inside the engine. And you're a monkey. So, the first thing you can think of to do to find out is to blow it up. *Kabloom!* You slide a little bomb down the dipstick hole and stand back." Sky seizes pieces of tree around her and rises. "*Kabloom!*"

Forward is startled by the intensity of Sky's explosion. He tightens his squeeze on the big limb he hugs. She brought him up here. The top of the tree. For training. He has dutifully followed her, despite the fact that moving through the tree still terrifies him. He hugs a major limb of the narrow trunk in the top of Sequitur. Sky back-walks out onto the branches. Forward is trunkward, loosening his grip for a moment so he can swing his arm around the thin tree that remains at this altitude. His posture is clingy, certainly, but also something more than that. Forward leans his forehead against the trunk of Sequitur and makes a vow … a solemn vow … an aspiration.

Forward has been recruited. The cause has found him. And he has found his cause. He understands now that it was Sequitur who called him up this mountain. More fundamentally, it was Mother Nature. She recruited him. She is under attack and needs his service. She has called a magical sixteen-year-old girl to be his trainer.

Sky channels Gaia. Once Forward realized this, he understood the source of the girl's magic. And her role. Forward also understands that he is here to learn this magic. It's a necessary skill in Gaia's army.

Forward knows he will be up in this tree for some time. He has much to learn. First, Sky is teaching him how to tend the cameras. To do that, he must learn to move through Sequitur. He must gain the ancient tree's respect.

Forward shakes away his fear. He leans boldy out from the tree. He looks up at Sky, who is backlit by the sun. "You gotta surf the wave you gayt," he says in a bad Australian accent. His ruggedly handsome grip suggests he is now holding the tree up rather than supporting himself.

PLANETARIUM

Bacon And Bananas

The attractive lady greeted Marley in her driveway, on her way out, with two quarreling kids, late for the weekly Webelos meeting. Somewhat suddenly, Marley stood alone in her kitchen. "Just wait a little, and he'll be with you," she said as she backed out the kitchen side door. She may have sort of blown him a kiss through the glass, right before she hurriedly pushed the door shut. There was the sound of an automatic transmission screwing in reverse ... a double *kaplunk* as the station wagon crossed the gutter ... a moment to put it in drive ... and then acceleration into silence.

Now Marley sits alone in her kitchen and listens to a clock. It's behind him. The only major appliance he cannot see in front of him is the stove, and so the stove must be behind him. That sound must be the stove's clock. He has heard such stove clocks before. The clock does not tick; it whirrs. An electric clock. Probably an electric stove as well.

Moaning. Now Marley hears moaning. It seems to come from the walls ... or maybe the floors.

He listens, steps quietly over to the cellar door.

The moaning comes again. He gently pushes the door. He slides a finger into the latch bolt to muffle the sound of its recoil. He stops when the door is a foot open; the hinges are squeaky. And now the moaning from below is repeating: "Dowwwn heeeere..."

The voice alarms Marley. It's too soft.

"Dowwwn heeeere..."

It sounds like the voice of a man who has been shot and lies bleeding.

"Is that you, Edison?"

"Yessss. Come dowwwn."

The stairs under Marley's feet creek as he descends into the cellar. He stops when he sees Edison.

The cellar is sort of comprised of two rooms. Though ventilation ducts, pipes, and wires run through the joists overhead, confusing the spatial domain, the claw-foot tub clearly sits in some sort of center of a second room, up on a little platform.

Marley cannot see into the tub; he can only see the portion of Edison that rises above the rim. The room is damp and warm.

Edison is not relaxed, nor completely reclined. The upper part of his body is stiff, upright, forward. And motionless. Edison's face is turned toward Marley. His head gestures the invitation very, very slowly as the rest of his torso remains completely still.

Marley's ambi-ocular sharpshooter eyes take inventory, a methodical scan of the room. Until he catches himself doing this. He blinks deeply, then more simply walks the rest of the way down into the cellar.

Edison nods at a chair.

Marley picks up the chair and carries it toward the tub, setting it down at what might be the boundary of the tub room.

"Come closer." Edison's voice is less spooky now that less volume is required. In fact, there's nothing strange about Edison's voice; he's simply talking very softly, and slowly.

Edison observes Marley's perplexed face and begins to laugh. He fights to calm it. He also holds up a knife now. Marley can see only the tip of it above the rim of the tub. "Come over and take a look," says Edison very softly, very slowly, very motionlessly, "inside my tub." He's trying not to laugh.

Marley approaches the tub. And then he is looking down into the tub.

Edison butters his dinner roll. Floating precariously in front of him on two rubber ducks and a large sponge is his dinner plate.

"Sir. I thought you were dead."

"This is how my wife serves me dinner," Edison says, squelching his laughter. "God, I love that gal."

"I thought in—"

"I mean, she's got that ... that *playfulness*!" Edison turns his eyes directly toward Marley. "Without that playfulness, there'd just be no room for us to work our magic together like we do."

Marley's left eye moves forward of his right.

"Could you?" Edison's gesture is clear. As was the pause before it.

Marley stands, steps over, and takes the dinner plate from Edison's wet lap.

"You can just set it on the—yeah, there's fine too." Edison stands and towels off. He pulls on a bathrobe that is pink, woolly, and maybe his wife's.

Soon Marley is back upstairs in the kitchen. With Edison.

"I'll bet you're black?" Edison holds a mug up.

Marley nods. He receives the mug of coffee. Edison wears an apron now. It's a woman's apron. Marley looks around the kitchen for indications that this is not just the house of a woman and her kids. Marley wants affirmation that this is really where Edison lives.

"Three strips." Edison smiles. His fork has speared one fatty end, and he rotates the dangling bacon slice, modeling it before he lowers it into the skillet. "Four strips, and you're sick. Wisdom developed over generations of trial and error." He places the metal lid of a small saucepan incompletely over the basking bacon slices.

The bacon sizzles, and the smell soon surrounds them.

"Yawn said I should come see you. Did the Brotherhood send Walker to The Motel in Ashton?"

Edison stands, back turned toward Marley, his fork still raised. His left hand rounds his back and reaches for the apron knot. It's too far to the right; he pulls the knot back toward his spine. " 'Send' is not the right word. That's not the way the Brotherhood handles its agents."

"You are admitting then that Walker is an agent of the Pythagorean Brotherhood?"

"Admitting?" Edison's fork raises to eyebrow level, then descends. "I'm sort of trying to speak your language. I wouldn't myself call Forward an 'agent,' but I think you would. So, let's just call him an 'agent,' alrighty? Eight, too." Edison sets down his fork and pours some orange juice. He returns the carton of juice to the refrigerator. Then he picks up the two glasses, brings them to the table.

"What you want to know is who sponsored the hit at The Motel."

Marley nods. "True."

Edison sighs. "Long story." He touches his knees as he sits down. "I'm sure you've guessed that if the Brotherhood has agents in The Motel, then TOC does too. It's sort of an early battle ground in the war that has started. Split a bagel?"

Marley considers this. "Sure. Thanks." He has many questions and starts with this one: "What is TOC?"

Edison is standing again, tending bacon, back turned. Waves of vaporized pig waft through the kitchen when he lifts the saucepan lid. As he turns, the shrug of his shoulders is clear. "Oh! You've not heard of TOC? It's just what some of us call it, anyway. It's an acronym for 'Tragedy of the Commons.' " It is clear that Edison knows his description is still incomplete. "TOC is everywhere. Overgrazing the commons in fields all over the world." He lifts the lid. The frying bacon is loud as he turns the slices with his fork. "They profit from stealing Gaia's ring."

"Gaia?" Marley recalls hearing this name on the cassette tape recording. Baskin was ordering his man to hit Gaia at The Motel. And frame it on the Brotherhood.

Edison half turns and shrugs with his spatula. "Mother Nature, if you prefer."

"TOC steals Mother Nature's *ring*?" Marley's confusion is compounding.

"Sure. The harmony, the birdsong. TOC steals from the world's commons. And what they gain is always less than what they cost everyone else. That's sort of their signature."

"I'm not following."

"Ah. Well, let's back up a moment then. Although the meaning of the Tragedy of the Commons may have started as a Malthusian warning, the way it's mostly used can be described by the story of a village of shepherds. If a shepherd wants to be greedy, and if he's also shortsighted, he can overgraze his sheep. He gains a little, and the village loses a lot. But even the little he gains isn't for long. Others see him cheating, and so they overgraze their sheep too. Pretty soon the whole village collapses." Edison flips a bacon slice. "That's the tragedy part." He flips the others. "Nature was in harmony, and then everything gets driven absurd. Out of tune. That's the ring-stealing part."

One of Marley's eyes moves ahead of the other as he squints. "Hold on. In one case, you're talking about greed breaking a harmony among men, and in the other, you're talking about greed breaking harmony with nature."

"Ah! Very good! The two do seem a little different. But in the deeper sense, it's all one. Anything sustainable

235

requires harmony with nature. When man forgets nature is a relationship, not a resource, things kind of go to duck poop." Edison laughs. "When men start exploiting nature, they always wind up exploiting each other too." He moves the bacon to a plate. "They overgraze."

Edison removes his wife's apron. He brings the plates over and sits down with Marley at the kitchen table.

"Do you always make breakfast at dinnertime?" Marley's question surprises him; it feels playful.

Edison laughs. "Maybe…" His fingers run over his head, in the reverse motion of a claw collecting poker chips. "… maybe it's the third time. Yep, I betcha this makes three." He smiles and inserts a bacon end into his mouth.

"You just had your dinner, and now you're eating breakfast?"

Edison has food in his mouth, nodding, laughing. "Just the bacon." He pokes at the strip on his plate. "I mean, where do they mine this stuff? It's so good!"

"So, who sponsored the hit at The Motel?"

Edison straightens. He faces Marley and quickly chews and swallows the food in his mouth before responding. "I was really sorry to hear about your sister, David."

Marley's mouth tightens.

"Well, the shortest answer is what I've already told you: TOC. But I'm sure you want something more specific than a mention of a globally diffuse cabal of greedy profiteers, profiteering from environmental degradation. A bunch of overgrazers."

Marley nods. "Yes."

Edison is behind Marley now. He places his hands on Marley's shoulders and gives a few squeezes. "What you need to understand first, David, is that there is a world war starting. A new kind of war. A huge war that will last many decades. The stakes are bigger than in all the previous wars in this world combined. Far bigger."

Marley hesitates. "You mean the War on Awareness?"

"War on Awareness. Hmm. WOA! I like that. That's a good name. Yes, that's right."

"I've heard of it, but that doesn't mean I understand it. Who's at war? What are the big stakes you're referring to?"

"The stakes, that's easy: everything. Nothing less than life on this planet. The life as we know it, at least."

"You mean an existential threat to mankind?"

Edison laughs sadly. "No; wish it were only that. I mean nature. The whole living planet. Gaia."

"I guess you mean a nuclear apocalypse? That could kill off civilization, but I don't see how it could kill all the life on the planet."

"I *don't* mean that. Yes, nuclear apocalypse, that's very, very bad—but what I'm talking about is very, very much worse."

Marley is silent.

Edison points with his fork to a shrub on the other side of the kitchen window. "See that bush?"

Marley nods. "Yes." He sees the bush.

"That bush works for months, years, whatever, collecting sunlight energy and storing it in its parts. Then we take that bush, and we eat it, burn it, whatnot. One bite, and we get a whole bunch of concentrated sunshine."

Marley nods his provisional understanding.

"And when we start telling that bush where to live, so we can eat it better, we've already lost some harmony with nature, see?

"That's anyway small fries compared to the type of absurdity I'm going to describe next—where we send things *way* out of tune." Edison offers a fruit bowl to Marley. "Banana with your bacon?"

Marley takes a banana. He holds it with both hands on the table in front of him and waits for Edison to continue.

"Thing is, not every bush that grows gets eaten. Not every little plankton floating around the ocean soaking up sunshine gets slurped up by a whale. Some get buried, and over time they get pushed down deep into the Earth. They take a whole bunch of carbon with. Away from the surface, away from the atmosphere for millions of years. Okay?"

Marley nods.

"So, when some greedy money monkey grubs up that long-buried bush instead of growing his own, well, it's a whole different story than just farming. A whole, whole different kind of disharmony. Are you seeing where this is going now?"

"You're talking about the oil industry?"

"Yup. Fossil sunshine. Bushes you don't have to grow yourself. There's so much of it, and that's why it's so profitable."

"There's carbon being unburied and released into the atmosphere."

Edison nods.

"What's the harm in that?"

"Well, we're not yet sure. But to suppose that there won't be any is a little like wishfully thinking there won't be any problem in running your piano over with a train. Hard to say in advance exactly which parts of the piano will change the most. But you can strongly expect it will be out of tune."

"And the train is too big to stop." Marley has raised his banana.

The two men look at the raised banana. Their soft chuckle is a collective effort.

"Big Oil will soon become the biggest business on the planet. It will be at the base of everything. It will be hugely profitable." Edison's face carries sadness.

"So, Big Oil. B.O. You're saying they're profiteers of environmental degradation?"

Edison laughs. " 'B. O.'? Heya, that's much better than TOC! I'm going to say that from now on: B. O. instead of TOC. The only thing that can stop B. O. now is awareness. Awareness raised about the true cost, the tragedy of the commons."

"The absurdity."

Edison smiles. "Yes, the absurdity. B. O. will be working very hard to cast doubt on any worry we can state. Discredit any expert opinion. Have us believe that there's no way of really knowing what the train they're sending down the track will do to the piano. Nobody can even say whether the keys will play sharp or flat or just the same as they did. They will emphasize the uncertainties to distract from the view of the certainties."

Marley nods. "They will use disinformation to block awareness." He finally understands the inevitable war coming. His face carries sadness. He peels the banana.

Edison clears the dishes from the table.

"I have a tape recording," says Marley. "A man named Tom Baskin is ordering his man in The Motel to 'hit Gaia.' He wanted it framed on 'a Brother,' and by that I guess he meant the Pythagorean Brotherhood?

Edison sits back down at the table. "Sure. But the 'Gaia' in that case isn't quite the Gaia I was just referring to. They're related.

"David, in response to the approaching war, there is a group forming. It's called GAIA—all upper case. Stands for Global Awareness in Action."

"I've not heard of GAIA. And I've read plenty on the counterculture movements and environmental activism."

"You wouldn't have come across GAIA in your work in intelligence—not yet—because they don't have an organizational structure you'd recognize. No newsletter. No command hierarchy."

"No command hierarchy? How can that possibly work for an organization?"

"See what I mean? GAIA is completely off the radar in your intelligence world. You can't conceive of a powerful group that doesn't have a powerful man at the top of it."

Marley nods, accepting this. "The Motel is what, then? A safehouse, or a training ground, or something like that for GAIA? That's why it's under attack by TOC?"

"B. O.?"

"Yeah, B. O., I mean."

"GAIA doesn't really have a headquarters, but they're everywhere and growing fast. That's what has B. O. worried."

Marley remains puzzled. "How does GAIA recruit if they have no recognizable organization?"

Edison smiles. "Ask yourself. How has she recruited you?"

The wall phone in the kitchen rings.

Edison looks at Marley. He reaches over to the fruit bowl and raises a banana to his ear. "Hello?"

Marley's chest spasms. Edison sees this and laughs. And this causes more spasms in Marley, faster spasms. And the faster spasms in Marley make faster spasms in Edison. Which make faster spasms in Marley. Soon both men are laughing. The phone still rings.

Edison leans over to the wall phone. "Hello?" He listens, responds: "What do you mean, 'how'd I know'? ... No, dear, I'm laughing about something else. ... What? ... Ah, geez. Where? ... Alrighty, I'm coming. ... What? ... Ha, yes, I'll shine my armor.

Kiss."

Edison gets off the phone, still chuckling, maybe about something else now. He slurps the rest of his coffee. "I'm afraid I have to skedaddle, David. My wife ran over a soda bottle."

Marley starts to stand.

"No, no, you stay put. Finish your coffee." He smiles. "Have another banana. You can leave whenever you want, just pull the door closed." Edison's eyes widen as he pulls off his glasses to put on his sweater. "She and the boys are on a busy street. I got to go. It was really wonderful to see you, David."

Next, Marley sees Edison smiling through the glass of the kitchen door as he closes it with Marley inside. He kiss waves. Just as Mrs. Edison did.

Anonymous Tip

On the drive to Reno, Marley called Arnold, and what Arnold recounted then is concerning now.

Just as Marley asked, Arnold had been on the lookout for that dust snake. The angry snake he knows to be created by either a VW van or a VW truck driven by a city slicker: the arsonist.

When Marley spoke with him on the phone, Arnold reported that because the city slicker likes getting around using the dirt back roads instead of the paved streets, for whatever reason, he wasn't hard to find. Arnold discovered that what's at the head of that angry dust snake is a 1968 VW bus, and what's at the head of that bus is Kevin Martin. Ken Doll. Arnold reminded Marley that they had met Ken Doll while they were raiding The Motel.

Just as Marley asked, Arnold has been following that snake: the snake of Ken Doll. And he has been careful not to get too close. Arnold understands that who they really want is not Ken Doll, but Ken Doll's handler. Or maybe his handler's handler. Who they really want is the sponsor. And the best way they'll get to the sponsor is by watching where Ken Doll's snakes go. See what snakes those snakes hook up with.

Arnold saw the snake across the ridge. He descended on it in his patrol car. He followed it, suffering its dust. The closer he got, the more he suffered. It was exciting but awful being behind it.

And then he lost the bus ... for a while. It came back onto the pavement up by the Coulot campground. Arnold drove through the campground looking and looking and looking for the bus. But he couldn't find it. He wound up helping two cars that both got flats right at the same spot, where there was a bunch of broken bottle glass in the road. The broken bottle glass punctured the tires of both these men. And that's why their cars wouldn't go. Arnold then got sidetracked with his critique of litterbugs, and Marley had to interrupt him and remind him of the cost of the call.

"Two fully grown men, and neither knew how to change a tire!" said Arnold. "Good thing for them I came along." Arnold pointed out that it was also good that the two flats they got were not on the same car. "Because even though they had two spares between them, the rim size and lug nut patterns were different, so the car with the two flats would have just been stuck."

"Why would one loan their spare to the other anyway?" Marley asked. "You think the two know each other?"

"Oh, yes, sir. Because they were both wearing suits. And even more than that, when I pulled up, one was in the trunk of the other, trying to figure out what to do. He couldn't even figure out how to unscrew the jack strap. And the other man, he was just inside his car with the windows rolled up, waiting for his flat to be fixed."

"Did you get a look at them both?"

"Well, sure. The one man, anyway. I made him help me fix the two flats. He wanted to just get back in his car too, and have me do everything. But how can that be fair? Sir, I told him that if the both of them were going to just sit inside their cars, then the best I could do for them is radio them a tow truck."

Arnold's description of one of the men matched that of Baskin. Arnold could only give a partial description of the other man. He caught some glimpses when he was knocking on the man's car window, when he was encouraging the man to get out and help, or at the very least, get out of the car while it was getting jacked up. "He wouldn't, sir. Just kept turning away from me when I came up to the window. I tapped some more, and I told him it's not about the little bit of extra weight, you know. I told him that it's more about how it's just kind of, you know, snobby to expect me to jack him while I'm already changing his flat for him."

Marley reminded Arnold again to try to be brief.

243

"And the first man…" Arnold chuckled. "Well, he didn't seem to like me tapping on the other man's window like that. But does that seem right to you, sir? Can't even get out of the car when someone's jacking you up to fix your flat?"

"What were the car models?"

"1971 Cadillac Fleetwood Brougham, black," Arnold said immediately. "I think those were fifteen-inch rims on that boat."

"The car of the man that wouldn't get out, you mean."

"Yes."

"How about the other car?"

"The other? Hmm…" Arnold paused to think. "Well, it was a rental, sir."

"How … how do you know it was a rental?"

"Oh, I don't know. You can just tell. Everybody can."

"Everybody can tell when it's a rental car? How?"

"Ah." Arnold chuckled. "I don't know, sir. You can just tell. Everybody can."

"Do you mean…? Do you mean that maybe the car gets washed so regularly that the paint gets a certain look, or—"

"Sir." Arnold's pause suggested his assembly of confusion, sympathy, and respect. "It's just a fact. Some things don't need a reason to be a fact."

Marley paused to think about this. Then, "Model and year? Color?"

"Sorry, I don't know about that kind of stuff, sir. Whatever model they use for rental cars, I guess."

Then Marley's change ran out, and the line went dead. If this meeting of men Arnold witnessed was Baskin meeting his own handler—or whoever is sponsoring the attacks on The Motel—then this could be dangerous for Arnold. The man in the Cadillac would not like being seen with Baskin. Baskin and his organization were paid well not just to coordinate hits, but to take the fall if need be. The higher the sponsor, the higher the cowardice. The biggest sponsors insulate themselves with telescoping layers of men doing their dirty work.

From what Marley learned from Edison, the ultimate sponsor of the hit on The Motel is as big, rich, and cowardly as they come. If B. O. is so future-thinking as to start a disinformation war this early in the environmental movement, then they are also future-thinking enough to eliminate anyone witnessing contact between their own elite and the likes of Baskin. That meeting at the campground is a piece of information they will want to not get out.

Marley was absorbed in these thoughts until just a moment ago, as he crossed the California border. His sister's voice awoke in his head: "Uh, hellowuh? Earth to Davey? Davey Davey Davey? Remember Arnold? Your friend, Arnold?" Marley hears his sister now from inside the car. "Aren't you worried B. O. is going to get him?"

Marley feels tears, wet tears, and a harmonious train of spasms in his chest, one after another, *bababababababa*. He swerves in front of an oncoming truck and crosses the road to halt before a service station pay phone.

Deputy Jaspers answers. "No, sir. Arnold's not here right now. Sheriff sent him up the mountain. Why? Because somebody called in with a tip. Yeah, a tip. Said they saw that Sherpa kid headed up to Quarter Horse. Pardon? No, sir. Anonymous."

Underwater Feet

Of course, from the sniper's perspective, it made little sense. How could a raised canteen have so effectively deflected that perfect head shot? Kalmut had waited to take the head shot until the deputy bumbling across the creek with his boots around his neck stopped moving for a moment. Whether his feet were soft or the riverbed rough, he was a hard target while his head bopped around like that.

When the deputy stopped, Kalmut got his shot. Looking through his crosshairs, Kalmut supposed that the canteen the deputy suddenly raised to his face would just add to the splatter of the exploding head behind it.

But that's now what happened.

A precision rifle like Kalmut's is single-shot and Kalmut is slow to reload. There are suddenly so many thoughts in his head. And the calls he has been hearing from the nature around him are loud. Especially right now. Somehow, these sounds seem related to the freakish miracle he just witnessed through his rifle scope. Some kind of godwork or good luck is going on. Maybe a tree fairy. No canteen could have possibly deflected the bullet that way. Kalmut is reluctant to reload and take a second shot at a man who has been blessed in this way.

He stands and lowers his rifle. Kalmut closes his eyes and listens to the sounds around him. The creek. The river further away. The wind in the trees. The birds. He is good at what he does. He has usually taken pride in that. But his hits have always been in urban and residential settings. This venue of mountains and nature is confusing. Somehow, it makes him feel that his pride is misplaced.

Kalmut could not kill the hippie girl. First job ever that he couldn't do. Baskin already had Martin under cover inside The Motel. Martin was just supposed to show Kalmut the skylight and signal him when the time was right. Kalmut was supposed to be the one to climb down through the skylight and strangle the girl. But he couldn't. When the time came and Martin waved for Kalmut to climb up onto the roof, Kalmut had been waiting in the night of nature just too long. The sounds and the smells were too beautiful. Interrupting that to go strangle an innocent young lady was something he found he just couldn't do. Or maybe it was the stomach flu he got from the local diner. That's the excuse he gave Baskin.

Kalmut is sure that it wasn't the flu. He has carried out a hit before with broken legs pinned under a burning car. Climbing down through a skylight to strangle a hippie would have been nothing, if Martin hadn't had him wait so long in the forest first.

Baskin was not happy about Kalmut not doing his job. Martin had to do the job instead, and that could have risked Martin blowing his cover. Kalmut told Baskin that he was embarrassed, and he really meant that at the time. He told Baskin it would never happen again.

Per their agreement, Baskin always pays Kalmut for the hit in advance. And Kalmut performed this hit flawlessly. If not for the magic canteen, Kalmut would now be square with Baskin, his professionalism restored. Instead, Kalmut observes a butterfly that has landed on his rifle case.

Kalmut has a code. A hit has been paid for; a hit must be delivered.

Grapefruit Spoon

It is a special property of David Marley's eyes that the more directly he looks at something, the more firmly it becomes riveted in place. The first time he hears the oinking and looks over into the adjacent booth, the three punks become stapled to their vinyl bench, suddenly quiet. He then turns his back on them—both in the sense of finding their talk from now until forever uninteresting, and also in the sense of seating himself in a position that makes their whole booth disappear from his view.

Deputy Marley is reading the funnies. Waitress Boo Boo likes this about him: that he is reading the funnies. They're from the Sunday paper; the only part she saved for him. Now she slides herself into the booth and her coffee orb onto his table, both at the same time, sort of a *swoosh*. She faces the deputy, and therefore, she has a very good view into the adjacent booth of punks. She tells the boys to stop oinking at the deputy. She tells them to stop the stupid bacon jokes. She tells them to stop dressing like hippies so hard, like they're cool cats or something. She knows they're not. She tells the deputy it is amazing that he can ignore this.

"It's like you're working in a pet store," she says with a building laugh. She's looking at Marley. "Just sitting at your register, all *la la la*, and 'May I help you?'—and what? No, you don't even hear anymore the tank of screeching monkeys behind you."

Marley's chest spasms ... and again. His face is almost smiling.

"How do you do it?"

"..."

From Boo's vantage point, she describes to David how the boys take turns sitting in the spot in their booth that is back-to-back with him. "That's where they say the rudest things; it's the spot closest to you. They're daring each other to sit in that spot closest to you and say it smells like bacon." Her voice raises: "When you shoot these punks, Deputy, I'll tell everyone it was self-defense."

Boo Boo and her coffee orb slide out. She has food up.

But she's immediately back, with the food that was up: Italian onion rings. "Alfonzo is sending this as your starter. Are you really going to let him decide your dinner, David? That's brave."

"He insisted." Marley's chest spasms.

Boo Boo looks into David's eyes. The shade of blue shifts, and his chest spasms again.

Boo Boo's chest spasms. She laughs, a second spasm. Then she cries. Very briefly. Just a tear.

Marley's eyes become dark blue—dark blue and dedicated to Boo Boo. She sees this and lights a cigarette. Marley slides over the ashtray. He hands her a napkin.

"She did that imitation of you perfectly. She called it your 'underground laugh.' " Boo Boo exhales smoke. "I didn't believe her. I didn't think anybody could laugh like that."

Dark blue and dedicated to Boo Boo. It is the deputy's eyes that are providing the ashtrays and napkins and anything else that might help her. Boo Boo sees this. She sees the severity of his pain and desperation. She sees that his sister was everything to him. She sees that he has collapsed into his suit of armor. She snatches his car keys clipped to a belt loop of his pants.

The oinking in the next booth is still going on. With volume, she says, "I'm going to help you shoot these boys in self-defense, Deputy."

The neighboring booth goes wild; they are boiling over with new potential and directions. Anything they do now is on top of the background of oinking and bacon jokes, which they sustain.

"She loved the way you raised her, by the way."

Marley nods.

"She just wished you would laugh. Laugh harder, I mean."

"... Harder?"

"Yeah. Be more playful." Boo Boo slides out of the booth. "Who's paying you little shitholes?!" She passes the punks. "Is this you guyses' job now—just sitting around the diner and oinking at cops?"

Somebody is paying the boys...? Marley's eyes take inventory. But Boo Boo and the boys are all in back of him now. This is the way he chose to sit. He stares instead at eight unoccupied tables before a wall hiding the men's and women's toilets. He faces empty restrooms, not Boo Boo, nor boys.

... Until he does face them. Marley has suddenly turned, head and shoulders supported now on elbows and forearms placed flat on the head cushioning between the booths. He hovers above the boys now like a gargoyle on a cathedral. His voice is black. "Who hired you to oink at me?"

Marley is indeed menacing, but the booth next door is just too excited now, too much momentum, and each of the three boys is at least as big as the deputy, and the deputy doesn't even have a gun, he's like Andy Griffith, so what's he going to do, huh? "Oink oink, what are you going to do, little piggy?"

"Your belt, Deputy." Boo Boo swings and flops the deputy's holster belt atop the cushion Marley has mounted.

Bringing the deputy his gun doesn't have the intended consequence. The booth next door becomes shrill and ever more delighted.

"Oooh oooh. Watcha gonna do, Andy? Shoot us?"

"Can't fight good enough, Clouseau, so Cato bring you your gun?"

"Cato!" The booth squeals. The punks have turned to attack the waitress now.

"Hwoyaaa!"

"Saaaaah!"

"Chinese, Japanese, dirty knees, look at these!"

Boo Boo rolls her eyes. "Vietnamese! My parents are Vietnamese, you ignorant butt hairs!"

Marley watches her as she walks off to ring up an order. Even as he turns again to face the booth of screeching monkeys, he remains lost in thought. Playful? Hmm...

Boo Boo returns and suggests aloud to Marley that he shoot at least one. Maybe that will make the others shut up.

Marley, still in his gargoyle stance over the booth, nods his head in consideration of this plan. Playful, hmm? Looking down at the boys but speaking to the waitress, he says, "Shooting them seems too much. Maybe instead, something a little less. Do you have those, those little spoons with the—"

"Serrated tips? A grapefruit spoon, you mean?"

Marley's chest spasms. "Yes. Could you bring me a grapefruit spoon?"

Boo Boo affirms that she can, and she will. She does.

"Here it is: your grapefruit spoon."

Marley's head lowers on his shoulders as his gaze turrets down into the booth. The gash in his forehead, the burn scar on his head, his broken front tooth—these things seem now so much more visible to the boys below than they had before. The deputy's eyes turn from dark blue to the color of an acetylene torch bead. He stares into the face of each boy. The grapefruit spoon slowly wags as he points it down at them. "Each of you..." he says calmly. "... each of you owes an eye."

The booth is silent.

One Chair Away

It is immediately clear that in the past, things were black and white and changed more slowly. The frames on the hemispherical movie screen above melt, overlap, trade places, merge, and disappear, always maintaining a background of the full panoramic view seen from the perspective of an old tree on the cliff of Quarter Horse. The projectors at the center of the Big Igloo are assembled in the same way as the cameras in the tree called Sequitur. From Sequitur, the cameras have watched the visible half shell in front of them—the river, the mountains, the sky, the stars and streams alike—for nearly a century. On the inner wall of the Big Igloo he has built, Fray has taken that half shell seen by Sequitur and simply rotated it skyward for the convenience of the moviegoer. From their reclined seats, they see what Sequitur has seen.

Motion is big in the early years—black and white and big. Mountainsides of snow-covered trees, and the light in the little theater is bright. In spring, the theater dims, but becomes more colorful, in a black-and-white sense. As the years go by, the forests in aerial view resemble growing penguins, fields of huddled penguins rocking on webbed feet as they grow taller. Older trees collapse sporadically, or in clumps during a storm. A time lapse at the new moon captures the whimsical path of a lightning bolt as, searching for a way from Heaven to Earth, it finds and electrifies a gangly spruce. The scars left by the fallen are quickly absorbed.

When commercial logging starts, something new appears. In a blink, trees no longer just fall; they vanish. It's like the penguins are being snatched by something under the ice. The forest now displays sections that look like patches of hair pulled out from the inside of the skull. Soon this simple plucking is lost in geometric patterns of denuded mountainside. Such an ugly color has been rare in *The Movie* so far, but now it is twinkling toward explosion. The polygons of this unusual color fatten, multiply, and become interconnected by curvilinear scars. The town of Ashton grows. In fall frames, when the weather is right, the smokestacks of the homes clustered down there in the little river town combine to create a giant jellyfish in the sky—the sky below Sequitur. A jellyfish above Ashton, but below Sequitur.

By the time color fully arrives in *The Movie*, the curvilinear scars have become thicker and less compliant, seeking to widen and become straight. Some scars can't be straightened and are abandoned. The forest heals over them, while deeper scars form elsewhere.

At night, it has mostly been just the moon on the wrapped screen, sometimes wading across the sky. But with time, the resolution increases to show the individual streaks of stars across the sky. And in the town, among the stoplights that flicker between green and red, headlights and taillights stretch luminous lines to and from points of departure and destination. Some of these frames of the town are magnified on the screen. Fray has looped sections into mini movies embedded in the wider view. There are multiple mini movies going on at the same time, so the audience must select which one to watch from the screen wrapped over them.

One of the loops shows Fray himself riding atop a lumber truck, from a place in the high forest where the trees were felled, all the way to the Ashton lumber mill. And then out of the mill, Fray riding the stacked lumber off to a destination where photos indicate a new phase for this wood as a pool deck or some other construction by man that will last for a time span that is fleeting compared to how long the wood could have remained alive in the forest. Over and over in a loop, the old man rides the logs, creating a sense of some kind of evacuation from nature.

There is a loop of Deputy Marley mowing the lawn of the town library. It shows him carefully setting his folded shirt and holster belt on the library stairs, and then in his V-neck T-shirt, he attacks a strip of lawn. Over and over, he cuts the same streak, while so much grass around him remains untouched. The audience laughs. Boo Boo leans over to Marley during this to whisper, "You did that for Annagrette? That's so sweet! My cigarettes are in the car." Just as his sister used to do, she kisses him clownishly on the ear as she unclips his car keys from his belt loop.

Telescopic views of the letters on vandalized signs come forward—pow, pow, pow! Letters disappear from one sign and appear on another. The signs transmit messages to the high cliff face of Sequitur.

Some in the theater sit up and even stand when Cupid suddenly goes dark. Cupid's bow, arrow, and glowing hamburger remain, but the cherub has disappeared.

East of Cupid, a dust snake grows from the edge of town to a spot in the forest just before The Motel. This dust snake is not the short rooster tail of a slow and heavy lumber truck as it grabs gravel in its wide tread and tosses it up to soon fall back to earth. This snake reaches even higher than the dust from an empty rear-wheel-drive pickup truck driven by a busy foreman. This snake is angry; its turbulent cloud suggests a launch by thin wheels after many collisions with the vehicle undercarriage. As if this dust snake were not already distinct enough, Fray has tinted it red so that the loop shows all of this dust snake's travels and connections: The Motel, the mill, meetups with other cars in the campground.

One of those other cars, obviously a rental, is shown then in a separate loop meeting with a long black luxury car. The rental arrives first and parks at the far end of the Coulot campground. It backs into a campsite and waits. The black car comes later and brings its driver's window to that of the rental car.

After they talk, the black car leaves first, then the rental.

But both cars are seen together again a short distance away, still in the campground. Both remain stranded there until a sheriff's deputy comes along to help them change their flattened tires. There is laughter from those in the Big Igloo theater who are watching that loop.

Mr. Fray is not only Ashton's baby-shower and funeral photographer, he also develops the town's film. This is perhaps the reason some in the theater facing a certain direction get to see again the man with the flat tire—the one with the rental car. In the new photos, the man with the rental car still wears his suit, but he is reclined, faceup. Rods and strings in the forensic photo help to recreate an instance of the man holding his Styrofoam coffee cup to his mouth. A solid arrow traces the path of the bullet through the cup and then the head.

Heads in the theater begin turning again to the loop of the vanishing cherub at Cupid's Diner. With magnification, a loop of The Motel appears right beside it on the screen. Just before the cherub's light goes out, the lights of a VW van go out. It has parked in the forest near The Motel. Its angry dust snake stretching a mile behind fades and fattens in the moonlight. Frames of The Motel blow up to show an instance of a man standing on a section of the roof. He has exited an open skylight. He is wearing a stovepipe hat—a hat just like the one the man in the front row of the Big Igloo is wearing. The man in the front row is the only one of the twenty-four moviegoers who does not see double stovepipe hats. He has also been watching a different loop than everybody else, and so he does not see the loop that shows his own VW bus parking in the forest near The Motel. He does not see how the others in the theater dome have left their chairs and backed to the Igloo's exit, blocking it.

Instead, the man in the stovepipe hat has remained focused for the whole latter part of the movie on a raunchy loop playing at a spot at the edge of the dome, which he views almost between his own knees. The clip of the sudsy cheerleaders holding their fundraising car wash in the parking lot of the local gas station is short, and yet endless in its loop. Despite so much else going on over the giant dome screen of the Big Igloo, the man in the stovepipe hat has not lost his focus on this single soapy event.

The photo loop opens the skylight and murders the girl inside eight times before Kevin Martin, Ken Doll, notices anything amiss. He lifts himself to sit up, pushes up the brim of his hat, and sees the empty chairs around him. He stands and sees the audience facing him, most backed up to the door, the deputy in the foreground.

Kevin, Ken Doll, he laughs and asks something about "Where's the fire?" He asks why everyone got up. He says they're freaking him out. And that he needs air. He says he needs them to make a path for him to get out.

"I'm arresting you," Marley says softly. His sadness over this choice seems evident.

Ken Doll pauses. Then his voice changes, falling back to his real one. A charade is dropped, and the hippie imposter speaks for the first time in his own ugly voice. "Better just get out of the way." He nods at the deputy's missing belt, and then to his right. "I got a Glock in my coat right there. Just one chair away." He grins. "Think you can get to your car and back bef—"

Ken Doll may surely wish later that he had been more observant, more quickly observant. Quicker to see the movie frames everyone else was already seeing. Quicker to notice Boo Boo standing behind and yet beside the deputy, pack of cigarettes in one hand, the deputy's holster belt in the other.

Marley's eyes have not blinked as he observes Kevin Martin. He blinks now, turns toward Boo Boo, lifts his belt from her hand. He motions for her to step back to the door with the others. Then he turns back to stare at his sister's killer: Kevin Martin, the dickless Ken Doll.

A short spasm starts in Marley's chest. It diesels, rises, and leaves through his mouth like a puff of black smoke lifting the rain cap on a tractor's exhaust pipe. Without shifting his eyes, he tosses his gun belt down onto a seat.

"One chair away," he says to the man.

Smashing An American Standard

Major David Marley struggles through the Vietnamese jungle. He's tired, hungry, bleeding ... and jubilant. Mosquitoes drink his blood. Flies carry away his flesh. Sinewy plants grab his feet, shred his fatigues, and drown his stride. His body is wet, red, pulpy. Along the way, his flesh has become raked and rasped into osmotic contact with the swamp around him. The wide pupils set in his beard stubble remain mystified over this sweaty communion.

The major rocks forward another step through the mud, grunting and cursing—and grinning, because he can make noise now. His slow, two-footed sex with the wet earth is awarded only rude sounds to acknowledge his deposits in her deep ecology. And his burden, he holds it differently now—just a sloppy bear hug. He's no longer uptight about the jungle slapping the ceramic; he's no longer worried about the nicks; he's no longer protective of the fixture like he was before. He has come down the river and out of the water. He breathes air now.

But the major hasn't eaten in a long time, and his body now burns the muscles that transport it. Extrapolations from his recent expenditures show him disappearing soon, simply vanishing with a little *poof*, the last calorie of his rest mass giving his load a final forward shove through the mud, then winking out.

Fortunately, Major Marley can expect to eat soon. He has seen the planes. American planes. Through the night, he floated down the river, unsure of whether he was headed toward safety, or toward even worse than what he had escaped. And then, at first light, he heard them, then saw them: the caffeinated buzzes and flying specks that revealed the location of an American hive.

If the river has a bank at all, it's a wide compromise. The swamp seems to go on forever. But now at least his feet touch bottom, and this is a relief. If he had stayed in the river much longer, his waterlogged resolve would have flaked away like carp flesh and sent him back to the bottom with his cargo. His hours in the river had been a balancing act—a balancing act between life and the last bubbles of death. By any natural evaluation of density, his load should be below the water, and him with it. The fact that he was able to keep the load at the surface for so long was a fraud perpetuated by frantic bailing, one mouthful from the bowl at a time, and daunting attention to orientation. Nature surely suspected the unstable equilibrium but held back, because Marley maintained the toilet in a stance that threatened to take a piece of the sky with it if it should sink.

He escaped that watery death. With his feet in solid mud, what David Marley thinks of now are rocks—hard rocks. As he pushes forward, he fantasizes over them, all different sizes and shapes and compositions. He will reach the air strip soon. He imagines the moment he'll stagger out from the swampy mess and into the disciplined clearing, suddenly in site of them— all those rocks of different sizes and shapes and compositions, runway markers lined up like a ceremony of sailors on the deck of a battleship. He imagines straightening his back and disguising his recent history as he walks down the line of them, looking at each one carefully, examining weight, shape, size, composition, maybe even color. Finally, he'll choose one, carefully kick it from the line, and shuffle it onto the packed gravel of the landing strip. He imagines a deep breath, perhaps a skyward sniffle, maybe a glance toward some frantically converging jeeps... Then he'll loosen his hug on the American Standard, carefully reposition the small slack of chain between his wrist shackles, and with the drop-slam of a Mexican wrestler, come down on that chosen rock and smash the fucking commode he has been chained to into pieces.

ABOUT THE AUTHOR

Robert Tyler

 Professionally, Robert Tyler is a scientist working to understand the dynamics of oceans and atmospheres on Earth and other planetary bodies. Unprofessionally, he promotes artistic approaches to raising awareness on the rapid changes taking place on beautiful Earth. He lives in Greenbelt, Maryland, USA.

Author website: roberttyler.me

Made in the USA
Middletown, DE
06 May 2023

29550092R00158